M000311335

Readers love the Dirty Kiss series by RHYS FORD

Dirty Kiss

"This is a great romantic suspense novel with a gritty film noir atmosphere and a sexy, heartfelt romance."

—The Book Vixen

Dirty Secret

"Another outstanding book by Rhys Ford."

—On Top Down Under Reviews

Dirty Laundry

"From the first page until the last *Dirty Laundry* held my attention… Fans who love mysteries must really give this book, as well as the other two a try."

—Top 2 Bottom Reviews

Dirty Deeds

"Rhys Ford is a master of story telling, and I enjoy how the overall story arc in this series builds around the mystery arc in each book."

—3 Chicks After Dark

Down and Dirty

"Definitely a must read for fans of the author and the series, or anyone that is looking for a strong read with lots of passion and story."

—MM Good Book Reviews

By Rhys Ford

Clockwork Tangerine
With Poppy Dennison: Creature Feature 2
Fish Stick Fridays
Grand Adventures (Dreamspinner Anthology)
Murder and Mayhem

Cole McGinnis Mysteries
Dirty Kiss
Dirty Secret
Dirty Laundry
Dirty Deeds
Down and Dirty
Dirty Heart

Hellsinger
Fish and Ghosts
Duck Duck Ghost

Sinners Series
Sinner's Gin
Whiskey and Wry
The Devil's Brew
Tequila Mockingbird
Sloe Ride

Published by Dreamspinner Press
www.dreamspinnerpress.com

DIRTY HEART

RHYS FORD

Published by

DREAMSPINNER PRESS

5032 Capital Circle SW, Suite 2, PMB# 279, Tallahassee, FL 32305-7886 USA
www.dreamspinnerpress.com

This is a work of fiction. Names, characters, places, and incidents either are the product of author imagination or are used fictitiously, and any resemblance to actual persons, living or dead, business establishments, events, or locales is entirely coincidental.

Dirty Heart
© 2016 Rhys Ford.

Cover Art
© 2016 Reece Notley.
reece@vitaenoir.com
Cover content is for illustrative purposes only and any person depicted on the cover is a model.

All rights reserved. This book is licensed to the original purchaser only. Duplication or distribution via any means is illegal and a violation of international copyright law, subject to criminal prosecution and upon conviction, fines, and/or imprisonment. Any eBook format cannot be legally loaned or given to others. No part of this book may be reproduced or transmitted in any form or by any means, electronic or mechanical, including photocopying, recording, or by any information storage and retrieval system, without the written permission of the Publisher, except where permitted by law. To request permission and all other inquiries, contact Dreamspinner Press, 5032 Capital Circle SW, Suite 2, PMB# 279, Tallahassee, FL 32305-7886, USA, or www.dreamspinnerpress.com.

ISBN: 978-1-63477-026-2
Digital ISBN: 978-1-63477-027-9
Library of Congress Control Number: 2015918969
Published March 2016
v. 1.0

Printed in the United States of America

This paper meets the requirements of
ANSI/NISO Z39.48-1992 (Permanence of Paper).

The final book in this series is for Lisa Horan, who has held my secret the entire time.

And for Mary Calmes, who has spent the years trying to pry it out of me.

A special warm thank-you and many hugs to Greg Tremblay, who brought Cole's voice to life.

ACKNOWLEDGMENTS

I OWE a world of gratitude and then some to the following people: Mom, without whom I'd still be unformed cells; the Five, Jenn, Tamm, Penn, and Lea, who have walked with me on this writing thing for a long, long time (don't do the math. It'll just hurt your head); Ren, Ree, and Lisa.

There are NO words I can give to say enough thank yous to Elizabeth North, Lynn West, Grace and her editing team, lyric, and everyone else at Dreamspinner Press. You guys rock me like a rocking thing.

And once again, I want to thank Harrison Ford. Because I can. And let's face it, he shaped as much of my world and imagination as anyone else I can think of. I owe him a hell of a lot.

GLOSSARY

All words are Korean unless otherwise noted.

Agi: Baby, as in infant. This word is used between Jae and Cole as a teasing affectionate term, referencing to when Cole called Jae baby in English.

Aish: Common Asian-centric sound denoting exasperation or disbelief.

Ajumma: Older middle-aged woman. Sometimes considered to be an insult in some circles as it denotes the woman has aged enough for it to be noticeable.

An nyoung ha seh yo: A general greeting. Can be used at any time of the day.

Beom joe ja: Criminal or criminal element.

Bulgogi: Thinly sliced steak marinated in a sweet, soy sauce mixture.

Char siu bao (Chinese): A steamed or baked bun made of bread and stuffed with a sweet, barbequed pork mixture.

Chigae: A stew-like Korean dish, made with kimchi and other ingredients, such as scallions, onions, diced tofu, pork, and seafood.

Dongseongaeja: Homosexual

Enceinte (Latin/French origins): To be pregnant

Halmeoni: Grandmother

Hangul: Korean alphabet / lettering system

Hanzi / kanji: Logogram characters used in Chinese (hanzi) and Japanese (kanji) writing. Sometimes used in Korea but less frequently as hangul replaced it as Korea's formal writing system centuries past.

Harabeoji / abeoji: Grandfather

Hyung: Honorific used by a younger male toward an older male he's close to.

Ibanin / iban: A different type person, a lingual play on the Korean word *ilban-in*, meaning normal person.

Jagiya: A term of endearment similar to baby or darling.

Kalbi: A sweet, soy sauce marinated short rib dish.

Kimchi / kim chee: A fermented Korean side dish made of vegetables with a variety of seasonings. Usually refers to the standard cabbage variation, which is the most common form of kim chee. If another vegetable is used, the dish will be referred to by the vegetable used, such as cucumber kim chee.

Kimchijeon / kimchi buchimgae: A griddle pancake made from kim chee and flour. Sometimes, other vegetables or meats are mixed in as well.

Kretek (Indonesian): A clove and tobacco blended cigarette originating from Java. The word comes from the sound the cloves make when burning.

Kuieo: Korean slang for queer.

Mandu: Fried or steamed dumplings made of rice or wheat flour wrappers and stuffed with a variety of ingredients.

Musang (Filipino): Wild cat, most commonly used to refer to a civet.

Ne / de: Yes

Nuna: Hyung: Honorific used by a younger male toward an older female he's close to.

Omo: Common Asian-centric sound denoting disbelief.

Oniisan (Japanese): Older brother

Oppa: Honorific used by a younger female toward an older male she's close to.

Panchan / banchan: Small dishes of food served along with cooked rice at Korean meals. Traditionally, the more formal the meal, the greater the amount of panchan.

Papas (Hispanic usage): Fries. Preferably covered with carne asada, cheese, and sour cream but plain is okay too.

Saranghae / Saranghae-yo: I love you

Sunbae: Senior or teacher. Someone who is considered a mentor.

Tatami (Japanese): Flooring mats either made of straw or other materials covered with straw rushes.

Unnie / eonni: Honorific used by a younger female toward an older female she's close to.

CHAPTER ONE

I HATE clowns.

To be fair, nobody actually loves clowns except for the sick fuckers who want to be one and those deranged weirdos who collect harlequin dolls, but in this instance, my hatred of painted-faced, floppy-shoed assholes was at an all-time high.

And after the hard kick to my shin I'd just taken from a bald guy sporting a bowler and a handlebar mustache, my general hatred for human beings was headed to new heights.

It was supposed to be a simple job—they're all supposed to be simple jobs—or so I'd been told when I'd agreed to take the case. Very simple because Esther Markensburg reassured me her soon-to-be ex-wife, Dawn, would be easy to find.

What Esther didn't share with me was Dawn ran away to join the circus. Well, a carnival. And a traveling one at that, so finding her was a bitch and a half. After a month of chasing down leads, I finally found Dawn, aka Miss Bubbles Bloo, peddling overpriced balloon animals to little kids in the sweltering California heat.

Asking around for Dawn in the first place was like running full tilt in a maze while totally blind. For every rushing inch forward, I got a pounding headache from slamming into a brick wall a step later. Carnival people are close-mouthed and odd. Flat-out, hands-down odd. There were rules only they understood, and while most of them would betray their own mother to turn a dime, they were intensely loyal when it came to rousting one of theirs over to the cops.

I learned that much after a month of digging around.

Since I was less of a cop, the said apprehension of Dawn Markensburg was rife with problems. Mainly, I merely had to serve her with her divorce papers. Nothing more. Esther was more interested in getting the divorce and keeping custody of their jointly owned poodle than anything else. Her lawyer suggested sharing the poodle's vet bills, but from the sagging state of the carnival, Esther was probably going to be paid in Circus Peanut candy and popcorn.

And fuck me if I knew how Dawn could run so fast in those damned green wobbly shoes.

The hot sun baked the carnival grounds to a crisp, and the drought we were suffering through wasn't helping a damned thing. Forecasters promised rain thick enough to make an ark builder cream in his shorts, but so far the only thing Los Angeles County had falling from the sky was more heat.

I'd nearly lost her, mostly because my alleged best friend, Bobby, shouted that he'd found her as she stood cattle-calling parents to shame them into buying a balloon. She'd taken one look at him and then at me—who he'd thoughtfully been waving down—and bolted, leaving a trail of half-inflated wiener dogs in her wake.

I gave chase, and Bobby stood there laughing his ass off while I dove into a cluster of flashing lights, ringing bells, and rigged gaming booths.

Desperation and frenzy scented the air. The carnival's gaming pavilions were set close together, creating slender walkways and packing its sparse crowd into a tight space, hoping to give the illusion of being busier than it was. Slightly faded stuffed animals stared down from their clotheslines perches, lifeless black eyes and curving grimaces mocking the few people bored enough to try their hand at a game. The pavilions' once bright red and white canvas tops were bleached from exposure, dull pink and creamy tea stripes patched together with thick dark jute.

The tents cut out a lot of sun, diffusing the light, and the large bulbs strung above the walks and around posts weren't lit yet, leaving me and the rest of the rabble soaked in steeped gray shadows.

Popcorn and wrappers crunched under my sneakers as I ran. My side ached, an adhesion under my skin tugging at my ribs. The bullet wounds were painful in the beginning, puncture holes in my body deep enough for my soul to ache as well, and they'd not healed as expected.

One of the thousand doctors I'd seen during my rehab gave me some song and dance about how my Japanese half lent to greater internal scarring, but he didn't quite explain I'd eventually end up with Cthulhu-like ribbons stretching from my skin down into my guts. The nerves wrapped into the scars were touchy today, probably in sympathy with my stomach's complaints about starvation and the sole cup of bitter black coffee I'd had that morning.

My stomach and Buddha-hand scar tissue were going to have to suck it up. I had a clown to catch.

Dawn's cotton-candy-blue afro made her easy to spot in the crowd. Unfortunately, there was also actual cotton candy, and I'd feinted more than a few times at the sight of a bobbing robin's egg floss in the crowd.

"Do you see her?" Bobby shouted at me as he pushed his way out of the masses near a toss-the-ring booth. "How the fuck did you lose her, Princess?"

Hooking up with my half brother, Ichi, did Bobby a world of good and gave me an ulcer. This was the man who routinely beat me into the mat during boxing sessions and could run me to the ground when we went out on a jog.

He'd already been a massive machine before Ichi entered his life, but my Japanese brother's food preferences were responsible for Bobby's peeling away the last bit of fat on his muscular body, or he was compensating for the decade-plus age difference between them. Either way, it was frustrating. A big brother's duty was to pound a guy's face in if he mistreated a younger sibling. I had no chance in hell of doing that to Bobby unless I got in a sucker punch… with a two-by-four.

Now he was yelling at me from across a tight walkway, startling people with his booming, growly voice. Sometimes bringing Bobby with me on a case was like taking a bear to a tea party and telling it to dance on the tables. No one has fun but the bear.

I scanned the crowd and spotted the guy who'd tried to trip me up earlier. He was barreling through a group of kids at the end of the walkway, and it looked like he'd brought a friend. The two of them were a wall of thick arms, furrowed brows, and mean looks. Since they were all sporting a variety of Happy Fun Times Carnival shirts, I gathered they were Dawn's coworkers. Avoiding them was at the top of my list… right after finding her and leaving.

"There!" I pointed at a frilly curl of blue hair bouncing up and down near a wall of stuffed animals. "By the goldfish place! Watch out for the guys behind us!"

"Go get her. I'll take care of them." Bobby craned his neck and was on the move to intercept the gang heading my way. "Meet me by the car!"

At some point in the last five minutes, the carnival had a buy-one-ticket-let-ten-people-in sale, because where I'd been able to see through the crowd, it was now like walking through an overgrown cornfield. The smell of sugar and peanuts thickened the air, giving me a contact high. The hay strewn through the walkways was damp in spots, dark and sticky from spilled sodas. I avoided a lake of melted something, probably ice cream and a bucket of iced tea.

I didn't have any qualms leaving Bobby behind. He just needed to stall them long enough for me to nab Dawn and shove court papers into her hand. The crowd jostled me, eagerly responding to a tall, ebony-skinned woman at a shooting gallery announcing a deep discount on how many ducks needed to win a big prize. She flashed me a wicked smile from her perch on the counter, knowing she'd fucked me up a little bit, and I grinned back, determined to break free of the causeway and find Dawn.

The sea of people shifted, and I popped free of the mass, gasping for any bit of virgin air I could drag in. Dawn was slipping around one of the rides, waddling as fast as her shoes would let her.

My prey was now easy to spot. Even without the hair, her oversized multidotted clown suit was bright and impossible to miss now that we were out in the open. The carnival's attendance was definitely increasing by leaps and bounds, and I edged past a woman with a pack of children, their wrists tugged upward by massive cartoon-character balloons. A plump Totoro hit me in the head as I went by, grazing my hair, and the white plastic weight dangling from the end of its string nearly poked my eye out when I slapped it out of the way.

The rides seemed to go on forever, and Dawn wasn't making good time in her slap-dash waddling. If clowns weren't already the scariest fucking thing in the world, a crazed, fixed-grin one pushing through lines of people was one butcher knife away from a horror flick. One kid began crying when Dawn's hand slapped his head as she penguin-hopped past. Then another joined the first, and the Great Wailing of the Carnival began in earnest.

I was in a Keystone Cop foot chase with a Gregorian monk soundtrack.

Elbows dug into my sides, and I almost ran over a little girl in braids. The unicorn plushy she held clutched to her chest nearly bobbled free, and I lost precious seconds making sure it stayed in her arms. Her mother gave me a thank-you or a fuck-you. I wasn't sure which, but I didn't stick around to find out.

Dawn made better headway than I did. Or she did before she ducked around a temporary barricade marked No Entry every few feet and the uneven ground hobbled her pace. I shook free of a streamer wrapped around my shin and headed to the fenced-off area, only a few strides behind my target.

Beyond the gap in the barricade, a small village of campers and trucks huddled together, some so close there was barely enough room to walk between them. The green-rotten scent of large animals hit me in the face, and I huffed a breath through my open mouth to mask the scent. It was strong, eye-watering strong, and I could see the edge of a temporary paddock, but not much else other than a long trailer painted with the carnival's red-and-yellow logo on its metal sides.

I'd stepped past the gap, and a long shadow fell over me. Heavy black boots crunched into a straggle of weeds, and I looked up to find a bowler clone with a Bozo haircut. This one was as large as the others and had a frizzy red mop nearly as wild as Dawn's wig, his gold front tooth winking at me when he snarled.

It was like the carnival was making these bruising assholes out back where they cooked up batches of scrapple and funnel cakes.

"Hey, fuckhead. You've got no business being back here," he barked. "Employees only, asshole."

"Sorry, Bozo, but I've got business with the lady over there." I nodded to Dawn, who'd somehow gotten snagged on a ground stake. She tugged at her onesie's leg, tearing the fabric, but she remained caught.

"Can't say I give a shit," Bozo spat back. "Want me to break this guy's pretty face for you, Dawn?"

"Go for it, Harvey!" Her voice was honey and dark, a sweet, dulcet roll men would pay four bucks a minute to have talk dirty to them. She tugged again and the spike gave way, pulling up from the ground. The hooked spike tangled into the fabric, and Dawn gave up trying to get it free. "God fucking damn it!"

I eyed Harvey, formerly known as Bozo, warily. His hands were the size of my boyfriend, Jae's, cat, Neko. And while I'd promised Jae I'd avoid getting shot at, things were a little unclear about an actual physical confrontation. Harvey reached for me as Dawn took a few steps, tripped over a cable, and landed flat on her face in a pile of something so foul I could smell it when she broke its surface.

Dawn's blue wig pitched off of her head as she struggled to right herself, and Bozo took my distraction as an opportunity to bash my face in.

I ducked the first swing. It whistled past my temple and glanced off of my shoulder. Glanced being the operative word. His fists were like stone, rattling my shoulder blade and spine. The yoga I'd been attempting to do with Jae for the past year helped with some of the dodging, but my aching scar tissue had other plans. A shot of sheer anguish ripped through my rib cage, and I gasped, doubling over.

He must have thought I was a professional soccer player or something from my reaction, because Bozo quickly mocked me. "I didn't even fucking touch you!"

His fist came at me again, this time driving into my stomach. The wind left me, and I did the only sensible thing I could do bent over my own knees. I punched him in the nuts.

Apparently his nuts were stone too, because he barely even flinched.

"Fuck this," I growled as he grabbed my shirt, tugging to haul me up. I went for the knees, swinging wide to catch the sides of his legs, and pushed all of my weight forward, throwing him off-balance. We went down—or rather he went down since I was already halfway there—and I punched again, aiming for a kneecap.

Something crunched beneath my knuckles, and he began to howl. Struggling to get loose of his grip, I twisted around to the chagrin of my already painful side. Another whack at Harvey's head and he went down, slamming his chin into the ground.

A few feet away, Dawn was now sitting in her own personal pile of shit and struggling to get her shoes off. With her wig gone, she seemed even crazier, a half-clown, half-blonde beach bunny mutant clad in a polka-dot vomit-inducing jumpsuit and smeared white makeup. She swore at me and grabbed a handful of steaming crap, probably to fling in my general direction, and that's when I noticed a very fuzzy, extremely grumpy face peering at me from behind an open paddock gate near Dawn's right side.

There were actually more than one, several past four, maybe even five, but it was hard to tell with their heads weaving about. They were tall, with elongated necks and disgruntled furry faces looking directly at me and Harvey. Without a damned thing between us but a formerly blue-wigged clown.

The only thing I knew about llamas I learned from a Monty Python song. They certainly were bigger than a frog but didn't have a foreboding beak or fins for swimming. All in all, I'd have been disappointed except for that line about a llama being very dangerous. Because from the looks on their collective faces, they were going to fuck up Dawn's shit. And possibly mine.

"Shit! Who left the gate open! Dawn, turn around! Don't show them your back!" Harvey screamed in agony when he tried to get up. He flopped back down, his knee giving out from under him. "Oh God, my knee!"

It was too late for Dawn. The llamas appeared to be led by the devil himself. An enormous black-and-tan beast rushed out of the paddock, his long fur sun-bleached at the ends to a caramel brown, but there was blood in his eye. Dawn was literally a sitting duck, basted in llama shit and tangled in her own shoes.

The others seemed content to mill about, a kung-fu fighting team, waiting for their turn at the main character in the movie. Or like lions, they waited for the strongest of the ravenous pack to have its fill of the prime cuts of meat before circling around to eat their dinner. Either way, Dawn was about to be introduced to four-hundred-plus pounds of wooly fury.

His ears were laid back, streamlined against his long skull, and he led with his jaw, two broad bottom teeth jutting up from his lower lip. Charging, the llama let loose a scream Tarzan would have envied and then struck Dawn with his chest.

Dawn, all one hundred and twenty pounds of her, went flying, a shit-covered, dotted bocce ball rolling across the hay-covered ground.

From El Llama Diablo's disgruntled look, I was his next target.

"Okay, McGinnis, don't turn around. No showing it your back," I muttered to myself, keeping my shoulder down in case I needed to do a Kirk and drop-roll out of the way.

The llama stamped, bucking his head down and swaying. He surged forward, trying to get at Dawn, who was lying on her back a few feet to my left, but stopped when I put myself in front of him. Up close, the thing smelled worse than I'd thought it could. Or that could have just been his breath. A diet of white-clad virgins consumed raw with a side of fava beans could do that to a llama.

"Dawn, you okay back there?" I got a groan, but I wasn't sure if it came from her or the now incapacitated Harvey. It would be my luck to wipe out the one guy who could herd these fucking things back into their pen. "Harvey! What the fuck do I do here, man?"

There was only silence to the right of me, and I risked a quick glance, keeping one eye on the llama. Harvey lay sprawled on the ground, fainted dead away. Good to know. If I survived the llama massacre and ever ran into Harvey in a dark alley, his knees were made out of glass.

"Okay, just you and me here, Bucky." I didn't know if I was supposed to make eye contact or not. Dogs were a no, but cats liked it when their pet human blinked slowly at them. I had little experience with horses other than a carriage ride in New York, and the llama didn't seem inclined to share any llama-whispering secrets with me.

The thing was tall. I wasn't short, over six feet, but the llama stared me right in the eyes. Up close. Personal. In all its snorfling, foul-breathed badness. Then he spat, nearly taking my head off with a globule of gunk, so I acted on my gut reaction on how to deal with an enraged, spitting hell-beast.

I went with a song. "You Are My Sunshine," to be exact.

I'm not the world's greatest singer. Hell, I wouldn't even put myself in the top five billion, but I could mostly hold a tune. At least good enough for a llama. I could only recall one chorus, but it seemed to be enough for the furry demon from hell. A few head weaves and a massive chest bump, hard enough to bruise my already sore ribs, then his ears came up.

He probably thought I was insane, but his teeth looked sharp and deadly. Getting my face peeled off by something called up from Satan's hairy balls wasn't my choice of how I wanted to go. I'd already laid out plans for that. Expiring after a long bout of old man sex with Jae was the last thing on my bucket list.

The llama stamped furiously, then chittered at his brethren. The herd... flock... reckoning... whatever a group of llamas were called... murmured back, shuffling about behind their demonic leader. The summoned hellspawn stepped back, shuffling a foot away, then turned his shoulders. I didn't want to break eye contact with him, not when I had a good round of choruses built up, a sunshine string of rosaries laid over one another like I was warding off a sickly vampire.

It seemed to work. Which was great because my throat was feeling raw, and I was concerned about Dawn. Harvey was on his own. I needed the man to stay conscious long enough to help me with the damned llamas, and he'd passed out like a three-year-old coming down off of a two-pound bag of M&M's.

The llama from hell trotted off, heading to rampage Downtown Los Angeles or maybe catch a beer with his buddies. Either way, he was off into the paddock, and my throat was rawer than a glory-hole addict's.

I did one final chant of sunshine. Then Dawn hit me across the face with a shovel.

"WELL, AT least your nose wasn't broken."

Bobby's consolations needed work. I was still tasting blood, but my right nostril seemed to be working again.

"And hey, I served her with the papers. There's that."

"Yeah, there's that." I took the towel off of my face. It was clean, and I balled it up, satisfied my nosebleed was done. "Fucking llamas."

"Damned clowns," he corrected as he pulled up in front of my house. "Here you go, Princess. Time to get out so I can go home and fuck your brother."

My blood, what little there was left in me, boiled.

Since Bobby could still hand me my ass and Ichi loved him—for whatever reason—I said nothing, getting out of Bobby's truck.

I did, however, slam the door as hard as I could, rattling the partially down window.

"Watch it, Princess. I might be a grandpa, but I can still fuck you up," he growled at me.

"Sure, gramps. I can't touch you. You can't touch me. Works both ways, old man," I teased back. "Thanks for the ride."

I stood in his dust for a moment, taking in the early evening. The old two-story Craftsman I'd bought after the shooting stood proudly on its large lot, the countless hours I'd spent renovating it worth every second and drop of blood I'd shed doing it. Tall oaks and red maples framed the house, and the hedges in front were recovered from their torching. I'd portioned off an enormous living space into an office for my investigation business, and a walkway led to the home part of the Craftsman—a home I shared with Jae.

Jae, who was coming down the sidewalk and heading right toward me. He simply took my breath away.

American born, Korean down to the bone, Jae'd struggled to be with me. His culture's distaste for homosexuals and being disowned by his family were enormous obstacles for him. I'd tried not to push, but I'd wanted him. In my life. In my bed. In my heart. I'd been all in almost since the moment I'd seen him. Needless to say, Jae took a little while and a lot of heartache before he decided he loved me too.

Thank God for that, because I couldn't handle losing someone else I'd fallen in love with—especially since it would've meant I'd have to watch him walk away from me.

Jae was a slinky, sensual length of muscle and pretty. His black hair was longer than when I'd first met him, pulled back into a ponytail at the base of his elegant neck and exposing his high cheekbones and full mouth. His honey-brown eyes were warm, full of love.

And something else, something troubled, and I wondered if Bobby'd called ahead to tell him I'd been clocked by a clown with a shovel.

"Hey, *agi*," I murmured, giving him a kiss.

He laughed into my mouth, amused at my affectionate butchering of an endearment.

"Your nose, Cole." Jae pulled back, skimming his fingers across my face. "Why do you always lead with your face?"

"Remind me to tell you about the llama," I replied. The trouble was still in his eyes, and I held him close. "What's wrong, Jae? What happened?"

"Animal Services called. About half an hour ago."

"What? Neko got loose and Godzillaed the neighborhood?" Frowning hurt a little bit, so I tried to smooth out my expression. "Okay, not funny. You're not laughing. Why would they call us?"

"They didn't call us. They called you. And Rick." Jae's voice was flat, a bit shaken. "They called to say they found your dog."

CHAPTER TWO

THE HOUSE—OUR house—was warm and inviting. I'd taken the large front space as my office, but the rest of it was massive enough to house a family of four comfortably. Or two gay men and a tiny demanding diva of a black cat.

The same black cat who now kneaded at my lap as if she were making a latch-hook rug with inferior yarn.

The call from Animal Services came in the middle of Jae cooking dinner, probably minutes before Bobby dropped me off. Half-chopped vegetables were still on the butcher block in the kitchen, but he'd turned the stove off, leaving whatever'd been simmering on the burner to cool.

He hadn't wanted to have *this* discussion out on the street—not in front of the hipsters rattling their cups at the bohemian coffee shop across the street or the nosy old woman a few doors down who took her dog out for more walks than it needed. Most of the time I was half tempted to get her one of those toy dogs on wheels so she could drag that around and let her aging basset hound stay home to rest.

We'd left all of that outside, and I'd come into the house to choke down the pieces of my past. Problem was, the plate I'd been served was overflowing, and I didn't know which poisonous morsel to pick up first.

"Tell me what they said." I went with the basics. We'd settled in the living room, and uncharacteristically, Jae's cat chose my lap to sit on. Of course, Neko might have sensed a cold front from her favored slave and gone with my warmth. "They found the dog. Where? Who found it... her?"

It was a her. I was pretty sure of it. It'd been so long, and the canine wasn't something I'd kept in my mind. At the time, it'd seemed like another time bomb lurking in my psyche, and I'd been halfway grateful but somewhat pissed to find she'd been taken.

Now I was all pissed, because it seemed like she'd been abandoned.

When Jae sat down next to me, I was confused. Not unhappy but confused. The sitting down next to me was nice. Definitely a good sign Jae wasn't pissed off at me. It was hard to tell sometimes. His face ran to beautiful but aloof, with a rare husky laugh and sweet, slow smile to lighten my heart. This burdened him. I could see it in the flatness of his expression. Hell, the *dog*. *Rick's* dog. It was almost too much to deal with.

"A rescue group found her by the train tracks in Torrance a few days ago. She was in poor shape. Hungry. Very dirty and matted. They got her to a vet, and they scanned her for a microchip." Jae turned toward me, crossing his legs to sit sideways on the couch. "Animal Services was notified, and they called the house, asking for Rick. I didn't know what to tell them. Apparently I've been answering a dead man's phone for a year now."

I deserved that. Mostly. There'd been good reasons... at the time. Now I questioned them significantly.

"In one way, it's good the number is the same." Jae studied me, an exact mirror of the look I often got from his cat. "But you didn't live here when Rick passed. You bought this place afterwards but kept the number. I'm confused a bit about why. Was it important to you to keep it?"

"Mostly because I... shit...." I rubbed at my face, still a bit sticky from the run through the carnival's thoroughfare. "I didn't want... I guess I kind of hoped Rick's family... or Ben's family... would change their minds and stop...."

There were no words for the emptiness I'd had inside of me then. My entire world had been Rick, Ben, and Sheila. I'd been estranged from Mike for years, and my friendship with Bobby came after the shooting. My friends were mostly Rick's friends, and I hadn't needed any other brother but Ben. I'd died in a hail of fire and pain, and when I'd been resurrected, the garden I'd built for myself was gone, and I'd been left standing alone in a desolated, vast blackness.

So I'd clung to the one thing I thought I had left... a crumb of hope someone—something—from my past would reach out and tether me to the world I'd lost.

"It sounds stupid. I know," I admitted. "But I wanted their families to be able to find me. I didn't want to disappear, I guess. Even if I felt like they were fucking erasing me out of their lives, I wasn't ready to let them go. Then after a while, I forgot about it. Guess it didn't matter anymore. Not once... I never heard from any of them again. Not until Sheila came up that walk."

I left out the part where she'd tried to murder Jae, but we'd both been there. It didn't need repeating.

"I can understand that." Jae nodded, his face relaxing from its stillness. His hand stroked at my thigh, a calm reassurance of his presence. Neko took it as a tribute and scrubbed her tiny face against his knuckles. "I do, Cole-ah. It was just a... shock, you know? I wasn't... prepared for it. The bigger question is, what are we going to do about the dog?"

We. Not you. *We.*

I didn't know what we were going to do with the dog. She'd been mostly puppy when Rick died, or at least that's how I remembered her. I'd asked Mike to see about taking care of her when I'd woken up from my coma, and he said she'd be okay. It wasn't until later that week that I'd found out Rick's parents swept in to erase him from my life... from our house... and they'd taken the dog with them.

I couldn't even remember her name.

"How the hell did she end up in Torrance?" Of course that was the first thing that came out of my mouth. "Rick's family don't even live in California. Fuck, do you think they dumped her? And she's only now been picked up?"

The enormity of the dog loomed over me. She was more than a small ball of fur. She was that damned tether I'd hoped for back when I was broken through, and now... staring at the man I loved and a cat I'd dug out of a bombed-out building with my bare hands... I didn't know what to do with the sudden reappearance of my past.

Of a tether I'd not been expecting.

"I don't know," Jae replied softly. "But there she was."

"We should at least pay her vet bills," I ventured. My gut told me what I should do, but common sense was screaming for me to wash my hands of the whole thing. I didn't want the past to come up out of the grave and eat my brains. I had enough trouble with the living. I didn't need the dead to hunt me as well. "God, Jae. I feel like... fuck... I'm sorry, but I feel... responsible. I need to figure it out. But the bills... I'll pay them—"

"I've already done that," Jae murmured softly. "I gave the vet the house card to pay her medical bills. They wanted to keep her one more day, and then she can be released."

"I—thank you." I wasn't surprised. Not really. Jae was a good soul. It was one of the reasons I loved him. "You didn't have to. I'd have—"

"It's what you'd want. I didn't have to think about it. It just *is*."

He patted my leg, smiling when I grunted at him in disgust.

"We can pick her up tomorrow after eleven in the morning."

"Pick her up? Like bring her here?" My gut did a happy dance, and my common sense threw its hands up in the air, disgusted at its second-guessing Jae. "You're okay with this? Because—"

"Because I know you, Cole-ah. You'd no sooner walk away from this dog than you walked away from Neko. You're good inside. You rescue things… people." His mouth was a warm, soft burr on my lips. Then Jae pulled away. "I told the vet we'd come get her. Now I will finish making dinner, and you go bathe. You smell like shit."

THE NUMBNESS I'd covered myself in from the moment Jae said Rick's name lasted until the hot water from the showerhead hit me. Then my world shattered, its sharp ends slicing through my sanity and leaving me weeping on the shower's tiled floor.

The pain was back. In my side. In my heart. Deep down in my soul.

It was so fucking stupid. A dog. The fucking damned dog showing up brought me back to that night when I'd lost every goddamned person I held dear.

And the hot water felt like blood on my skin.

I couldn't stop my mind from plunging back into the memories of that night. Fragments of scents and faces flashing through my brain, a zoetrope shudder of images I didn't want to see. I didn't want to recall the last kiss I'd given Rick, the feel of his mouth on mine, or the sounds of chatter and dishes clinking in the bistro's outdoor dining area.

My body still bore the marks of tearing metal. I didn't *need* to feel them again, but the damned dog brought it all back to the forefront. The pain'd been incredible, and I remembered finding God in the space of time when Rick went slack in my arms, his mouth filling with gurgling blood and the light slowly fading from his grassy-green gaze, the white lie he liked to tell with tinted contact lenses. I hated not remembering what color his eyes really were, then recalled their guileless hazel brown. I hated myself with a passion of a thousand fiery suns because my last kiss with him tasted of blood.

I'd known we'd been shot. I heard the boom, saw the flash, then the fucking goddamn agony. I knew we were dead in that forever-lasting few seconds it took for the bullets to pierce our bodies. Out of the corner of my eye, I'd seen Ben in the car, and I'd opened my mouth, begging him to stay down, to stay back, because someone was killing me and Rick... because I didn't want him to die. I didn't want my best friend, Ben, to die.

It took another flash and a report of thundering booms for me to realize it was Ben who was killing me. My Ben. My own fucking brother-in-blue and beyond.

That hurt more than any bullet, but I was gone into the darkness before I could chase the tail of that poisonous dragon any deeper into my soul.

I felt the cracks of my sanity begin across my face, shattering away the numb mask I'd somehow put on downstairs without knowing I'd tied it on. Something sharp punctured through my chest, shards of a broken heart I'd kept hidden for years.

I clutched at the shower wall, digging my fingernails into a fine line of grout, demanding myself to hold things together, but the deep pain was too much to fight, and it rose up, a lick of cold fire set free from the dark place I'd hidden it.

The tears in my eyes were scalding, hotter than the water beating my skin. My breath caught on a sob I tried to shove back down, but the sound escaped anyway, a childish whimpering scream I couldn't bite back.

I didn't want to cry. I didn't want to remourn the two men I'd lost, but the dog—Rick's fucking animal—let loose the demons I'd buried, and they came roaring back with a vengeance, hungering for any bit of my mind they could consume.

"Fuckers. Goddamn fucking sons of a—" I couldn't stop the hard, racking sobs. They shook my spine, folding my stomach up around the scars, and twisted thousands of little knives in my gut.

I didn't know who I was mad at. No, that was a lie. I was done lying to myself. Ben—I'd fucking loved Ben nearly as much as I loved Rick. Maybe more because we didn't have to delicately balance each other out. We didn't have to work to compromise over things like fucking white dishtowels or keeping track of dinner parties we owed to other couples. I didn't have to worry about birthdays or anniversaries with Ben. Instead I'd found a brother who welcomed my boyfriend into his life as if Rick was a part of me.

Not like Mike. Not like every fucking nice word I'd had to squeeze out of Mike about *anyone* I dated.

The resentment was too heavy to carry anymore. I hated them for leaving me. Hated them still for dying together. Hated Ben taking Rick. And I hated Ben the most for taking himself away from me.

Just as I hated myself for living.

I pounded at the tile, needed the solid thwack of stone to remind me I was alive. I wanted to tear down everything around me, loathing how the world continued to turn when my own life'd stopped short. And just when it felt like I'd found my way back into the light, I was dying all over again.

The shower floor was hard on my knees when I fell, the strike of stone twisting at the bruise I'd somehow gotten chasing Dawn through the carnival. I sat back on my haunches, my shoulder blades pressed into the shower's glass door, and wept.

It hurt so much. It still hurt. So did the guilt eating me up inside. For living. For loving Jae. For even falling in love again.

I hated me the most. Because Jae… goddamn Jae who made me feel again. Jae who took the fragments of my heart I'd scraped up off of a blood-splattered parking lot and reluctantly patched it together so he could love it. I was angry—so fucking angry—at loving Jae after Rick died underneath me and feeling like I'd turned my back on Rick, as if he never mattered. Not like Jae mattered now.

The door opened, nearly spilling me onto the bathroom floor. Then Jae slipped in under the water with me, kneeling in my pain.

"Cole-ah." Jae slid into the shower, his worn jeans going dark as the denim soaked up the water.

My eyes burned from crying, and I couldn't stop my jagged sobs from tearing out of my chest. A cramp ached along my ribs and down my chest, the scars from Ben's betrayal seizing up when I tried to twist away from Jae.

His touch burned nearly as hot as my tears.

"Don't…." I didn't know what I was warning him not to do. Not to hold me? God, if ever I needed someone to hold me together it was now. In that moment when I was shattering, a too hot piece of glass touched by icy cold memories, *that* was when I should have welcomed Jae's touch.

But I couldn't. It felt wrong to feel the comfort of his hands sliding across my bare shoulders or his fingers running through my hair, slicking it back from my face. He was strong. Despite me having a few pounds of muscle on him, Jae's lanky build held a granite-hard resolve. He pulled me into the curve of his body and held me, tightening his arms around my shoulders and burying my face into his chest.

I tried to protest, tried to shove him away, but my soul clung to him, and my body gave way.

Clutching Jae's T-shirt, my fingers locked on to the fabric, kinking my knuckles until they ached from being frozen in place. My joints were on fire, strained from being folded together, and at some point, the water'd gone cold.

I cried harder, thankful the stream no longer felt like blood. I was surprised to find it tasted clean, washing down my throat in a rush of Los Angeles's whiff of chemical flatness and not the searing metallic gush I'd been expecting.

"It's okay, *hyung*," Jae whispered at me under the water's shush. "I am here. We're here. Right now. And everything will be okay. I promise you."

He said other things in Korean. Coddling, soothing things I normally only heard in the deep of night after we made love. In the bright splash of the bathroom, those words almost seemed profane, a too intimate stab of affection in a place I'd crushed my heart into pieces.

"*Saranghae-yo*, Jae-Min."

I loved him so much, too much perhaps. I'd loved Rick. I'd always love Rick, and Jae understood that. Knew he was loved as much if not deeper than I'd loved Rick. I didn't deserve him. Didn't deserve his compassion or his touch or even the gentle kisses he gave the corner of my mouth when we woke in the morning and I reached for him because my cock was as glad to see him as my heart was.

"I love you very much, Cole-ah," Jae replied, softly stroking my heart with his gentle words. "We will get through this. Promise, *agi*."

THERE IS a point to crying when the body can't produce any more pain. Even as it simmers beneath the skin, no more can break through the thick mucus and sweat hardening on the surface. I'd reached that point more than an hour ago, but the *ache* of it all remained.

Lingered.

Throbbed.

I didn't poke at it, a sore spot in my heart I needed to avoid. I sat in the living room with Neko to keep me company as Jae rattled about in the kitchen. It was late, nearly nine, but Jae insisted it wasn't too late to eat. Mostly he needed to cook. It centered him like yoga or his photography. I sat on the couch, stroking Jae's tiny black cat, and stared down my life, wondering what I used as a touchstone before I had them.

The beer Jae'd left me was still full, water beading into a thick sleeve over the brown bottle's side. Neko's breath smelled of tuna—people tuna—a mostly bribe, somewhat treat for her not peeing in my shoes because we'd taken too long to get her dinner.

It was always safe to bribe the cat. One can never go wrong with a can opener and white albacore.

If only I was so easily satisfied.

"Cole-ah, do you want potato—" The doorbell rang, breaking off Jae's question.

My nerves were running too close to the surface, with too many fears brittle under my skin, and I was up off the couch and into the foyer before Jae could reach the door. He walked out of the kitchen and into the long hall, wiping his damp hands on a towel.

"What is wrong?" I'd put the worry there in his honey-brown eyes. It was there more for me than who was at the door. "Did someone call? Is that Ichi?"

The bell rang again, insisting and pushy. There was a gun in the hall closet. Locked up tight in a box and put away. I'd not touched a weapon since I'd handed my Glock to Mike because I was scared to carry it—frightened I'd shoot and kill Ben's wife, Sheila. She'd tried to kill Jae. I had no idea why I was panicking. It was stupid, but there I was, throwing reason to the wind.

Rule one about life—someone tries to kill you, you try to kill them right back. I extended that little law to those I love. For some reason, the people in my life didn't agree.

"No, no one called." I put my hand on Jae's shoulder, holding him in place. "Let me answer the door."

We battled there. In the middle of the hallway, we waged a silent argument. I didn't want him to go forward. I wanted him as far from the front door as possible. He wasn't going to cower behind me. It wasn't who he was. I knew that, but it didn't mean I didn't want to swaddle him up and carry him off.

And he'd gladly hand me my ass if I ever tried.

"I'll see who it is. Maybe it's one of those magazine things they scam kids into selling." I tried to lighten my words with a smile, but Jae wasn't buying it.

"Get out of the way, Cole." He pushed my shoulder, jostling me back. "Go sit back down. If it's not anyone we know—"

"Jae, *please.*" My voice broke, strained until it cracked into pieces smaller than what was left of my soul. "I can't... not tonight. Just let me get it. I won't risk something happening to you. It might be nothing, but I just... can't. Jae... *no.*"

The bell sang out, strident and hard. Jae met my eyes and sighed, "I don't know why—fine."

Flicking on the outside light illuminated the front walk, and an outline of someone shimmered behind the door's inset frost panes. The person was shorter than either of us and held themselves up, ramrod straight, unwavering under the bright floods. Butterflies fluttered about in my stomach, their wings sharpened to razors to cut into the soft lining of my belly. Edging up against the door, I peered through the peek hole, and my blood ran cold.

"It's not like there is anyone who can hurt me, Cole-ah," Jae continued to protest. "There's no one left who can do that."

"Really? Don't be so sure about that, *agi.*" I took a deep breath and unlocked the front door. "Because that's your aunt outside on our front porch."

CHAPTER THREE

I WAS not fluent in Korean. Not by a long shot. Neither was the cat, but I'm pretty sure she understood every single spit of hot anger being laid down on the cold tin roof of Jae's relationship with his aunt. Too wrung out from the day, I stood and wondered if I could somehow slip past them as they argued in the foyer. It would be difficult, because if there was one thing I'd found out about Kim Jae-Min, it was that he gestured and stabbed at the air when he was angry.

Apparently his aunt did too, and since I didn't think they were actually blood related, I gathered it was something one picked up when entering the family tree. All I knew was I could one day look forward to standing with my chest forward and stabbing at the air like a demented blind octopus knitting an invisible sweater for a snake.

I slid in between them when they drew in tighter, and Jae's eyes went hot and dark. It was a far cry from how he'd been when I'd first met him. Close on the heels of his cousin Hyun-Shik's funeral, he'd been rigidly polite and quiet as his aunt flung razored words at him from every direction. She controlled lives, orchestrated the movements of her little dynastic clan, and it'd been good for Jae to break free.

My biggest question was what brought her here. To our door. Tonight of all nights. When I already had the past lurching up at me with broken, rotten teeth and a hunger for my soul's flesh.

"Time out." My voice was rough. Seeing as I'd just torn it open while screaming at myself in the shower, I was going to cut it some slack. Jae's aunt, however, merely looked stunned, as if I was a chair that suddenly came to life next to her. I didn't take offense. It would be like being pissed off because a scorpion stung me when I picked it up.

"You don't need to deal with this, Cole-ah. Not her. Not now." Jae's accent thickened when he was angry. Or in the middle of sex and sometimes even when he cooked. Whenever his passions were stoked, his voice turned milky with Korean. Right now he sounded like we'd just spent the weekend naked and on sticky sheets. This did not bode well for his aunt. Whatever she came by to sell, he was not only not buying, but he was willing to burn her at the stake for crossing our threshold.

I hoped he didn't remember I'd been the one to let her in.

"I would speak with Mr. McGinnis before I leave. I didn't come here for me—" She drew herself up, an elegant, brittle woman with as poisonous a soul as I'd ever met.

"You don't do anything unless it is for *you*," Jae shot back.

"It is for your *uncle* that I am here. After all he has done for you. For your family—"

"He has everything he's ever wanted from my family, including me being out of it." My lover pointed at the door, a hard purl in his crafting. "The door is there, *Auntie*. Tell the man I once called uncle I wish him luck. May he survive whatever he's brought down on himself."

Jae was close to breaking. He was stiff, holding himself in, and his aunt was going to lose her hand if she reached for him. I caught her wrist before her fingers could touch his arm. It'd cost her to come to us. Anyone could see that, hear it in her voice as she strained to reason or barter with Jae in our main hall. I took a good, hard look at the woman who'd once turned Jae's life upside down. She was battered, her pride and ego bruised and shattered from unseen blows. Something big dragged her to our front stoop, pulled her hand up and made her push her finger against the doorbell, and then held her there as I opened the door.

"Jae?" This was going to be his call. In the sear of his anger, I knew he wasn't seeing straight. He'd probably said things he'd regret later. Okay, maybe years later, but he'd regret them. I had my own regrets I was dragging around like Marley's chains. I didn't want Jae to start forging his own.

He stared at me, a hard, cold look I normally caught when blocking his light when he lined up a shot. Unfortunately, I couldn't move a few feet away to make him happy. This one was all on him.

I didn't need to be a mind reader to know the thoughts going through his head. Reading Jae's still face was easy for me. His heart and soul lay in his gaze and the set of his mouth. The burnt-sugar anger in his eyes faded to a sweet amber, and his lips softened as he worked through his turmoil. Finally he scrubbed at his face and sighed.

"I'll go make some coffee." The next look I got was one that promised a long discussion. Possibly with shouting—or at least quiet muttering—but the slide of his hand over my stomach as he went by told me it was okay.

MANNERS KEPT Mrs. Kim's face prim and tight when she walked into the living room. Some of Jae's photos were on the wall, a few nude studies and a couple of urban landscapes I'd really liked. The nudes were black and white, pulled in close to follow the form, but lacked any facial features. One was of me, lying on my stomach with very thin white sheets draped over my ass. Unless she knew the scar patterns on my ribs, there was no way his aunt would know it was me, but I felt a blush shoot over my face anyway.

None of our friends gave us shit about that print, but I'd caught Bobby's smirk and a remark about fine asses running in the family.

I stood until she sat down, then took up a corner of the couch, unsure if I was supposed to wait until we had coffee or if it would hurry her out the door if I began the conversation now. His aunt took matters into her own hands and cleared her throat.

Then there was silence as her gaze flitted about the room again.

She was a hard woman, drawn tight and pinched. At some point she'd been a little girl, laughing and playing or perhaps not. From what I'd heard about the *chaebol*, South Korea's dynastic families, love had little to do with relationships and even less to do with marriage. Jae's immediate family lingered on the edge of a *chaebol*, but the tendrils of that particular Kim clan were insidious, slithering through every single person and tangling up their lives.

Mrs. Kim was near the top of it all, or at least in Los Angeles. Her husband had power and influence, something she wore around herself like a coat. Except now the garment was thin in spots and certainly missing a few buttons. Still, I'd never have thought that given how she held herself, despite her tugging on the hem of her skirt.

She'd come for battle, armored in a pink tweed suit with a pale yellow blouse under her jacket. For a gay man, my fashion sense wavered between everything being clean and letting a drunk toddler dress me in the morning. Living with Jae helped. Before that I'd trot over to the front office only to have my office manager, Claudia, turn me right back around to change.

Who knew all greens did not go together?

Despite the brightness of her wardrobe, Mrs. Kim looked sad and tired. She was done dragging around her familial burden and, for some reason, felt like the only one she could turn to was me. Considering what she'd done to Jae in the past, things must be totally fucked.

"You know my husband, Kim Min-Shik, yes?"

She'd softened the harshness in her voice, but the crackle of censure was still there. I wasn't sure if it was for me, Jae, or her spouse.

I nodded. I knew of him. We'd never actually met. He'd hired me for a case suspecting his son's suicide was not all it seemed, not knowing it would turn out their daughter murdered her closeted gay brother. In the end, the family lost both of their children. Hyun-Shik to the grave, while Grace, their daughter and Hyun-Shik's killer, lived in a small jail cell that no amount of wealth could open. She'd been left with her grandson, Will, and Jae's older half brother, Kim Min-Ho's illegitimate son, was moved in to take Hyun-Shik's place in the family.

I'd gotten Jae out of the whole thing—well, after a hell of a lot of emotional turmoil and work but still, *Jae*.

And no amount of money would get me to eat at their dining room table come Thanksgiving time.

Jae came with the coffee and saved both of us from small talk.

She took the cup he offered and sipped at it without asking for cream or sugar. He probably remembered how she liked it, or perhaps her poisonous tongue made everything bitter, and doctoring it did little for the taste. Mine, however, was perfect.

There was clear evidence he was not pleased she was in our house. Jae didn't ask her if she wanted anything to eat. The tray came with just three cups of coffee and a stone-faced Kim Jae-Min.

His aunt took a few more sips, then thanked Jae with a quiet nod. "My husband... Jae-Min's uncle... is in trouble."

"I do not call him uncle," Jae muttered sternly.

"Trouble how?" I asked. Jae shot me a look when I leaned forward, doing all of the tricks the police department taught me on how to get a witness to feel connected to an interviewer.

"Someone is trying to kill him," she stated flatly, as if people came after her family all the time. But then having been in the middle of a gunfight with her daughter, that wasn't outside the realm of possibility. "Your brother Mikio—Mike—has protection around him, but there is no one on his staff who can investigate the matter. They can only protect. Not—"

"Investigate," I murmured. My older brother's security firm promised discreet protection and skilled guards. He'd wanted to open up an investigation branch, offering it up to me to head. I'd turned him down, so the division lay stagnant, a dangling, withered carrot he waved in front of me every once in a while.

Usually right after I got shot at.

"He's up in San Francisco, right?" Jae frowned over his coffee.

"No, he is in Los Angeles now. In Koreatown. In the same building as Seong Min-Ho." Her face flattened, caught in an expression she almost let go before remembering where she was. A bit slipped out anyway, disgust and revulsion at the thought of her husband's gay friend.

Jae had no such qualms. "So he is near *hyung* and *nuna*?"

"On another floor. Not so close."

She was determined to keep the family separate from Seong Min-Ho and his *katoey* lover and Jae's adopted older sister, Scarlet.

"He lives there for work. It is easier than driving down to the house every day. It's too much traffic. Too much...."

She trailed off, leaving the obvious pink elephant in the room. Her husband had no intention of ever coming home.

"Someone shot at him. Twice. First in San Francisco and again here, in Los Angeles. The first time, no one was hurt, but last week, your uncle's driver... he was killed. They shot up the car. At a stoplight and the police... they are useless."

"I'm not sure what *I* can do for you, Mrs. Kim." I eased her back to the present. "If Mike is protecting him—"

"Your brother said he would talk to you when I asked if you could help, but I came here myself to ask. I don't know where else... who else to go to. We need to find out who it is, Cole-ah," she replied, and Jae stiffened when she spoke my name.

It was too familiar, too intimate, a stretch over the formal honorific she could have used, but the tears in her eyes made me leery to make an issue over it. I also had no fricking idea how to bring it up, so I kept my mouth shut.

"I cannot lose my husband too. My grandson cannot lose his grandfather. Haven't we already lost so much?"

Tears always did me in. It was the major reason I never wanted to have kids. One little lip quiver, and they'd all be riding unicorn ponies and owning Disneyland. "Mrs. Kim, this is something for the police to handle."

"That is the problem, Cole-ah." She sniffed, taking a tissue out of a pocket in her suit. "They think I'm the one trying to kill him."

"Do you believe her?" I asked. Jae's eyes met mine in the bathroom mirror, his mouth full of water as he rinsed his teeth. Neko'd joined me on the bed, stretching out against my side, offering up her belly for a rub. I complied, ruffling her soft black fur. "Your aunt, I mean."

Jae spat, then replied, "I did not think you were talking about the cat. I don't know what to believe or... I just don't know, Cole-ah. I am... *angry* at them. Still."

I didn't blame him for being angry. Hell, I cut my father and stepmother out of my life like the cancerous growths they were. My teenaged half sisters and I communicated as often as we could, but the relationship was strained at times. An outburst from Mike during the last visit they'd made put him in the same doghouse as I was, but at least the girls were allowed to stay with him. It was a game of hot potato all of us were becoming very skilled at playing.

"Do you want me to *not* help them?" That was a harder question to ask, but I had to put it out there.

Jae flipped off the bathroom light, then padded into the bedroom. There were enough moonbeams and street light coming from the long windows set high on the wall to illuminate the room, and it turned his skin to ivory. Shadows tickled the curves of his cheekbones, and his mouth ripened under the soft glow. Supple and lean, his chest was marred by a tiny rippled scar, a reminder of how close I'd come to losing him when Sheila'd shot him. He moved gracefully, water flowing around rocks on a lazy, misty afternoon. The things he could do to my body... my mind... were extraordinary.

I loved him. Flat-out. Full-on. No holds barred. He was beautiful, complicated, quiet, with a streak of stubborn too broad to swim through when he was angry. I was lucky to have fallen in love with him, doubly so when he finally admitted he loved me back and was willing to do so out in the open.

Now his aunt circling back around muddled things, bringing old memories and hard grudges back up to the surface. I was going to be selfish and man enough to say I didn't care if his entire family fell into the fires of hell if it meant he was safe and happy.

"Let's talk about this." He climbed into the bed next to me, his cotton pants rubbing at my bare legs as he made himself comfortable. Reaching across my belly, he stroked at the cat's head when she mewed from her sprawl on my other side. I was tired, too worn out to do anything but talk, but my cock tingled a soft hello from its nest beneath my briefs, happy to have Jae near it. "I wasn't expecting to see her. It's odd when the past I've locked away comes jumping out at me."

"Pretty much how I felt about the dog," I muttered. "Thing is, she's a lot easier to deal with than your aunt."

"The dog I can handle. I like dogs." Jae rested his chin on my chest. "I do not like my aunt."

"So back to my original question… talk to Mike in the morning about your aunt? Or blow her off?" His sigh ghosted over my nipple, and my dick did another tingle to remind me it was awake. "It's really your call, babe. If you want me to help your family, I will."

"I'll feel like shit if I say forget about them. I know I will. *You* knew I would too. So yes, tell Mike you'll help her, but don't get shot doing it."

Jae gently eased Neko away from me, then slithered up my body to press his mouth against mine.

"Now, as for blowing off, I have you for that."

"That's a blow *job*."

Jae's smile was wicked and promising. "Ah, you will have to show me the difference."

CHAPTER FOUR

AFTER A brief conversation on the phone, I agreed to meet Mike and Mr. Kim in Koreatown. It was a short drive from the Craftsman, a few turns and a long stretch of streets, and since Jae'd come into my life, I spent a hell of a lot of time down in Koreatown, so I mostly knew where I was going. What I didn't plan for was a drastic sale at one of the Korean grocery stores and the thousands of people who flocked to the corner of W. 6th for cheap napa cabbage.

Actually, I should have planned on it, because Jae'd told me he was avoiding the place, even though he was tempted by a crate of mangoes for three bucks. I'd asked him if he wanted me to stop and grab some on the way home from my meeting, and he gave me a look that clearly questioned my sanity.

Having spent over half an hour sitting behind the smoky exhaust of an orange Mitsubishi filled with old Korean women and a very patient-looking young male driver, I conceded to Jae's assessment of my mental health. An opening cracked in the traffic, and I slid the Rover into the other lane, leaving the carload of *ajumma* behind.

Koreatown ebbs and flows, expanding and contracting into its surroundings as the months go by. When I'd first moved to Los Angeles, Koreatown was still recovering from an exodus of its population following the riots. It was honeycombed with various non-Korean businesses and residential areas, but over time, it oozed back into its old areas, filling itself in before spilling out. With growth came a bit of gentrification, but for the most part, Koreatown remained entrenched in its traditional closed-door roots. There were plenty of hidden treasures, but you had to know someone who knew someone to find them.

I now happened to know a lot of someones, so I was aware of what I was walking into, even if Mike hadn't told me what to expect.

Finding a parking space took me nearly as long as it did to drive to the tall glass building across of the Korean embassy, but the universe took pity on me just as I was about to give up and put the Rover in a parking garage down the street. A sleek black sedan pulled out of a spot near the front door, and I nearly wrenched my shoulder hastily getting my SUV into the space. I kept my car door slightly open while a bus zoomed by, the hot wind of its exhaust catching me in the face. Then I headed into the building, nodding at the short man who pulled the door open for me.

From the outside, the building looked like a typical LA skyscraper. Clad in mirrored panels and with a lobby weighted down with veined marble, it smelled of paper, long hours, and office workers desperate for Fridays. Many Asian interests held suites behind heavy wooden doors marked with discreet gold letters, mostly in Korean, but there were smatters of English and Japanese as well. The halls off the main lobby led to two banks of elevators and were covered with a lush moss-hued carpet, while a pleasant-faced older woman manned a reception desk set in the middle of the marble ocean.

"*An nyoung ha seh yo.*" My greeting took her aback, but other than a brief flinch of a confused frown, the receptionist recovered quickly, returning my hello. She stood up, probably intending to intercept me when I headed to the far set of elevators behind her, but holding up the sleek metallic black card I'd had in my pocket stopped her.

It was kind of like playing a Black Lotus among a pack of newbies. She stuttered, backpedaled, and grabbed at the desk when her low heels slid on the marble. I paused to help her, but she waved me off, telling me she was fine.

"Have a good afternoon."

She gave me a bow, much deeper than I deserved, and turned pink when I bobbed along with her. The woman was about to go into round two, but I headed to the elevator. I'd already been caught more than once in a lengthy courtesy game. Longer than playing Monopoly with drunks.

A large, thick-bodied Korean man dressed all in black was the only sign there could possibly be an exclusive club behind the door by the back elevators. His muscles bulged out from under his short shirtsleeves, stretching the material to the point where I worried for the stitching. I had my card ready for my approach, and he smiled tightly when I got near, showing me a gold-rimmed front tooth. The tooth was familiar, but I didn't recognize him. For all I knew, the tooth thing was a uniform of sorts among Korean bodyguards. I'd met a lot of those since knowing Scarlet and Jae.

My card was scanned, and the door clicked open for me. I thanked him with enough curve on it to seem sincere, then stepped inside, right into the Simjang Club.

I'd never met the club's owner, but it only took three steps into the door the first time I'd visited to realize he loved Vegas, the Rat Pack, and a brightly colored drink, because there was enough neon to light up the Strip. Jae and I were given a membership by Scarlet's lover, Min-Ho, and went a few times with them, mostly because it was someplace Min-Ho did business at and they made a mean steak. Prices were steep, the drinks were potent, and the waitresses were gorgeous Korean women wearing red halter dresses and tottering around on nosebleed heels.

Taking up most of the first floor's back half, the Simjang's windowless walls ran to honey oak wainscoting and cream plaster, and the booths were wide, circular monstrosities ringing the club's restaurant area. A few larger tables took up space in the middle, covered with starched white tablecloths and heavy place settings. There was another double door on the far wall. I avoided that room, mostly because I didn't gamble. I also couldn't afford to lose the millions shuttling around on the poker and *godori*.

I spotted Mike before he saw me, and I was glad for it, because it sure as hell looked like he was sitting with Scarlet's *hyung*. A younger version of the man who'd been a bit of a protector to Jae and certainly someone we both considered a good friend, so I knew him pretty well. Unlike Kim, whom I'd never actually met.

To say I was confused was an understatement. Jae and I never spoke of his family. He wasn't much of a sharer where they were concerned, and I sure as hell wasn't going to push. We had his sisters over every once in a while, and that was pretty much the extent of our involvement. I'd never met his mother or his older brother. His genetic lines were a tangled fishing net of treachery and subterfuge, and I had no intention of sticking my foot into it unless he asked me to.

Which was why I was at Simjang meeting a man who paid me to find out who killed his son. I'd been asked to stick my foot in, but I wasn't sure how it was going to go down between us. I'd handed his daughter over as the murderer and banked my own rage at his neglect in taking care of my lover when Jae was underage and living in the Kim household.

I was going to go with civil politeness. Hopefully he'd do the same, and we could both walk out of the club alive and well. I wasn't carrying anymore, so the chances of him being shot were minimal, at least from me.

Mike caught sight of me and waved me over, standing as I approached. Kim remained seated until I was nearly on them, then slowly rose, brushing at the front of his dark gray suit. Up close, he looked even more like Seong Min-Ho than before, with nearly the same placid expression Min-Ho wrapped over his face when meeting someone new.

My brother and I were going to have a little discussion of our own after we were done with Kim.

Mike looked the same, dressed in a dark gray business suit that screamed security detail. There was a bit of weary to his face, but I'd expected to see that. His wife, Maddy, was entering her last trimester, and impending fatherhood hung on him heavily, a chain-mail tunic of worry he forged link by link with every passing day. His hair was longer than I'd ever seen him wear it since we were kids, nearly flopping over his forehead and down the sides of his square head, a very different look from the severe hedgehog bristle and fade he preferred. The rest of him was as it always was. He was still shorter than me and stockier, more bulldog tough than graceful, and for the most part, the bossiest, most caring person I'd ever known.

Until I met my mostly mother and sometimes office manager, Claudia—then Mike fell to a distant second, but still, he gave it his all. He just couldn't hold his own against a Southern-born black woman who'd single-handedly raised eight sons. But then, who could?

"Cole, this is Kim Min-Shik. Min-Shik, I'd like you to meet my brother, Cole McGinnis." Mike smiled warmly at both of us, as if we'd never spoken on the phone or his daughter hadn't tried to aerate me with a hail of bullets.

"It is a pleasure to finally meet you, Mr. McGinnis." He held his hand out, squat fingered and broad. "Thank you for all you've done for my family. I know it has been trying at times, but I am grateful for your perseverance in the matter."

The man was tanned and about six inches shorter than me, with a few silvering strands running through his short black hair. Kim's suit was trimmed neatly to his triangular torso, and he was more legs than chest, different from Seong's nearly even body ratio, but his dark brown eyes were almost identical, down to the crow's-feet creases at their corners. He wore Bleu de Chanel, an oddly fruity, sweet scent for a man who wore his power as tightly buttoned to him as his shirt, and as I shook his right hand, I noticed his left was missing a wedding ring. And from his fingers' even skin tone, I'd have sworn he'd never put one on before.

"I was glad to help. Anything for Jae-Min's family." It was a small dig and childish on my part, but I took a bit of satisfaction in his used-car-salesman smile faltering for a second. Okay, so I hadn't quite forgiven the Kims for tossing Jae out the first time, then trying to ruin his life later, but I owned my pettiness. I waited for Mike to slide in, then sat down next to him. "My brother tells me you're having some difficulties. And my condolences for the loss of your employee."

His chin went up, and his eyes flicked over to Mike, who frowned at me.

"I wasn't aware your brother filled you in on so much. We'd agreed to discuss everything here."

"Full disclosure, then. Your wife came to our house last night and asked me to investigate." I might have heard a groan come from Mike, but there was a definite hiss on the Kim side of the table. "She didn't have a lot of information to give, but I figured I'd get that today."

"I'm sorry she went to you. It wasn't…." Kim was struggling with his words, brief flashes of emotion roiling under his expression. He flattened his lips, then took a sip of his bourbon, licking at the corner of his mouth to catch a stray drop. "Ha-Eun shouldn't have bothered you. I know she's been… difficult with Jae-Min."

Difficult. My brain nearly broke into guffaws at the word. I stopped a snort from slipping out of my nose.

"Don't worry about it. I'm here because Jae asked me to be. Regardless of what's happened, you're still his family," I said as pleasantly as I could. Mike shifted on the green vinyl seat next to me, and I prepared my ribs for a jab from his elbow. "Why don't you tell me what's going on?"

"Someone is trying to kill me. That is all I know. The police suspect my wife, and to be honest, I'm not sure she wouldn't have a hand in it." He held up his own hand, the one lacking a ring. "Yes, she might have come to you, but that would be a manipulation on her part. Her family is very… ruthless. She and I are very estranged and have been for years."

"I'm confused as to why you're still married to her, then." This time I got the elbow, and I muffled a grunt so Mike didn't know he got the hit in.

"We have… connections, deep ones. Ones we cannot sever. Our families arranged our marriage. In the beginning, it worked out well, but after… Hyun-Shik's proclivities emerged, it splintered. I did my best to patch things as I could, but Ha-Eun had other ideas on how to fix things."

His shrug was small, and I wasn't sure what blame he was trying to erase, if any.

"I left the family to her. We were… pulling at one another. It was better for us to go our separate ways, even if we cannot break our marriage. I'd expected her to go on with her life. I've gone on with mine."

This was the man who'd bought his son, Hyun-Shik, a membership to a gay sex club so Hyun-Shik had a place to go and be deviant, as Jae's aunt'd put it. This was also the man who'd let his wife toss Jae to the curb so he'd end up working at that exact same club. The shrug wasn't helping me forgive him for that.

I took a deep breath and asked for an iced coffee when the waitress sashayed up to our table. Unlike Jae's uncle, eleven in the morning seemed a bit early to begin altering my senses.

"Let's clarify a few things. Why would she—Ha-Eun—try to kill you? What does she gain from that?" A chilled bottle of milk coffee appeared before I even had a chance to blink again, and the red-dressed waitress left refills of Mike's soda and Min-Shik's bourbon on the table. "Lay this out for me. Is she seeing someone else? Another guy who'd want you dead?"

"My estate is split into two, with monthly allowances set aside for Ha-Eun. Everything is split evenly between Hyun-Shik's son and Jae-Su, my son with Kim Bo-Yun." He picked up the bourbon but didn't drink it. Instead he swirled it about, clinking the ice against the glass. "Will is still a toddler, and Jae-Su isn't strong enough to run my business. My wife could make a good case to the board of directors that she should take over, at least until the boys are old enough."

"She's been a housewife for what? Almost thirty years? Unless I'm missing something," I replied. "Why would they hand over control of your company to her?"

"Because she's from a very powerful *chaebol* family and has been… I'm not sure what they call it—" He looked to my brother.

"Social engineering. Backdoor stuff," Mike supplied softly. "She's set herself up as an unpaid liaison for her family's electronics business. Ha-Eun isn't a housewife hosting Tupperware parties. She's been brokering deals for the past decade or so."

"Most of the board are related to her or owe favors to her family, but she's based here. If she's found someone to kill me, she'd have to find them here, in Los Angeles. The man who blocked our car in and killed Derek Park, my driver, screamed at us in English. I gave my description to the police and to Mike's sketch artist, but I don't know who he was. He wasn't Korean."

"I don't see how I'm going to be able to help. It's not like I have connections to Killers 'R Us." The coffee was cold against the hot of my throat, soothing a bit of the anger I'd held in.

"You do to this one, Cole. It's why I debated bringing you in. Sketches came back with a few mug shots. Cops ran Min-Shik through a photo lineup, and this is who he picked out." My brother took a small tablet out of his inside suit pocket. A few taps on the screen called up what he wanted to show me, and he tilted the tablet so I could see it. "Looks like our shooter was Jeff Rollins. Your Jeff Rollins."

Jeff *fucking* Rollins. Certainly not mine, per se, but at one time, he certainly had been.

The on-screen photo was a chilling slice of my past coming up to slap me across the face. The man staring back at me with cold, hard blue eyes was familiar. So very familiar. He was older, understandably so, because I'd not seen him in over ten years, but the firmly set jaw and hawk nose was pure Jeff. Unforgiving, judgmental, and most of all, unwavering in his beliefs.

The last time I'd seen Rollins, he'd been walking out of the squad room with all of his possessions in a brown cardboard box used to ship printer paper. Despite being stripped of his badge and gun, he'd held his shoulders up, his spine ramrod straight as he strode out of the police station. He'd been my mentor and senior partner while I'd worn a rookie uniform, and it'd been a shock to see him ousted from the one job I'd thought he'd been born to do.

He'd also been my biggest secret, one I couldn't share with anyone on the force. Not then. And after he'd left... the station and my life... it no longer mattered, so I'd buried Jeff away, much like I'd buried Ben and Rick.

My ex-lover was back, and it looked like he was trying to kill Jae's uncle.

CHAPTER FIVE

WE TALKED out the shootings with Kim Min-Shik until my head hurt. He was either the most unobservant man in the world, or he was hiding something. Since I knew the Kims' behaviors fairly well, I was going with the latter. When I'd first met Jae, getting information out of him was like pulling teeth from an unanesthetized gator. Improbable, dangerous, and very unlikely to yield anything of use.

He'd since warmed up and trusted me. The same could not be said for his uncle.

A stern-faced black man approached us after about an hour of going through the roundabout of Min-Shik's memory. His suit was cut generously around his shoulders, hanging a boxy line of fabric down his hips. His bald head gleamed with pink and green stripes when he passed near the neon martini glasses on the bar wall, and I stiffened, not liking the determined look on his face.

"He's one of mine, Cole," Mike said softly as the lean man stood by the table and gave us a curt nod. "Min-Shik, your detail's ready to take you to your afternoon appointments. This is Martin Frazier. He'll be heading the team assigned to you."

"Mr. Kim." Frazier shook Min-Shik's hand, then moved aside to let Kim out of the booth. "Car's parked across the street, Mr. McGinnis. If you'd like to wait in the lobby, I can bring it around to the front so Mr. Kim's exposure will be minimal. If that's all right with you, Mr. Kim."

It took me a second to realize he wasn't talking to me. I was used to being the only McGinnis at a table where men with guns stood announcing their plans. Mike nodded, all business, and pushed at my leg, urging me to get out.

"That'll be fine, Martin." Min-Shik drained the rest of his bourbon in a swift gulp. I admired his ability to hold his liquor, because if it were me, I'd be a slithering mess after the first two tumblers. Min-Shik stood without a quaver in sight, buttoning his suit up once he was out of the booth. "I'll see you in a few minutes. If you all will excuse me, I'll use the restroom before I go. It is a long wait through downtown traffic right now."

Frazier left us with a turn of his heel and a smart nod at my brother. By the time I slid over the green vinyl seat and got up, he was gone, swallowed up by the shadows pooling by the club's entrance. Min-Shik was less stealthy but nearly as quick, smiling at a waitress before he ducked into the men's bathroom.

"Swear to God, it's like you hold auditions for guys to play Batman," I muttered at my older brother. "Or Mange. He looked like he could hiss and slither with the best of them."

Mike barely looked up as he signed the tab for our drinks. "Frazier is one of our best. You'd know that if you worked for me. I'll even throw in a free Batmobile if you want."

"No, I'm good. Last thing I need is for Jae to have access to something with jet engines." I shuddered at the thought. "Although if you're talking about the Tumbler from the last movies, I'd reconsider."

"If Jae doesn't need jet engines, you certainly don't need something that can roll over other cars."

Mike shook his head when I snorted at him.

"After this, you're going to go get the dog, right?"

"Yeah, down in Torrance. Why?" I'd told Mike about her when we spoke earlier. Normally I'd have waited to share something like that, because as usual, my brother had his own opinions about what I should or should not do with my life.

"You sure? About bringing it home?" He tossed a twenty down on the table for a tip, then turned to face me. "And Jae's onboard with it?"

"Jae's the one who told the vet we're bringing her home." I didn't want to talk about this with Mike. Still tender from the stabbing my soul took the night before, I needed him to leave things alone. At least until I was ready to take a good hard look at them myself.

"There are other options, you know. I can ask around to see if anyone wants her. Or you could pay someone to foster her. I'm just worried you're taking her in because… hell, I don't know why you're doing this. Guilt over Sheila? Because you couldn't help her? Guilt over Rick?"

Mike put a hand on my arm when I tried to step away.

"Cole, the thing with Sheila nearly drove you over the edge. Do you really want to open up that can of worms again?"

"Mike, I know you're worried, but it'll be okay." I didn't tug away. Instead I patted Mike's hand and said quietly, "She deserves someplace where she can be loved and be safe. Because out of all of us whose lives went to shit because of Ben, she's the only one I *can* bring home. So yeah, she's coming home."

WE MADE it as far as a foot outside of the building's front door when hot bullets sprayed the sun-warmed glass. The noise of gunfire ricocheted off of the tall skyscrapers around us, a pop-pop noise booming loud enough to rattle my hearing. It seemed to go on forever, a strike of noise slapping at us as soon as our shoes hit the long strip of concrete sidewalk near the street, and then my brain kicked into action.

I grabbed Mike first, shoving him down. He'd been more security conscious, still on the job and his mind focused on Min-Shik. My lizard brain apparently didn't work that way. I was more focused on keeping my brother alive. Jae's not-quite uncle could apparently go fuck off and take care of himself in the middle of a drive-by as far as my mind was concerned.

A long second later, my common sense overrode my instincts, and I grabbed at the oddly reluctant Min-Shik, helping Mike pull him behind a round planter.

"You carrying?" Mike shouted at me.

It was hard to hear. The gunfire was sporadic and seemingly chaotic. Car alarms were going off, and people were screaming, adding to the waterfall of sound pouring over us. I shook my head, and Mike cursed.

"Hey, you're the one who suggested I don't carry my Glock on me." I checked over Min-Shik. He had a cut across his cheek, beading blood over his now pasty skin. Shock widened his eyes, his pupils blown out, and I wondered if he'd struck his head somehow when we'd dragged him down. Then I remembered the constant river of bourbon he'd downed inside the club. "Do you see Frazier? Is the car you sent armored?"

We'd seen the car pull up, and Mike's phone burbled to tell us it was good to come out. There hadn't been enough time to make a visual of Frazier, and part of me wondered if it was even him who'd driven up. I couldn't tell where the shooter was, but the gunfire seemed concentrated on our side of the street.

A shuddering pop of bullets followed my train of thought, and the building's remaining front windows shattered, spraying us with tiny clear pebbles of safety glass. Leaves rained down on us as the large planter we were hiding behind lost part of its treetop.

"Someone's in the car. On the passenger side."

Mike looked like he was about to stick his head out to look, so I grabbed his collar, jerking him back.

"I need to check on Frazier."

"Some asshole is shooting at us, Mike."

He glared at me, and I played the one trump card I would now forever have up my sleeve. "Do you really want me to be your kid's sole masculine influence in its life? Keep your fucking head down."

"I hate you so hard right now," he muttered back but thankfully remained behind the planter. Glancing over his shoulder, Mike frowned. "How's Min-Shik?"

"Fine." I kept crouched but scooted back a bit, raking my palms on the rough sidewalk. "Bit shell-shocked."

"I think the shooting's stopped. Calling the cops. Check on Kim, okay?" Mike was already on his phone before I could answer him.

The planter was long and hip high, raised up from the sidewalk by a cement step, and it gave us a nice stretch of cover to hide behind. If the shooter'd been thinking straight, he'd have waited until we were next to the street to start his spree. A quick check of the surroundings reassured me there weren't any major injuries, or at least none that I could see.

"You doing okay there, Kim?" I pivoted, keeping my head down, and got a better look at Min-Shik. The cut on his cheek was closed, but his eyes were still glassy. Patting him down, I searched for any wet spots, scared he'd been hit and I hadn't noticed. His hands were shaking, and his face turned a sickly green as I checked him over. "If you're going to puke, turn your head. Don't get any on me, okay? Are you hit? Are you bleeding anywhere?"

"No, no. I'm—"

The vomit came hard and fast, a torrent of hot gushing sick stinking of liquor and bile. He got my shoes and a bit of my leg, but I shuffled back fast enough to avoid getting any of it down my shirt.

Bending him over to empty his guts on the pavement, I listened to him making wet gacking sounds I'd sooner expect from Bill the Cat than a powerful Korean executive, but being shot at could do that to a guy. Patting his back in sympathy, I murmured, "Don't worry. You get used to it after a while. Trust me. The first two times are the scariest. After that? Getting shot at is like a walk in the park."

TORRANCE IS an odd city. It sits in the county's crotch and is pretty much the smallest if even existent blip on everyone's radar when they think of Los Angeles.

It's also exactly what anyone who doesn't live in California thinks the state looks like.

Draped over a twenty-mile lip of white sand beaches, Torrance is less like a blonde beach bunny and more like that one hot cousin third removed at the family BBQs who'd sneak you a shot of tequila when your mom wasn't looking. Kind of pretty. Way out of your league. And you never knew existed until just that moment. So, beyond the crystalline beaches, palm trees, ocean views, and low crime rate, Torrance didn't have much going for it.

"Are you sure you are all right?" Jae eyed me from the passenger seat. He looked a bit grumpy at not driving us down, but I'd had enough revelations to last me a few hours, and I didn't need to see the Gates of Hell as well, a common occurrence when Jae took the wheel. He drove like he fought, aggressive, succinct, and with a precise knowledge of how to skewer into a tight space.

Suffice it to say, his driving scared the fuck out of me.

"I'm fine, babe. Promise." Other than a scuff on my palm, I was okay. Rattled a bit, which was surprising considering how often I'd been shot at in Koreatown, but that was probably par for the course. "Just my hands where I scuffed."

"And Uncle is okay?"

"Yeah, *Uncle*. Let's talk about your uncle." I risked returning his side-eye with one of my own. "He's really a cousin, right?"

"Older, so I call him uncle." Jae made a face. "He's also my brother's father. It's… complicated, so uncle seemed like the most respectful at the time."

"Want to tell me about why he looks like Seong?" The crease between Jae's eyebrows was slight. "Like exactly like Min-Ho—that *hyung*?"

"They're half brothers. I thought I told you. It is how he knew about Dorthi Ki Seu and where Hyun-Shik could go to be… *gay*." As creases went, this one was deep. "They share a mother. *Hyung's* older. His father died in the war, I think."

"I'd always wondered at the connection between the two of you. Min-Ho's always lurking there, kind of like a giant head floating in front of a curtain."

"Any connection I have with *hyung* is because of *nuna*. Without Scarlet, he wouldn't know me," Jae clarified. "Not really. My mother isn't… our last name is Kim because it is her last name. We don't all share the same father, so she is not very… welcome in the family as a whole."

"That woman gets nicer and nicer with everything I hear about her." I reached over and patted Jae's thigh. "Well, I got the best of the batch she's cooked up. Just so you know."

We drove in silence for about half a block before Jae poked back at me. "So this Jeff, he was your boyfriend before Rick?"

"Boyfriend's a strong word for what we were." It seemed strange to discuss Jeff, especially after so many years had slipped by since I'd seen him last. "I was partnered up with him, and he took a lot of shit for it. He was kind of the epitome of a rough, masculine cop, and there I was, a rookie who wasn't going to be in the closet. I had a bit of a chip on my shoulder back then. He kind of helped knock it off.

"One night he came over to the little box apartment I had and we got drunk. Next thing I knew, he was fucking me and telling me I was driving him crazy." I shrugged at Jae's hiss. "I was a kid, and Rollins was… kind of what I needed then. It lasted about six months. Then he was off the force, and I was partnered up with someone else."

"What did they kick him off for?" Jae'd heard me talk about the wide spectrum of cops I'd worked with. "Was it bad?"

Most of them were solid, good guys like Montoya and Bobby's ex-partner Camden, but for every ten good cops, there was one who was a little sticky, and Rollins seemed perilously close to dancing that line.

"He shot a kid." I held my hand up at Jae's disgusted sneer. "To be fair, this kid had a gun on him. And not a plastic toy gun. Gangbanger up from Long Beach looking to score some brownie points with his crew, so he decided he was going to hold up a taco truck. Thirteen-year-old kid caught a bus up to Echo Park just to hold up a goddamn taco truck. Gun went off, and he winged a woman working inside, then took off down the street. Practically ran right into us.

"Jeff told him to drop it, and the kid shot at us. Blew out our squad car's front window. He returned fire while I radioed in. Got the kid in the leg and chest." It'd been one of the first times I'd heard a gun go off on the streets, and the sound rippled terror into my soul, reaching down to places I'd thought were safe from harm. "HQ was following procedures when they took his badge and gun. Shoot someone, and you're going to be pushing papers for at least a week. Everyone goes through that. No matter how many years they're on the force. Rollins felt like they were singling him out for something, so he walked off, left the job behind him."

"Did the kid live? The one he shot?" Jae asked softly.

"Yeah, well, until he did it again. Next time he went out looking for trouble, a bigger trouble bit him back. I got word about six months after Rollins walked that the kid was killed in a drug dispute. Seems like he picked the wrong pair of dealers to try to shake down for money." It was hard looking back at the times when I'd worn a uniform. In the beginning, I'd wanted to change the world. Little did I know it would end up changing me a hell of a lot more. "Jeff would have had his badge and gun back. It was a righteous shooting. But now I don't know, Jae. It looks like he's gunning for your uncle. Rollins was a dick, but he wasn't… evil. That's not the man I knew."

"Just be careful, Cole-ah. If I have a choice between you and Min-Shik, I'd rather you be the one to walk away, okay?"

"Agreed." I snuck a quick kiss to his cheek. "Hey, we're here."

There was a whiff of coconut oil and salvation in the air when we drove up to the vet's parking lot. The wood slat building was on its third or fifth life, but it seemed to be thriving. The animal hospital embraced its '50s-style roots, going a little bit crazy with a mural of black, pink, and yellow polka dots on its alley-facing side. A young girl wearing blue scrubs played with a gamboling Great Dane puppy on the greenscape behind the parking lot, one of its front legs sporting a cast as blindingly pink as the spots on the hospital wall.

A straggling pack of spandex-clad bikers zipped by, a stream of bright colors over the dark strip of road, helmeted rainbow trout focused on staying between the white painted lines of a bike lane. I slowed the Rover to let a pair of older women in sensible, crepe-soled loafers meander past, their flowery-print summer dresses nearly as bright as their smiles. The one closest to me, a cotton-candy dip of silver hair and pink cotton, waved at me when they shuffled past, her companion's eyes fixed on the cement journey in front of them, her coral-painted thin lips moving rapidly in a long-winded story.

The whole place was so fricking bucolic, I half expected Snuffleupagus to dance out of the hospital tossing glitter and rose petals on our path.

Nothing happened when I got out of the SUV. No birds alighted on my shoulder to sing me through the door, although Jae did get a bit of a halo from the sun shining behind his head when he walked around the front of the Rover. I had no sign from God that we were doing the right thing. I'd spent a good part of the wee hours of the morning sitting on the couch, sipping coffee and contemplating if I was doing right by bringing the dog into our house.

Our house. Rick's dog.

There were a bunch of other solutions. All of them viable. Paying for it—her—to be fostered was one. Giving her to a friend who already had a dog. Hell, I almost called Maddy at 3:00 a.m. to see if she knew anyone who wanted to take in a cute white-golden barky thing, because the thought of the *dog* was making me sick to my stomach.

Neko on my lap reminded me it wasn't the dog. Just like me digging her out of building rubble had not been about her. Not all of it. Mostly it'd been about Jae. Needing to be the man Jae needed me to be. Someone to turn to if he reached out.

That's why we were there. Because the past was reaching out to me—I was reaching out to me—and I needed to rise to the occasion.

I was still sick to my stomach and kind of disappointed to discover the greenscape was actually a wide swath of expensive fake grass, because tossing my stomach up on it seemed like a really good idea.

"We don't have to do this, *agi.*" Jae touched my arm, his fingers trailing down to the back of my hand. "It is up to you."

He was touching me in public. The man who'd once asked me not to stand too close to him because I set his nerves on fire and he was scared to be outed. We'd walked to get a pizza, and the terror of my touch sent him shaking under his skin. He'd held my hand that day. Or at least I refused to let it go once I'd gotten hold of him.

That was us in a nutshell. Never letting go once we'd found one another.

"No. If you're good with us taking her home, then let's do that. Vet said she was sweet and liked cats." I clasped his hand, drawing on his strength and warmth. "I still don't remember her name. It's been bugging the shit out of me."

"It'll come to you. If not, she'll get a new name." Jae grabbed for the door. It creaked when he opened it, a tiny shrieking hello accompanied by the jingle of a bell above the frame. "It'll be fine."

The inside of the vet's office was as much of a throwback as its exterior. Speckled blue and white tiles checkerboarded the floor, and a wraparound counter cut the waiting room off from a pair of hallways leading to what I imagined were examination rooms. Thick plastic sling-back chairs lined the outer walls, and off to one corner sat a pair of industrial scales in front of a partition nearly covered with animal stickers.

An old man sat in a red chair, his leg providing support to a chocolate lab nearly the color of his owner's skin. Both had a grizzle of gray hair on their faces and a dignified air about them, as if they could wait all day if necessary because each other's company was all they needed. The man nodded a silent hello. Then he and the dog went back to staring out of the window, watching the world go by.

Jae was at the counter talking to a perky young man with a Brian name tag and blue eyes sparkling with interest. For a twink he was cute, bubble gum sweet and lithe. He slid a glance over me, and his smile didn't falter one bit, but his body language shifted away from flirty to professional when I sidled up to Jae. We did a shuffle of driver's licenses, credit cards, and paperwork to prove I was the owner of one Maltese-mix female dog, just in case anyone else wanted to stroll in, pay the last thousand dollars on a vet bill, and take her home.

"If you hold on a moment, I'll bring her out. Doctor Chang would love to talk to you before you go. The doctor's very excited to see this little girl finally go home." Brian gave me another flashing grin. "I bet she'll be so happy to see her daddies after being lost."

I didn't correct him. Neither did Jae. I also wasn't sure I liked being called Daddy.

Shit, I hadn't called Bobby to tell him about the dog. Mike and Maddy knew, but not Bobby or Ichi.

There wasn't time to think about what I'd done or not done, because a second later the young woman we'd seen with the Great Dane was in the waiting area with an apricot and white shorn fur ball dancing at her side.

They'd clipped her hair short. I'd expected that. I'd been told she'd been living rough for quite a long time and had been fearful when the rescue people first approached her. Much like any McGinnis, she apparently was guided more by her gut than her brain, because she'd trotted into their arms in exchange for a hamburger. She'd become a favorite in the first few hours of her hospital stay, trading cute head cocks and tail wags for belly rubs and snacks.

Our girl was easy. A slut for affection, cheap food, and a pretty word.

She also recognized me. Something in her wee little brain clicked, fired up a roman rocket, and fixated on my presence.

Her name was Lady Butterfly Meg Murry. It hit me as she scrambled across the tile floor to get close to me, dragging the vet tech with her. Rick'd called her Lady. I'd called her Meg. She'd been a surprise breeding off of a woman's prize Maltese, and the only one left after her more robust brothers and sisters were sold. Some sort of poodle crossbreed with a face like a plush teddy bear and a tongue long enough to reach the back of my sinuses, which she'd tried for every chance she'd gotten.

Jesus Christ, I'd forgotten so fucking much of everything, either shoving it away behind a wall or maybe lost in the pain as I'd recovered, refusing to look back at the life I'd had and lost. But here was Meg, excited and happy to see me because I'd take her home.

She *knew* I was there to take her home.

And I broke down crying as soon as I picked her up and buried my face in her lemon-scented short fur.

CHAPTER SIX

"So Jeff Rollins, huh?" Bobby popped the cap off a Tsingtao and caught it as it flipped up. The evening was nice, a pleasant, cool night, and we'd come out to the yard to talk. "Jesus Christ, you were partnered with that crazy asshole? No wonder you're fucked in the head. And to think I'm letting you hold my granddaughter."

One of the reasons I'd bought the Craftsman was its backyard. The house was huge and set on the front half of the property, leaving nearly half an acre behind it. I hadn't done much with it at first, but after Jae moved in, the yard sprouted an enormous concrete pad and short walls, forming an outdoor living-dining space. I'd gotten a BBQ grill big enough to roast a couple of turkeys and paid someone to stretch triangular shades over the entire space. It looked a little bit like we were planning to host a Sydney opera, but surprisingly, they kept the area a hell of a lot cooler than I thought they would.

The perimeter already had a massive hedgerow around it, but the kid quotient was going up quickly, and the street out front was busy. We'd finally decided on a seven-foot-tall horizontal slat fence with Craftsman-style posts. A wood and wrought iron gate was set on the walk after our front door, and it looked like something a hobbit would special order out of a catalogue. Jae loved it. I kept expecting a gray-robed wizard to come rap on our door and ask us to take care of a ring for him. All in all, the fence was open enough between the slats so we had a good airflow and could see out onto the walk but not so big a kid's head could get stuck.

Bobby's son had some ears on him, so I'd imagined the grandbaby would end up looking like Dumbo when she was born. Sadly, I'd been right.

"How *is* V doing? Learned to fly yet?" I teased. "Found her a feather she could use?"

"She's doing fine. And fuck off, her ears are fine." Bobby kicked at me from the chaise he was sprawled on. He missed, but only because he didn't put much effort into it. "Jesus. Seriously, what kind of name is Venona? Sounds like something you'd name a squirrel."

"It's a good strong name. Good enough for a counterintelligence project. So maybe she'll be the princess of squirrels. Hiding secrets and shit." I countered Bobby's sour expression with a salute of my beer. "And back to your original question, Rollins wasn't that bad. Just... intense. At the time, I wasn't really paying much attention to anything other than his dick."

"And now he's killing people for a living?" He whistled under his breath. "Gotta tell you, Princess, you sure know how to pick them. How'd the two of you hook up?"

"He was one of my first partners. You know how that is. That rotation they do until you settle in—"

"Nah, I got a partner, and he stuck with me for years. Shit like that only happened to you, Princess."

"That's because dinosaurs roamed the earth when you were a rookie. The force evolved since then. I wasn't the only one on rotation, asshole," I countered. "And the thing with Rollins started when we were drunk one night, and then... shit happened. He showed up at my place with a bottle of whiskey, and next thing I knew, I was up against the wall with my pants down around my ankles with him telling me I was hot. I didn't know what was going to blow first. My dick or my mind."

"Shit, Rollins. Gay. I knew of him but didn't really know him, per se. Never would have guessed gay in a million years." He shrugged, then took a drink. "But then I guess people used to say that about me too. How deep was he? He didn't hit you, did he?"

It was a fair question, especially with some cops. I hadn't been the only gay guy on the squad. I knew of at least two others besides Rollins who'd slip into dark corners at clubs to get themselves off. They were the most violent, needing to prove themselves beyond the closet door they were standing behind. Gay cops in the past were often statistics, eating their guns or going sour.

Things changed slowly behind the blue line. No matter how many parades were marched or rainbow flags were waved, it was shitty being gay or lesbian and wearing a badge. Wong, a good friend and a detective out of Central, tells me things are different, but I had to wonder if it was really that easy for some guys to step out of that darkness.

Rollins certainly hadn't been one.

"No, he didn't hit me," I replied softly. "Came close a couple of times. Or at least that's what it felt like. It didn't last long. We hooked up maybe ten or twelve times. Then he was off the force. He was so fucking angry inside, Bobby. I mean, at the time, I didn't realize it. I was kind of pissed off too. Mike was pissing me off. I was angry because my dad and Barb didn't come to my Academy graduation. It felt like things were going to shit no matter what I did."

"When'd you realize your dad wasn't going to get his shit together about you?"

Bobby never pulled punches when we were in the ring together, and I didn't expect him to do any less outside of the ropes, but this time he was almost tenderly probing at the edges of a long-picked-over scab.

"Probably the last time I saw them. Shit, Mom—Barb—surprised the fuck out of me, you know? I guess I'd always thought Dad was the asshole about it. I didn't…." The pain was still there, raw and prickling in my soul. My emotions were running too hot already, and I couldn't… didn't want to… revisit that night. "I'm not exactly the sharpest spoon in the drawer when it comes to people."

"Gotta give you that one, Princess. Your heart's always in the right place." Bobby smirked at me. "Pity you're never in your right mind, though."

"Funny."

"Yeah, I'll be here all week."

"What? My brother tossed you out of his bed already? Too old to keep up with him?"

Another kick came my way, and this time he grazed my shin. We sat together for a moment, drinking beer and watching the bug zapper bring death to at least four insects before Bobby spoke again.

"You going to take this job why? Shouldn't the cops be handling Rollins?" He cocked his head at me, scratching at a peek of skin showing through the torn knee of his jeans. "You're a private investigator, not some rogue SWAT force. Rollins is a loose cannon, and you sure as fuck don't need to become his target."

"Mostly Mike wants me to see if I can find out where he is and who hired him," I confessed. "Rollins knows Koreatown, but back then—

before he left the force—he never even went into that part of town. Now he knows the layout, knows the traffic. If that was him today, he knew we were heading out. Knew Min-Shik… Jae's uncle… was there. Someone's getting him information. I've got to find out who."

"So that means he knows someone Min-Shik knows. Maybe hooked up with some guy, you think?" Bobby grunted. "And getting info in K-town is a bitch and a half. Like prying barnacles off of a rock."

"That's where I come in. Cop connections and Koreatown ties." It sounded good on paper, but I had my doubts. I knew a lot of people casually, on both sides of the law. "Mostly Mike wants to know who is behind Rollins. If I find out where he is holed up, I'm calling up O'Byrne or Wong. They can come take him down. I'm not getting shot up by some crazy ex-cop because of Jae's not-quite uncle. I don't think I even *like* Min-Shik, to be honest."

"So, you want help? Or are you going in alone on this?"

We finally came down to the reason Bobby pulled me outside. He laughed when I gave him my most patient, withering look.

"Don't give me that, Princess. You know Ichi's going to shove at me until I offer myself up for sacrifice. He doesn't seem to think you can handle shit on your own."

"I can totally handle my own shit." My protests were weakened by Bobby's burst of laughter. "Fuck you. If you help out, you've got to let me do things my way."

"If I do that, then we'll all be sitting at God's table wondering why the angels are laughing their asses off," he shot back. "How about if I let you think you're doing things your way and cover your butt instead?"

"That'll work," I agreed.

"*Agi!* I'm letting the dog out. Will you watch her?" Jae's voice pulled at me from the back door.

He stood in the light coming from the laundry room and peered over to where Bobby and I lounged. Before I could answer, the Creamsicle mutt we'd rescued from her stint in Torrance wiggled out from between his legs and bounded into the grass.

She spotted me and bounced toward us, her tongue lolling so far back from her open mouth I was afraid she was going to smack herself in the back of the head with it. Two ecstatic leaps forward, and her bladder took over, pinging some part of her brain to stop and pee. Her butt wiggled as she went, eager to reach me, with a goofy look on her face to tell me she'd be but a moment. As dogs went, she was sickeningly cute.

Neko had yet to be convinced.

"I got her!" I called back. "How long until dinner?"

"Maybe ten. More if Ichi doesn't get his face out of the fridge. I'll need time to kill him." Jae grinned at me, nearly the same expression as the dog's. "So maybe fifteen or twenty."

"You can take him. *Hwaiting!*"

He gave me a thumbs-up and shut the door. The dog finished peeing and gamboled over toward me, meandering about the lawn as she found small points of interest along the way.

"That dog is not right in the head. She thinks she's a cow." Bobby watched her munch a closed dandelion. "What are you guys calling her? Lady or Meg?"

"Neither. We're going with Honey." I snorted at Bobby's grimace. "New life, new name. Jae didn't like Lady, and well, Meg was out because we've got too many Ms as it is. 'Sides, Jae's dog when he was a kid was named Honey, so he likes it. She answers to anything. Not very particular."

"Exactly like you, then. Except she looks like she knows where to shit." He took another sip of his beer. "What's Mike think about the dog?"

"That I'm making a mistake," I confessed. "What do you think about her?"

"That you've made a mistake," Bobby replied sarcastically. "But then I said that about Jae too, and look how that worked out for you. They coming over? Mike and Maddy?"

"He was busy mopping up the mess with Min-Shik, and Mad Dog's not feeling too good. Dizzy." The dog finally made it to the cement but then took off after an erratically flying moth. "If she's off-balance, she doesn't want to walk around too much. She's afraid of falling and hurting the baby. So tonight it's just the four of us. She's going to throw something together at their house so we can all go over and visit them. Ichi's doing a mural in the nursery, and Jae's got some belly shot thing he's doing with her."

"Oh no, no seeing the future sister-in-law's bits." Bobby recoiled. "Too much. Too far."

"Don't think she offered to show them to us, but that's Jae's thing. I don't get involved. I just nod and say it's all pretty, then pass Mike something to throw up in. He's more nervous than she is." I snapped my fingers and got Honey's attention. She galloped over, her short ears flat against her head. I scooped her up and put her on the chaise, rubbing her belly when she flopped over onto her back.

"Think Rollins saw you? Today, I mean?" Bobby asked as he straddled his lounger. Honey wiggled down, arching her head so she was in his reach. Scratching her head, he studied me carefully. "Kind of funny a guy you partnered with ends up shooting at you and your brother. You'd think knowing you, he'd have done it way before now."

"No, not so funny. And not just that one partner. There was Ben too," I reminded him. "LA's kind of a small place, you know? You think it's huge, but it's not. Not really. We're all connected, some closer than others, but pull on one string, and you'd be amazed at how many people dance. Ben and Rollins knew each other. Shit, it was one of the first things Ben told me when I met him… that he and Rollins were pretty decent friends… but I never saw them together. I guess I forgot all about it."

"Fuck, that should have told you to get as far away from Ben as you could have gotten. Rollins was shit back then, and he's shit now." Bobby gave Honey one last pat, then stood up. "Just keep your head down on this one, Cole. You get killed, and then who am I going to get to be my best man?"

FOR BEING on the run for years, Honey settled in nicely. Or at least she let me think she did. The vet'd given us some spiel about how she needed to feel safe and to give her someplace covered to sleep at night. One stop at a giant pet supply warehouse on the way home, and we were the proud owners of a black wire kennel, several dog beds, enough treats and food to sicken an elephant, and oddly enough, a massive cat post.

Because apparently Neko would feel slighted if we came home without anything for her. Or at least that was my story and I was sticking to it.

We'd set up the boxy kennel in a corner of our bedroom, draped a towel over it, and left the door open for her to go inside to get that sense of sanctuary. Honey didn't seem to give a shit about what the vet thought she needed. Once upstairs, she dragged the dog bed out, then curled up into a wave of snores. In a matter of hours, Honey'd shed her mean life on the streets for a full dish of food, a soft, fluffy bed, and human pets, and she was out for the count.

But that could have been the big dinner and potty she had before we came upstairs.

"Are you snoring?" Jae asked from the bathroom. "Falling asleep on me is not good, *agi*."

"Nope, that would be the dog." I was toweling my hair dry when Jae came out, and what little I had left in my mind was gone in a rush of lust. I dropped the towel. Damp hair didn't seem like much of a priority anymore.

With the bathroom light doused, the bedroom was a dim wash of dark and gold, brushed with shadows from the wall sconces I'd turned on earlier. He stood at the edge of the bed, a hand's breadth away from me, probably waiting for me to say something about his naked body, slightly hard cock, and the wanton quirk of a smile he had on his face.

I growled and reached for him.

There was no question about how much I loved Jae, but there were times when he simply stole the breath out of me. Padding naked into our bedroom, wearing nothing but a few drops of water, Jae was more than enough to think I'd died and gone to heaven.

He wore my birth sign on his body, a prismatic Japanese-style rooster riding his hip and flowing down to this thigh. Brilliant blue and green tail feathers curled up against his lower spine, and the bird's flamboyant metallic head and chest glistened under his wet skin. The bird was fierce, talons out and proud, riding swirls of wind and *ume* flowers across Jae's body. He'd sat for hours under Ichi's needles, letting my younger brother ink the bold, aggressive bird under his pale skin.

Just as I'd sat for hours for the stone ox I wore on my shoulder and arm.

Jae'd wanted something vivid and passionate, saying it would represent my soul. I'd gone for a realistic fu-dog representation of his birth year, a bull carved from granite standing proud and firm at my side. He was my rock, a touchstone of sanity in the maelstrom of my life.

He carried me as I carried him, under our skin and without regrets.

So yeah, I loved the fuck out of him.

My hands were rough, callused from working on the yard and house, and he shivered when I skimmed my fingertips along the rooster's crest, tracing up the bird's spine and over Jae's hipbone. I eased him back onto the bed, then chased the streamers of goose bumps my touch left on his side with my mouth.

We both laughed when the dog gave out a loud, piggish snort, then settled down into soft wiffles.

"I can take her downstairs," Jae offered, but I shook my head.

"Nah, leave her alone." I laid down a soft kiss on Jae's belly button, my cock responding to his husky murmurs. "I like you right here."

We sometimes shared soap. By now I should have been immune to the scent of green tea on him, but I wasn't. Combined with the light musk of his skin, the earthy sweetness did something silly to my insides. There were times when I had to stop using the same gel because I got rock hard every time I showered. This was going to be one of those times.

I laved at his belly, licking off the drops of water I found there. His cock nudged my throat, begging for attention, and I rubbed my cheek against his shaft, looking up to meet his gaze. His eyes were hot, needy, and I took that as a yes to my silent question.

Pulling up onto my knees, I angled my head down and took Jae into my mouth, sliding his cock as far down my throat as I could go. He gasped, his hips rocking into me, and spat out a swearword I don't think I'd ever heard from his lips before.

Or at least it sounded like a swearword. Hard to tell in Korean sometimes, but there was enough scorch on it for me to believe he wasn't merely telling me what he'd like on his pizza.

Jae's cock was already primed to spill, a dip of salty bitter on the edge of his head, and I caught it on the roof of my mouth, spreading it around my tongue as I began to suck on him. His fingers dug into my shoulders, kneading me with light scratches. I liked the feel of him in my throat, a brushing of his velvety head at my soft palate before I drew him back out, scoring at his ridge with a light scrape of my teeth.

He growled and twisted his hips up, sliding back in. I took him in as I reached for the lube on the nightstand. My shoulder ached with the stretch, but I caught the cool bottle up on my first try. Another dig of his fingers, deeper this time, urged me on. Gripping the root of his cock, I sucked harder, pulling on his shaft when I drew off, slicking my hand with my spit. After flicking the cap, I dribbled the lube over my already damp fingers, making sure I ran some down the side of his balls.

The burst of vanilla hit my nose, and I inhaled quickly, loving the aroma of the sugary-tasting lube heating up on Jae's warm skin. Fanning my fingers under his balls, I cupped them, rolling them about while I licked at his shaft. His head was flushed, stretched tight and deep purple with his need.

"Cole-ah... *hyung!*"

He was begging, his knees rising up to let me reach any part of him I wanted. There was a lot I wanted, mostly to have him twisted up so tight in his desire I could push him to the edge and keep him there.

He pulled at his own nipples, tugging on the flat brown points until they were as hard as his dick. I ran my tongue around his slit, pressing past the tiny pout with the tip of my tongue when he rubbed his hands over his chest. Jae arched his back, diving down into the pleasure riding through his body, and with my mouth firmly over the head of his cock, I slid my fingers into his hot, grasping hole.

Jae bucked, opening himself up for me with a spread of his knees, and I clenched hard on the base of his cock, refusing to let him cum.

I kept at him, pulling him to the edge, then drawing back, slowly building up the pressure in his balls until he muttered darkly at me, needing the release. Taking one last suck of his cockhead, I pulled my fingers free of his heat and got up onto my knees between his legs. Putting my hands on his hips, I spread my fingers over his ink and lifted him up, angling his body so I could enter him.

My dick didn't need any more priming. I was so hard it hurt. My skin was stretched too tight over my body, over my cock, until I felt like if I moved wrong, I would split open and everything I had inside of me would gust out, spilling over my lover.

That was not where I needed it to be. I needed to be inside, filling Jae with my heat as he pulled himself around me, closing the circle between us.

I slid into him, slowly pushing past the tight ring of his body as Jae lifted his legs up to rest them on me. He held on, his hands on my shoulder and in my hair. Tugging my head down, Jae dragged me into a kiss, and I plunged deeper still.

There weren't words for how I felt with Jae around me. Or even in me. Our bodies were wet, sweaty, and surging against one another until our skin ran slick and hot. I couldn't tell where my cock ended and he began except for the flutter of his muscles when he clenched his ass.

"Love you," Jae whispered, his breath ghosting down my neck.

He held me to him, unwilling or unable to let me go. Tightening my arms around his waist, I pulled him up to me, fitting my hips into the curve of his ass. We moved together, slowing our rhythm until we were in time with Jae's tiny gasps.

I was engulfed, pulled in deep, so I felt the first shivering wave of his body's release when it hit. Driven by his need, I rode Jae harder, rocking against his body and drawing out every little moan and muffled scream I could.

"*Saranghae-yo*, Jae-ah," I growled, then closed my mouth over his. I needed the taste of him as I drove him over, and when another shaking tremor hit, I caught his gasping scream in my throat.

He came before I did, a lurching spasm ratcheting violently through his body. His limbs stiffened, and his ass clamped down over my cock, pulling and milking me on. The searing spill of liquid on my belly brought my balls up, curling up into tight rounds. I caught the spiced salt of Jae's scent. Then he sank his teeth into the tender skin under my jaw, and any control I had left was gone.

We moved still, both of us unwilling to let go. His hips rolled, taking me along for the final few strokes of our long, hard ride. The ache began as slowly as we ended, my muscles easing away from the rigid tightness of my climax to a languid molasses. Jae groaned when I slipped free of him, but I carefully turned him to his side, wrapping my arms around him.

I was sticky, a little bit sore, and possibly had a large hickey forming on my neck, but I couldn't name a time when I'd been happier. Jae lay next to me, his legs tangled in mine, and he sighed, brushing his fingers over my lips.

"Love you."

He gave me a soft kiss, and I nibbled on his lower lip, then let him pull away.

"I love you too, babe," I murmured as a rattling snort broke the quiet around us. "But your dog snores."

CHAPTER SEVEN

A DAY later, and Koreatown looked like it hadn't been caught in a reenactment of the OK Corral. Or at least at first glance. There were small signs of damage. The planter we'd taken cover behind was gone, and repairmen were replacing a span of windows on the building's exterior, but other than some shattered glass sitting in the gutter and glittering under the LA sun, the street continued along with its business.

I had to keep in mind this was the same district the riots spilled into back in the early '90s. K-town was an old hand at sweeping up the damage from gunfire and neglectful authorities. The area and its residents had been abandoned by the police department at the start of the violence, and Koreatown had a long memory. It'd been plunged into a war zone rivaling any in the Middle East and in many cases was still licking barely healed wounds. On the outside, its face was set, firmly Korean and put together, but beneath the mask of signs, sparkling buildings, and bustling storefronts, K-town held a grudge.

And its biggest grudge was against the LAPD, who'd turned its back when K-town needed help the most.

That's kind of what I was counting on when asking Bobby to meet me at the *soon dubu chigae* restaurant across the street from where the shooting took place.

He met me at noon, a little grumpy around the edges. I wasn't sure why. He'd been the one to cancel our run that morning, so the lack of endorphins running through his veins wasn't my fault. I'd done the slog anyway, returning home just in time to kiss Jae good-bye as he headed out, shower, then tell Claudia I was going back to the scene of the crime.

She'd purloined the dog.

"She and I will spend the day together," Claudia'd rasped through the end of her head cold. "Going to put my feet up and watch stories with Sissy. Dog might as well keep us company."

"So I pay you to put your feet up and watch stories?" I'd teased. "Thought I paid you to keep my head straight."

Her snort rivaled one of Honey's snores. "Boy, *God* ain't got enough money to pay me to keep that head of yours straight. Go do your thing, and try to come home in one piece."

The tofu house was a favorite date night spot for me and Jae. It looked like it'd been a Denny's or pancake house at some point, but with K-town, I was never sure. For the longest time I'd thought a day care down on Wilshire had been a dentist office, until Jae corrected me and told me it'd been a strip club.

Mostly now I just kept my mouth shut and took things at face value.

A porcelain-skinned older Korean woman greeted us at the door, her hair an immaculate helmet of black loose curls held together with a gallon of hairspray and sheer will. She was dressed more for church than playing hostess to a busy lunchtime crowd, but that's how she always looked. Her name tag was in Korean, but her name became a moot point about ten visits ago. Jae called her *nuna* once, and apparently that was all she wrote, because she'd been "older sister" ever since.

We were sat down, given iced barley tea and a pair of menus. I already knew what I wanted. Bobby grunted and tossed the menu back onto the table.

"I'll eat whatever you're having. You're a wuss."

Bobby scoffed at my outraged hiss.

"Dude, I know you. You're probably going to order the Korean version of a hamburger."

I had my mouth open to protest, but *nuna* slid the *panchan* onto the table and nudged me with her elbow. It was the standard fare: thin slices of fish cake, a few types of kimchee, and two small headless fried mackerel.

"He doesn't like eyes," she whispered loudly at Bobby, giving me a wink. "No worries, *dongsaeng*. I remembered. We take care of you. Same as always?"

I nodded, and Bobby told her the same for him. She left us to seat the next group, and Bobby laughed softly as I took my chopsticks out of their paper wrapper.

"Look, I don't like eyeballs. Sue me," I grumbled at Bobby under my breath.

Nuna was back, and she brought company. It'd been a few months since I'd seen Park Hong Chul, and he looked good. All things considered.

He'd cleaned up a bit from the first time I met him, chasing down an investigation so full of family secrets I needed a flowchart to figure out who was related to whom and why they wanted the last person I met dead. Along the way, Hong Chul, formerly known as C-Dog, introduced me to his little girl, gained himself a half brother, and ended up showing his metal sculptures in a few shows alongside Jae's shots.

He was stocky, built like a literal brick shit house under his pressed shirt and jeans. The tattooed gangbanger simmered beneath the surface of the shy, smiling Korean man thanking the hostess for bringing him to the table. Still, for all the neatly combed hair and pleasant manners, Hong Chul got more than a few disapproving glances from the group of older women sitting at the table across of us.

It was the neck tattoos. No matter how progressive and trendy the world becomes, some things and people are influenced by centuries-old beliefs. Jae's willingness to put the rooster on his body was a big fucking thing, probably more socially damning than admitting his love for me.

Hong Chul wore his ink now for his daughter, changing every line he'd had scribbled on his body into something beautiful in her name. Pity he couldn't do anything about his *don't-fuck-with-me* swagger.

The waitress bumped into our table, dumped a fish in front of Hong Chul, took his order, and whispered off. It was kind of like being served by a Korean roller derby girl, as she got her hits in before I was even aware she'd come around the bend. We did a round of good-to-see-you and settled in to do business.

"So you were part of the shit that went down yesterday?" Hong Chul barked a short laugh. "Should have figured it was you. You're like a bad luck charm, Cole-ah. Every time you turn up, fucking shit happens. Maybe you ought to go live on a desert island or something so the rest of us can be safe."

"Yesterday was *not* my fault." My protest was rebuffed by both of them laughing at me. I picked at my headless fish with my chopsticks and muttered, "Yeah, well fuck off. Both of you."

"Why don't you fill C-Dog here in on what shit you've stepped in so we can eat when the food gets here?" Bobby picked through the kimchee, snagging a thick clump. "And one of you can have my fish. That's a shit ton of bones to fight through."

"Cole, I'll split it with you," Hong Chul said, grabbing Bobby's mackerel. "Hey, what the fuck happened to the head?"

WE'D AGREED to eat first, then get into why I wanted their help. Bobby watched in part disgust but mostly amusement as Hong Chul finished off the last of his raw, spicy crab. I was down to sucking the last of the meat from my *kalbi*, scraping up the final grains of rice from my bowl. The hostess slipped us a couple more mackerels, sans heads, and Hong Chul sighed heavily.

"You know," he said, waving a crispy fin at me with his chopsticks. "I'm going to come in here now, and they're going to be all, look here's that poor Korean boy who won't eat fish heads. His poor mother. So much waste. You're going to get me kicked out of my house. My mom won't be able to come here no more."

"Shut up, eat, and listen." I refilled our iced tea from the plastic carafe the waitress left on the table. "I kind of need your help."

I gave Hong Chul a quick rundown of what happened, swearing him to secrecy before I revealed Kim Min-Shik's name. He blinked at me in a pretty good imitation of an owl and choked on something he had in his mouth.

"So you know him?" My fingers were sticky, and I was debating if I wanted to battle a package of wipes when Bobby tore one open and handed it to me. "Thanks, old man."

Bobby kicked me under the table, catching the support and rocking the *panchan* about. Hong Chul rescued the kimchee and kept eating, motioning me to continue talking with a wave of his hand.

"Yeah, I know him. Well, I know the stuff he runs. Well, maybe runs. Guy owns a bunch of clubs, here and up in Hollywood." Hong Chul snagged one of the wipes. "Lots of girls working through the one down the street."

"He has his fingers in a lot of pies—"

"Dude, puns." Bobby tsked.

"Pull your mind out of your ass, Dawson." I shushed him. "Mike says Kim's into a lot of entertainment stuff but a lot of investment properties and businesses. First time I dealt with the family, I wasn't paying too much attention to what he did. Didn't think it mattered, but maybe now it does."

"You're stretching, Princess. The wife's doing it." Bobby offered up his opinion.

"Rush to judgment much? And they let you make detective. All the evidence first, Dawson," I countered. "Ignore him, C. Thing is, *other* than his wife, I've got to look at anyone else who might want Kim dead. I need someone who can help me dig stuff up."

"From underneath." Hong Chul nodded. "No one's going to talk to the cops, and I've got people I can talk to. You think he pissed someone off, and they're coming after him for it? They'll want anyone around him too."

"No one's moved against the family down in Garden Grove," Bobby pointed out.

"Nah, too far. Anyone with a grudge is going to go local. You're going to hit the guy where he's around. No one's going to drop down to OC to shoot up a guy's wife."

"Especially since they live in a gated community. My worry?" I took a deep breath, sharing a trembling fear I had growing in my belly since I'd dodged bullets the day before. "I'm scared they're going to go after Jae. They're connected. So is Scarlet and Seong Min-Ho."

"The embassy guy?" Hong Chul whistled under his breath. "Nah, no one's going to hit that guy. Too many people owe him favors. Want your grandma in Jeju to come live with you? He's the guy you talk to. Way too much *chaebol* power there."

"Rollins wouldn't care. According to the cops, he's got no connection down here, but let's face it, they don't know shit about what happens down here most of the time. I can tap into some resources there 'cause they've got me on consultant status, but I'm thinking other than case updates, not much else is going to come out of that corner." The tea was smooth, and I sipped at my cup, easing the scratchiness in my throat. "I want to poke around. See if he's working for someone close to Min-Shik. *That* part I can do. But around the clubs, I don't think I'll be able to get anyone there."

"Yeah, that's me." Hong Chul pursed his lips. "Just so we're clear, I'm only asking around if Min-Shik's got someone on his ass? Or do you want me to dig into this Rollins guy too?"

"Rollins might be out of your league, there," Bobby interjected.

"You've got to be kidding me." The gangster was back, a roiling oil slick of violence under Hong Chul's smooth words. Looking at me, he jerked a thumb toward Bobby. "He's kidding me, right?"

LA's Korean gangs were small but deadly, operating under the cover of rich connections and able to slide away into a close-mouthed community. Hong Chul fought his way into the gangs, then fought his way out, but his pride was definitely sharpened by the experience. He bristled slightly, thick chest up and a bit of madness creeping into his eyes. Bobby tilted his chin up, and I had the unique opportunity of being center ring at a cockfight.

"Settle down, you fricking idiots. Look, Rollins's an ex-cop, and I know you can take care of yourself, but I don't want him honing in on you. You've got Abby to think about, remember?"

Hong Chul gave me a little irritated hiss but rolled his shoulders back at his daughter's name, settling back into his chair.

"If he comes up in any conversation, then see if you can push a little bit but not too much. We don't know where he's holed up. Talked to O'Byrne this morning, and all she could give me was the old pursuing all leads shit, and he doesn't have a permanent address listed."

"Which means no one knows." Bobby shook his head. "They're chasing ghosts, then."

"Pretty much. I don't know what they got from any witnesses yesterday, but shit was going to hell pretty fast. Shooter's angles looked like they were at street level going up, so O'Byrne said they were hoping the buildings' cameras caught a car or something." I leaned back in my chair, groaning when my stomach rebelled at the movement. "We know Rollins has guns. He used to talk about them all the time when I rode with him. Liked having an armory."

"You're going to have to do this two pronged. Dig out who hired Rollins but keep your eye out for him. Don't want him to catch us pissing against a wall because we weren't watching our backs." Bobby stretched and said, "He's one of those guys you have to worry about. Lots of weapons and a short fuse. We should see if we can hunt down anyone from the force who knows Rollins. Besides you, Princess, who did he hang with?"

"I've got a few guys I can get a hold of. There's also a couple of bars he liked to hang out at, but let's face it, it's been years. He might not have been to those places in years, but Bobby, you and I can hit those up. Might find something."

I made eye contact with the waitress, making the universal sign of needing our check with a few clam pantomimes. She nodded and turned to retrieve another table's food.

"If we catch wind of him, he's for the cops. Anything else for right now?"

"Am I doing this as payback for favors, or is there money in it for me?"

Hong Chul eyed me. I rattled off a daily rate I was willing to fork over plus any expenses he might need. Hong Chul whistled low, and the old ladies sitting across of us gave the entire table a dirty look.

"Shit, yeah. I'm in."

"You pay him but not me?" Bobby scoffed. "I see how it is."

"You've got my baby brother. You should be lucky you're still alive." I reached for the check as the waitress was about to lay the billfold on the table. "And I'm buying you lunch. If you're not an asshole, you might even get a coffee out of the deal."

"THEY HAVE any idea of where the shooter was?" Bobby paused at the tofu house's entrance, holding the door open for the three women coming up the steps.

Early afternoon on Wilshire meant people, car exhaust, and the occasional food truck squatting in hour slots with runners filling the parking meters and hawking demi-exotic meals meant to tickle the senses. LA has its own strange love affair with food, a curious dichotomy of sophistication and trash combined with a very jaded palate. Unlike the Midwest, where anything that can be deep-fried will be, LA's maverick chefs were more interested in wrapping things up, be it sushi, tacos, or flatbread.

A truck serving *kalbi* tacos was parked half a block down, giving off a sweet, smoky scent, and my stomach growled despite just having sucked clean nearly two pounds of the Korean ribs. The tofu house's parking lot was full, and Hong Chul motioned to a beat-up Toyota Camry slightly listing to the right near the entrance.

"Do you believe I'm driving that piece of shit? My mom backed into my Civic." Hong Chul jingled a set of keys with a plethora of small brightly colored plastic charms dangling from it. "I look like I'm collecting Pokémon."

"Bet your kid loves it." I studied the dangling animals. "Only one I know is the yellow one."

"Ichi can tell you each and every single one of them," Bobby groused under his breath. "Your brother's obsessed."

"Like you didn't collect GI Joes when you were a kid. He's from Japan." I bumped him as we walked to the Rover. "You're just old."

"There's like a thousand of them."

Bobby jabbed at me. It was a light hit, but it stung just the same, landing on a bruise I was still carrying from the carnival.

"Seven hundred and nineteen, depending how you count." Hong Chul shrugged when we both looked at him. "Look, it's a thing. I've got a kid. Just fucking shut up, okay?"

Bobby stopped short, and I nearly slammed into him. He pointed across the street to the building Rollins shot up yesterday. The way things were going in K-town, it was going to be easier to list the buildings where someone *hadn't* attempted to murder me.

"Hey, is that Mike?"

"You just saying that to distract from your doll collection?" I teased, trying to crane my neck over his shoulders. No, Bobby was right. It was Mike coming down the stairs, and he looked up just as I raised my hand to wave at him.

To say Mike and I had a complicated relationship was an understatement. We were stubborn, probably a legacy from our hardheaded father, and both of us had ideas on how life should be. Sometimes it was hard to reconcile seeing him as the influential CEO of an international security firm when I distinctly remembered him sliding down the curved banister of our house in Chicago and smashing his balls against the post at the bottom.

He'd definitely left that little boy behind. If I didn't know him, I'd have assumed the man in the trim dark suit and stern businessman face never got a red flush off of two beers or wept when he saw the wife's first ultrasound. He looked aloof and powerful. Until he spotted me, then his face broke out in a grin wide enough to touch his ears.

If there was a moment where I was sure my brother loved me, it was right then. In the middle of Koreatown's midday chaos, I felt our connection stronger than I'd ever before.

Which is why I felt his pain when a bullet ripped through his chest and he tumbled to the sidewalk, a boneless, helpless heap lying so fucking still amid the terrified screams rising up around us.

CHAPTER EIGHT

LIFE SHOULD go by in a solid line. From the time one is born to the time of death, with the exception of unconscious events like sleep and comas—having been in one myself—time should flow in one direction, forward. Sometimes it moves like molasses, and other times it is like shooting the rapids. But always forward.

Except when my brother is riddled with bullets in front of me and I can do nothing to stop it. Then time becomes a dashed line, jerking forward and backward in sharp, harsh stops and starts, and I can no longer tell *when* something happened or if it even happened at all.

I don't know why it was different when Jae and Claudia were shot. Maybe because it was only one bullet then. Maybe because I was all he had, and if I didn't hold my shit together, no one else would. It could have been because when it was all said and done, Mike was my older brother and the rock I clung to when the world tried to drown me with its shit and sorrow.

Was.

I wasn't ready for was.

And I was praying he wasn't either.

Literally praying.

Time'd turned sketchy. I didn't know what day it was. Fuck, I couldn't even tell anyone anything, but I needed something to anchor myself to, something bigger than the flesh and the now. My mind kept staggering between the hot flush of Mike's life pouring out of him from between my fingers as I struggled to keep him alive and the bumpy ride in the ambulance as I sat at his feet, begging a pale, freckled female EMT to save my brother.

Struggling to right myself, I had slices of memory. Jae arriving hot on the heels of me nearly slamming the emergency room tech against a wall. A very pregnant Maddy stumbling in on unsteady constructed legs and fighting Bobby as he shoved her into a wheelchair, her belly ripe and heavy with the child she carried for a life shattered by gunfire. Ichiro grabbing my arm when we watched yet another surgeon head into the room where they were carving up our brother. These all fought with the now I was living, drowning out my surroundings in a sea of stricken faces and fear.

There was a point past bitter coffee, murmured whispers, and pained looks, and I'd reached it. The day'd slipped away from me, unnoticed and forgotten. Cedars was a mass of windows, and Los Angeles stretched out beyond it, an earthbound universe speckled with moving lights and boxy lines on the horizon. I needed to breathe, to find something outside of the white walls and soft chairs, because I couldn't stand another second passing without doing something. Even if my something affected nothing, I needed to find someplace to spill out my fears and hatred against the world in general.

I found a space of peace and quiet between the hospital's two main towers, a sliver of deserted silence in the cacophony of people fighting to live or slipping under Death's heavy cloak.

The chapel was nondenominational, nearly rigidly so. A discreet sign at the door announced when services were held but reassured the wandering soul the chapel was open to any and all every single waking moment of the day.

It was empty, resonant in its calm, and I slipped in, searching out some place to sit to gather up the threads of my sanity.

That was where Claudia found me, caked in my brother's dried blood, wringing the last of my terrors from my broken soul and praying as if Satan himself was chewing on my ass.

I didn't need to look up to see who hovered at the end of the row. There was no mistaking her white and black ombré dress with large bright red poppies scattered about the skirt hem. She'd worn it once to work because she was going to a church thing afterward. I'd told her she looked pretty in it. She'd responded with something about not needing to look pretty for me but thanked me anyway.

Next morning she brought me a pie with cherries as deep red as the poppies on her dress and as sweet as her soul. I'd told her that too, but right now pie wasn't going to make the hurt go away.

"Praying isn't a bad thing to be doing right now, honey." She eased onto the long bench next to me, her warm, broad body filling the cold space to my left. Her hand found mine, Claudia's strong, heavy fingers wrapping across my knuckles tight enough to remind me I wasn't alone. "I'm just going to sit here with you, baby. Right here for when you need me."

She hadn't been upstairs when I'd left the waiting area. Or maybe she had and I just hadn't realized it, but she was there now, pulling me back from where I'd been floating and dragging me back down to the reality I'd left behind in my numbness.

For a big, fierce woman, Claudia could generate some serious calm. I steeped in her quiet, drawing in the scent of a perfume I'd bought her for Christmas, and stared at her crimson faux-alligator pumps as she stroked my back. I was bent over, curled up around the ball of pain radiating out from my stomach, while her hand soothed away the prickles along my spine.

I tried to breathe, but the air caught somewhere in my throat, and all I could do was gasp, choking on my own tongue. My eyes watered, and I was trapped in the stink of wearing my brother's blood on me while outside the man who shot him—a man who'd once fucked me and I'd depended on having my back while on patrol—continued about his fucking life as if Mike didn't matter.

"He's going to die, you know." I finally found the words I had buried in my throat.

"We don't know that yet, baby boy," she murmured, her voice hushed down to a melodic roll. "Only God knows what's planned for us, and sometimes—and not to second-guess our Lord—but I wish he'd be a bit more forthcoming with the good news bit of things. Mike is strong. You'll see, baby. He'll be okay."

"I don't mean Mike." In the middle of my numb senses was a solid truth, and I'd stumbled upon it, stubbing my brain on the obvious. I was tired of being taken from. Tired of losing people I loved because I didn't strike first. This time was going to be different, and there was no turning the other cheek or any of the fucking nonsense about letting the cops deal with things. "Rollins. I am going to find him, and I am going to kill him. Because the fucking son of a bitch needs to die for what he's done to me. My family. To Maddy. Everyone. Especially to Mike. If it is the last thing I ever do in my life, I am going to put him into the ground. I promise you that."

Her hand stopped in midstroke, and I glanced up to the left, staring into Claudia's soft brown eyes. There was so much pity in them, I'd have drowned if I weren't already soaked with my own tears.

"Don't look at me that way, Claudia." My voice broke, shattered like glass under the weight of her disappointment. "I can't do this anymore. I just fucking can't."

I don't know what I'd expected from her. Knowing how she'd raised her eight sons into adulthood, perhaps a sharp slap across my face to knock some sense into me, but the world is a crueler place than that. Instead she turned in her seat and folded me in, wrapping her arms around my shoulders, and buried me in the soft wrap of her body.

I'd rather have had the slap. I'd rather have had the violence. I needed something sharp to cut out the pain inside of me because I didn't want it anymore. I didn't want to feel it anymore. I was scared about having my brother's kid look up at me with Mike's owlish eyes and hedgehog hair to ask me to tell them about their father. I didn't want to hold Maddy's hand when we lowered Mike's remains into the ground. And I sure as shit didn't need to stare down my life without having to push back at my bossy brother's interference and fight with him over what flavor of Pop-Tarts was the best.

I shouldn't win our arguments because his voice wasn't around anymore. I couldn't lead that life. Even with everyone else around me, I *refused* to have a Mike-sized hole next to me when I reached for my older brother.

"I know you are scared. And I know you are hurt. But if the Lord decides to take your brother from us, it is because Mike needs to be free of the pain brought to him from that monster's hand," she murmured into my hair. "Be the man your brother knows you are, and do not become what did this to him."

How I had gone through my life without the woman hugging me, I had no idea. Claudia's encompassing warmth reminded me of that hole, and if I thought I was shattered before, then I'd yet to learn the word. She was talking, but I heard nothing but the stroke of her voice against my fractured heart. Claudia's velvet tones snagged on my broken edges, leaving tiny bits of fluff behind to dull my sharp anger. I was wrung out, tasting salt and blood at the back of my throat, and just when I thought I couldn't cry any more, she broke me open, lancing at the hot anguish I'd nursed inside of me.

"I can't… I can't lose him," I choked out. "Haven't I fucking lost enough? When is it going to stop?"

"I don't know, honey. I just don't know." Claudia rocked me back and forth, squeezing me hard enough to hurt, and whispered, "But you have to remember that I love you. Jae loves you. We all love you. And should you fall, I shall catch you and lift you up. Because no matter what comes of this, baby boy, Mama's going to be here for you. You can count on that."

I SCRUBBED down as best I could in one of the staff's bathrooms, then changed my shirt into one Claudia'd brought with her, stuffing the one I'd been wearing into a plastic bag. There was an incinerator in its near future, but for the moment, it went with Claudia, along with some of my grief.

Heading back to the waiting room, I found Jae standing a few inches from Maddy, his hand on her shoulder while she stared off into the distance, her skin drawn tight over her bones. I'd never thought of her as fragile. Never once in the time I'd known her would I have called her delicate, but as she stared Death down, her strength wavered, battered down to the core.

Maddy's belly was huge, swollen up under her full breasts, and she had one arm wrapped around herself, cradling the child she was carrying for my brother. Her eyes were the same shade as Claudia's shoes, blown-out blood vessels painting splatters across her whites, and looked huge with her long blonde hair pulled back into a tight ponytail. Her sweats hid her legs, so I couldn't tell what prosthetics she'd put on, and I had a passing thought to ask her if she'd brought what she needed to take care of them.

But then her legs were probably the last thing on her mind at the moment.

I touched Jae's arm when I went by, lingering long enough to ghost some of his warmth, then crouched in front of Maddy, breaking her vigil on the surgery's swinging doors. She stared at me for a long time, until I wasn't sure if she was angry or just lost. I'd understand it if she were both. God knew I was. But eventually she blinked and touched my face with her fingertips, trailing a nail along my cheekbone.

"You find the asshole who did this, and you wrap him up tight and hand him over to the cops, Cole." The steel was back, hammered down but tempered in a fierce rage equaling mine. "You find him for me, okay? For me and the baby, Cole. Do you promise?"

"Yeah, Mad Dog. I promise." I took her hand, kissing her fingertips, and tasted her tears on them. "Do you need something?"

"No more coffee." She shook her head, her lower lip trembling when she sniffed. "And I have to go take a piss, but I'm scared to leave, you know?"

"Let me see if the ward nurse has any idea how long they're going to be," Jae offered. "I'll be right back."

I pulled up a chair to sit in, angling it in front of Maddy's purloined wheelchair. I grabbed ahold of her hands and rubbed at them, trying to bring warmth to her palms. "Want me to tell you he's going to be okay?"

She eyed me with a look she probably used to cow CEOs and large rampaging dinosaurs.

"You know that for certain?"

"No, but I don't know if that's what you want to hear." I looked around. "Where's Ichi and Bobby?"

"They went to get me food. Like I can get anything down." Maddy's gaze drifted back to the doors. "I don't know what I'm going to do if he—"

"Can't go there. Claudia broke all the what-ifs out of me, so you can't use them either. We don't know what's happening. And—" I stopped talking when Jae came back out of the doors with a very tired surgeon in tow. The buzzing returned to my ears, and I nearly took Maddy with me when I stood.

"Cole-ah!" Jae held up his phone for me to see. "I'm going to call Ichi and tell him to come back."

"Mrs. McGinnis? Madeline, yes? I'm Doctor Branson. I operated on your husband, Mike."

The doctor was my age, maybe. It was hard to gauge, especially since he'd run his fingers through his short brown hair, making him look like a toddler who'd rolled out of bed on a Saturday morning. He sat down in the chair I'd just vacated, leaning toward Maddy to talk to her.

"First off, he's out of surgery and in ICU. He's holding steady, but there's some brain swelling—"

"But he wasn't shot in the head, right?"

Maddy's already pale face bleached to gray, and she dug her fingers into my wrist.

"You didn't tell me he was shot in the head. Oh God… no…."

"No, no… he didn't get shot in the head. But he probably struck his skull on the cement when he fell, so there's a bit of swelling there. For right now I'm going to keep him sedated so he can heal. His blood pressure is erratic, and there was some trouble when we had him on the table, but he's been stabilized." Branson glanced up at me, then continued, "I'm not going to lie to you and say that he's going to be okay.

"Things are still touch and go right now, but he's in good shape overall. I think we can be optimistic about him doing better over the next couple of days, but we need to watch him carefully for internal bleeding or infection. More importantly, how are you holding up?"

"You tell me. I'm out here, and my husband was shot up by a crazy man." Maddy struggled to rise up out of the chair, but the brakes weren't on, and it rolled slightly, tumbling her back down. Cursing, she pounded her fist on the frame and grabbed my arm. "Help me up. I'm going to go see him."

"Mad, don't." I pressed down on her shoulder, trying to keep her in the chair. "I can push you anywhere you need to go."

"I'm not fucking helpless, Cole. I'm not you. I don't run away when things get fucking—" She caught herself, eyes going wide with horror. Grabbing at my shirt, she hauled me back when I tried to pull away. "Oh God, I didn't mean that. I didn't—"

As if I weren't already battling the rage inside of me and hoping I didn't piss myself in relief at what the doctor was telling me, Maddy's words dug down deep through my throat and grabbed at my balls, squeezing them with a glass-shard clench. There was no holding back a sting of tears. Even as much as I'd already cried myself out, there they were, hot and ready at her verbal slap. Swallowing, I attempted a smile, and she held on to me even tighter, her cheeks wet and her mouth ugly with a sob.

"I didn't mean that, Cole. I don't even think that. I don't know what I'm saying." Maddy tried pulling herself up again, but I shook my head, knowing she was weak and unbalanced from the stress. "Please, honey. Oh God, I am so, *so* sorry."

The hurt slipped away quickly. Odd that. Before Ben threw my world upside down, I'd have held on to those sharp words like a badge, cutting myself with them over and over again until I practically became a martyr for the grudge I bore. Looking down at Maddy, distraught and torn, all I felt for her was affection, love, and a bit of fear she was going to hurt herself and the baby because she needed to be the strong one.

"You're tired. We're all tired, and right now I think we'd snap at anyone who got in our way of seeing Mike. We're good, okay?" I kissed the top of her head. Glancing up at Branson, I asked, "Can we go see him? Just for a few minutes?"

"Let me see if they've got him settled, but it can only be for a few minutes. Then he's got to rest, and the staff will monitor him for a few hours. Are you nearby?"

He nodded when I murmured a yes.

"Best thing to do is have a short visit, then get some sleep. I know it's hard, but if you're going to do him any good, you need to take care of yourselves."

"I can go to your house and grab some things for you, Maddy," Jae offered. "Ichi's in the elevator right now. What do you need, Maddy?"

She rattled off a long list of things. Then my heart broke when she asked him to bring her one of Mike's shirts to sleep in. Maddy accepted a kiss from Jae and wiped at her tears when Ichiro hurried toward her. "Oh God, he looks so much like Mike sometimes. Right now it hurts, you know?"

I'd never seen Mike in Ichi. Not until just then when she mentioned it. They didn't have the same build. Ichi was lanky to Mike's squared-off stockiness, but their hair and the set of their jaw were exactly the same. Mike was very conservative, where Ichiro was edgy and fluid. Both reminded me a bit of bulldogs, and I was pretty much bookended by two brothers who shoved at life until it did what they wanted it to do.

Ichiro gave freely, like the bone-crushing hug I got when he drew near, reminding me he was strong enough to hold us all together if we needed him to. Kind of like Mike.

"Yep, like twins," I groaned at Maddy.

I let her catch him up, taking the time to snag Jae before he left. Bobby hung behind Ichi, listening with his head canted, but he watched me out of the corner of his eye, probably waiting for a satellite to fall on me or for the ground to open up, revealing a Hellmouth created solely to swallow me whole. Since neither happened, I ignored him and kissed my lover fiercely, cupping his face so I could have him as near to me as possible.

When I pulled back, Jae huffed a satisfied breath and sighed, wrapping his arms around my waist to steady himself. Rubbing his nose against mine, he whispered, "You doing okay, *agi*?"

"I wanted to kill Rollins, but Claudia talked me out of it," I confessed.

"Probably better that way. I don't want to visit you in jail." He blew a bit of hot air at my nose, tickling my nostrils. "Scarlet is watching Honey at the house. I'm going to call *nuna* and ask her if she can make up the downstairs bedroom for Maddy, then go down to their house to grab her things. Bobby and Ichi will drive you and Maddy home, okay? Don't fight me on this. Let him."

I debated arguing but then realized I had no idea where my Rover was. For all I knew, it'd been impounded for overstaying its welcome at the tofu house. Nodding, I acquiesced. "Deal. Bobby's driving me home."

"Good. And no killing anyone. Bad karma." Jae stole another kiss, hugged me, then reluctantly let me go. "You don't need any more bad luck. Too much crap happens to you already."

"Not going to kill him, but I *am* going to find him. You can't ask me not to do that, *agi*. Not this time. Not after this." I was prepared for a fight, but Jae shook his head.

"I heard you promise Maddy. I understand that. I don't like it, but I understand it."

He smiled, and it was tinged with a regretful sadness I'd not seen before.

"Who called you Don Quixote? They were right, no? Always chasing after shadows and monsters under the bed, but sometimes, *agi*, the windmills do turn out to be giants, and there you are, battling them. Just… please be careful, okay? *Please?*"

"I'll be careful. Besides, Claudia told me to play nice. And I *always* listen to Claudia," I murmured into his ear. "Wait, if I'm Quixote, does that make you my Dulcinea?"

"So long as that wasn't his horse, then yes. Sure." Jae sighed, then bit my lip. "Now go see Mike, and you and Maddy come home. I'll be waiting for you. Both."

CHAPTER NINE

I WOKE up drenched in sweat, nightmares, and tears.

The night'd been a long one, struggling to come to terms with Mike and being unable to sleep for the helplessness plaguing me. I'd finally drifted off at four in the morning, my arms wrapped around Jae and the dog snoring in the bed she dragged about until she found the right spot to sleep in. I'd lay staring at nothing as she was mapping out the bedroom floor like she was looking for T-Rex skeletons in the desert, gridding out her preferences before settling down for a few hours.

Neko, as usual, was mostly unaffected by the whole disruption to her routine, but sometime after three, she curled up behind my neck and began to lick my hair. There's something oddly endearing but disquieting about a cat grooming you. I wasn't sure if she was feeling sorry for me or basting me to make sure I was tender enough for when tuna-and-egg surprise fell off her favorite foods list. I'd fallen asleep to the rasp of her tongue in my hair.

Then I woke up alone.

Stumbling downstairs after I washed the night sweats from my body, I wasn't surprised to find Jae in the living room, drinking a cup of coffee. It was still morning, the sun hadn't swung up over the Craftsman, and the pot was fresh, the sweet, bitter pull of roasted beans greeting me when I came in from the front hall.

What did surprise me was finding Detective Dell O'Byrne sitting on the couch, cradling a mug of brew and giving the alarmingly friendly Honey a belly rub.

Thank God I'd gotten dressed in old jeans and the Dr Pepper T-shirt Jae and I seemed to be sharing before coming downstairs, or I would have had a hard time explaining why I was wearing Batman underwear at my age. Oddly, "because I want to" rarely seemed like a rational adult thing to say in those kind of circumstances.

O'Byrne was a woman a lot of older people would call rawboned. She was lanky, a stretch of sinew, no-nonsense black bob, and firm square jaw, seemingly ready-made to be a cop. A recent import from another county, she'd taken the job as a senior detective in Robbery-Homicide. My heart skipped a beat when I saw her, and my first thought was Mike.

Actually, my only thought was of Mike. Jae's gentle smile calmed the rabid ferrets chewing at my stomach, and I relaxed. Jae wouldn't be smiling if O'Byrne was here with bad news.

"Dell stopped by to talk to you." Jae stood, dislodging Neko from his lap.

Dell. Sure, we could call her Dell, but my brain always defaulted to O'Byrne. Even dressed in worn blue jeans, white button-up shirt, and a leather jacket, she was all cop. In uniform or riot gear, she'd be terrifying.

Honey lifted her head, but apparently the detective's fingers were magic, and no fucks were being given about her favorite human leaving the room. Jae reached me in a few strides, then gave me a soft kiss, rubbing his knuckles on my unshaven cheek. "Are you out of razors? Or am I going to be scrubbing pots and pans with your face?"

"Actually, I just needed you, so I skipped the skin scraping." I rubbed at the scruff across my chin. "Mike? Any news?"

"He's okay. The surgeon said he's still under but responding well." He smiled at my sigh of relief. "Ichi came by to take Maddy over to Cedars. They're going to let her visit with him for a bit. Then her doctor wants her to check in with him. He's concerned about the stress on the baby."

I took another kiss from Jae and smiled as warmly as I could at O'Byrne. With as little sleep as I got, I might have notched it all the way up to lukewarm. "Let me grab some coffee—"

"I'll get you a cup. Then I'm going to get some work done." Jae tugged at the waistband of my jeans. "You have the evening shift with Maddy down at the hospital. They'll let you in to see him for five minutes every hour. One person only, but I think they're letting Maddy stay longer. She'll be home for a rest and dinner after her appointment. Then you guys can head up."

"What time can we see him in the evening?" I rubbed my eyes, scraping at the sleep still clinging to them.

"Maybe six? It's open twenty-four hours, but don't let her push too hard. She's not looking good, Cole-ah. Make sure she eats while she's down there, and then try to get her home by eleven. Okay?"

He tugged at my chin hairs. They were short, and he shouldn't have been able to get a grip on them, but no one told Jae that. He yanked once, and I winced.

"You eat too."

"Coffee first. Food later." After shaking Jae loose, I held my hand out to O'Byrne. "Surprised to see you but good to see you."

She took it, giving me a firm handshake without the ball-teasing crush most cops felt they had to give. It was what I liked most about O'Byrne. She was firmly on the right side of the blue line without being an asshole. Most of the time.

"Good to see you too, McGinnis. Heard about your brother this morning when I came in. Shitty fucking thing."

O'Byrne moved to the other side of the couch and sat down when Jae came in with a large cup of coffee for me. This time Honey oozed off of the cushions and waddled after him, her toenails clicking on the hardwood floors.

"Your husband... um... boyfriend told me about the dog. Sorry about that too."

"Dog's okay. She seems to fit right in. Kind of lazy and immune to the cat's bitching." I sipped at the coffee and nearly moaned. Jae'd broken into his stash of Puna District beans, giving me about twenty ounces of silky dark liquid gold to savor while O'Byrne tore me apart. I sat down before I fell to my knees from the coffee mana I'd been given. "What brings you by?"

"Actually, your brother." She picked up her own cup, turning it around, then hooking her fingers into its handle. "And you. Heard through the grapevine the shooter used to be one of ours. Or the alleged shooter, I should say, so I asked for the case and did some digging. Want to tell me what you think is going on?"

Giving O'Byrne a rundown on what Mike told me, including the attempts on Kim Min-Shik and the death of his driver, I stepped through the attack in K-town, going over as much as I could remember, then ended with Mike getting shot the day before.

"Sounds like Rollins got a line into your brother's schedule." She quirked her mouth to the side, thinking. "Or he's got someone else doing some of the shooting, maybe?"

I hadn't thought about Rollins having an accomplice, but then it made sense. Especially since he seemed to know Mike's movements and Kim's whereabouts at any given time. A small drop of alarm plummeted from my brain and into the hot scald of my guts.

"Son of a fucking bitch." I set my cup down, my anger boiling up hot and fast. "If someone's feeding Rollins information, then it's probably someone on Mike's payroll. But why go after Mike if the target's Min-Shik?"

"He runs a security firm. I imagine he'd do extensive background checks. Maybe the target's not this Kim guy. Maybe it's Mike. Was he up there in San Fran as well?"

"I don't think so. But if it was a day trip, he might have not told me." I shook my head at her questioning glance. "His wife's pregnant, so he keeps me tuned in to what he's doing just in case something happens. Any time Mike goes out of town, I'm on Maddy watch. I can ask Maddy if he was up there. Or get his assistant to tell me."

"Who benefits from Mike's death? Besides you and the wife? Or do we have to look at the wife?"

O'Byrne's query floored me, and I struggled not to get pissed at her for asking.

"Partners in his business? Ex-lover? You're his brother. Anyone who'd be mad if he tossed them aside? Before or during the marriage?"

The thought of Mike cheating on Maddy brought my brain to a stuttering halt. "You've got to be fucking kidding me. Mike? Fuck around?"

"Stranger things have happened. We always don't know what goes on inside of a marriage, McGinnis."

"You're off your rocker, O'Byrne." I sipped my coffee, then said, "She's got leg blades she could sharpen, and he'd be sashimi the second she found out. This slow burn shit isn't Maddy's style. Also, Mike's a pretty shitty liar. Maybe with business stuff he's all cool and collected, but put him with family, and it's like a game of Operation. He doesn't even buy Christmas presents early because he's too scared of blurting out what he got someone."

"Okay, if not the wife, then who? Only thing we have pointing the shootings at Rollins is this Kim guy, right?"

I nodded. "He's skeevy too. Don't like him. And not just because he and Jae have a history. There's something wrong about him. Oily. I got a guy who says he runs bar bunnies at the places he owns—"

"What's a bar bunny?" O'Byrne pulled a thin cop notebook out of her back pocket. She stole a pen from the cup on the apothecary chest we used for a coffee table and began to scribble in it. "That like a booth babe?"

"Guy or girl who works for the bar, kind of. Usually the owner or the manager. Pretty much goes around and gets guys to buy them drinks." I grinned, thinking of all the times in the past when Bobby talked himself into sliding a hot twink onto his lap, only to find out he was on the take with the bar. "Guy ends up paying top shelf, but the bunny's poured from a rum or tequila bottle filled with water or simple syrup so it looks like a real drink but it's a schooner of nothing."

"Yeah, I know that game." O'Byrne shot me a quick grimace. "Can't believe they're still pulling that shit."

"Hey, if it works, why change?" Even with my years on Vice, Scarlet and Jae upped my knowledge of bar scams to the point where I was even wary of places I'd been going for years. "Anyway, Hong Chul says Kim Min-Shik's places are known for that. Doesn't work on the locals, but the tourists looking for a hot Asian chick to dance 'Bar Bar Bar' with? Guaranteed moneymaker. What can they do when their hot piece of ass doesn't get drunk after five margaritas? Call the cops?"

"No, I get it. It's just stupid." She tapped her pen on her notebook. "But if he's pulling that kind of penny-ante crap, what else is he hiding?"

"That's where I was heading, because he might have crossed someone, but how did we go from K-town to Rollins? That's what I was poking at. Then…." I sighed. "Mike got shot. That blows everything I had laid down out of the water."

O'Byrne's cell chimed in its opinion from its nest in her jacket before I could continue. She answered the phone, then asked the caller to hang tight for a few minutes.

"Hey, do you mind if I grab this real fast? It's one of the tech guys I had digging for Rollins's contacts. He says he's got a couple of maybes he wants me to look at."

"No worries. Let me get us some refills. I'll be right back." I grabbed the coffee cups, then headed to the kitchen.

At the end of the hall, Jae's studio door was cracked open about dog-width, and Honey stood sentry in the space, her tongue lolling out when she saw me. Her nails clacked on the floor, scrabbling in a rat-tat-tat machine-gun dance across the polished wood. The dog caught up with me in the kitchen, panting excitedly at the dishwasher for some reason.

"You need to work on your begging skills, kiddo," I told her while I poured coffee into our mugs.

There was a small internal debate on making another pot, making one winning because Jae was nose down in his work and would periodically shuffle out like a swamp monster for some java when his brain shut down. Honey and I did a little bit of a tango as she tried to con me into giving her a dog cookie, but I told her to be strong.

From the look on O'Byrne's face when I got back into the living room, I was going to have to take my own advice.

"Yeah, he's back. I've got to go. Thanks for digging that up." O'Byrne tucked her phone away, then pierced me with a look honed by years of slicing apart criminals in an interrogation room. "Why don't you take a seat and tell me what you know about Rollins going to visit one Adam Pinelli in prison?"

"SO YOU never knew Ben had an older brother?" Bobby jabbed at me with a right hook, grazing my shoulder. "What kind of best friend were you?"

"Hey, we didn't talk about family. Probably because he was a cop, and his shithead brother was in jail. It was just him, Sheila, and the kids. Well, his parents were over down in Westminster, but it wasn't like I was going to their house for Thanksgiving or anything. Last I heard, the Pinellis split up after everything went to shit, so I don't even know where his mom or dad are now." I ducked, figuring a hospital cafeteria wasn't the place for an impromptu boxing match. Still, the smack stung. I'd gained bruises upon bruises over the past week, and Bobby seemed to uncannily know where each and every one of them was.

"No pictures around the house or anything?"

"Ben never said *shit* about having any brothers or sisters. I just figured he was an only child. Look how long I knew you before I met Jamie, and he's your kid."

"Mostly because I didn't want you to perv on him." Sliding into a chair, Bobby shoved my hip when I bumped into him, nearly spilling my drink.

"Watch it, dickwad." I set my iced coffee down on the table. "'Sides, you really want to give me shit about your fantasy of me eyeing Jamie up while you're fucking my brother?"

There were times when my brain and mouth forgot their surroundings and spilled out the worst possible things to say in public. Like right now, as a pair of ancient nuns tottered past us on orthopedic shoes. I couldn't complain about the censuring looks they gave me or the very audible sniff from the shorter one. All I could do was slink down into my chair and hope I wouldn't be needing their spiritual services any time soon.

Bobby had the good sense to wait until they were out of earshot, then muttered back at me, "I'm *not* fucking your brother. I'm going to goddamn marry him, which is a shit more than I can say about you and Jae."

That was not something I was going to discuss whilst among stale devilled egg sandwiches and burned rice pudding.

The cafeteria was quiet, with the exception of a group of nurses chatting in a corner over cupcakes and coffee. The rest of the patrons were taking things to go, shuffling from station to station in a familiar numbed-mind zombie lurch of semihunger and worry. Most of the hot foods were put away, but the cold cases were doing a brisk, steady business, and a bank of microwaves sang their own version of "It's A Small World" with every processed meal.

"Tell me about what O'Byrne told you." He leaned back in his chair, poking at the limp bean-and-cheese burrito I liberated from the cafeteria's cold case and nuked to bubbling. "And get some of that in your stomach."

"Eat or talk? I can't do both."

"Sure you can. Do it all the time. Usually in my truck and getting food all over the seats, so you can probably handle it now. Munch that down, Princess, and talk."

The burrito was a tasteless slag in my mouth. I wasn't sure if it was the food or just the ashen bitterness everything tasted like since Mike'd been shot. The beans were hot, with nuggets of cold spots icy enough to scrape the roof of my mouth, but I choked down the bite I'd taken. My stomach threatened to toss it right back up my throat in a defiant fuck-you to my best efforts even before I swallowed. When I finally did get it down, it lay there, playing possum in my roiling guts.

I put the burrito down and took another sip of my coffee.

"Hey, stay with me here, Princess." Bobby snapped his fingers in front of my face to grab my attention.

I knew what he was doing. He'd done this for me twice before. Once for Claudia and again for Jae. I was so tired of people I loved collecting bullet wounds I wanted to scream. Or I could just want to scream because I was so fucking scared deep down inside that I'd never hear or see my brother again.

It'd been so fucking hard to sit there for ten minutes and stare at his lifeless body. We were only allowed a few minutes each hour, and we stretched it out for as long as we could, passing the time along like a baton.

And I'd spent most of mine crying.

"I wonder if Mike felt like I feel right now. After Ben shot me." I couldn't talk around the chunk of emotion caught in the back of my throat. It was thicker and harder than the bite of bean-and-cheese burrito I'd taken down, slivered with glass shards of regret and pain. "How the fuck do you survive doing this? How did he do this? How am I going to fucking do this and not fall apart in front of Maddy?"

"Because he's strong. And because you're strong too."

Bobby reached across the table and grabbed my hands, his fingers biting hard into my flesh. I couldn't look up at him. He'd become so much to me. As dear to me as Mike and Ichi.

"He did it because he knew you were too fucking pissy to die on him. Just like he's going to come out of this because he's got a kid waiting for him. Because he's got Maddy, you, and Ichi waiting on this side of the fence for his short, stubby ass to get better."

"Mike wants a baby girl so badly, you know?" I stared at Bobby's fingers. They were so different from mine, broader and a bit more beat up. "Mike didn't want to know the sex of the baby, but she went and got a test. They were going to find out together. That's where he was heading. When he got shot. He was heading home so they could share that."

"Does she know what she's having?"

"No. She wants him to be there. When she finds out. Maddy's so stoked about this kid because she wanted some part of Mike, and now… he's got to wake up so they can find out together." An ache started in my chest, joining the others I'd already stored there. "Shit, Dad should know she's pregnant. I don't think they know. Maybe the girls told him."

"Did someone call him? About Mike being here?"

"Yeah, before Maddy got here. I called. When he answered, I couldn't even fucking speak. Jae took the phone and told him. Fucker just hung up after Jae was done talking. Didn't say anything. Just fucking hung up. And I feel like I've done this to Mike, you know? Because he stood behind me—"

"Mike stood behind you because it was the right goddamn thing to do. Because that's who he is. He'd stand behind anyone against the shit, your dad, and that bitch he married, Cole. Your dad is an asshole. He's got two really great sons. Okay, one's kind of screwed in the head, but still, a great guy."

I looked up to catch Bobby's smile when I chuckled.

"That shit's on your dad. You need to keep focused on your brother."

"I need to get Rollins and whoever else is running with him off the fucking street, Bobby. We need to find out why he's after Mike and keep Maddy safe." I eyed the burrito Bobby scooted closer to me and picked at its stale, dry tortilla. "I'm going to pack Jae and Maddy up and get them into a hotel. Someplace high-end so it can be locked down with security."

He snorted. "Oh yeah, *that's* going to happen."

"It's got to happen, man. I can't have them out there, vulnerable. Fucker shot Mike out in broad daylight. Mike'd met Min-Shik up there. The guy who died before? Used to work for Mike, and Min-Shik hired him away, but the guy was on shaky terms with Mike's company. Liked to use a bit too much force when keeping people back."

"Someone Rollins might like to know," Bobby grunted. "But this Adam Pinelli crap. Rollins knew Ben. A hell of a lot of people knew Ben. How the hell does O'Byrne think he's connected to this?"

"I don't know. O'Byrne's going to drop by and pay him a visit," I replied. "Might be nothing. Might be something. I just want to find Rollins and put an end to this, Bobby. I just want to keep Mike and everyone else safe. I say we keep to the plan and dig in deep."

A tall, skinny guy in scrubs ambled in, his long arms flailing about like octopus legs as he walked. I'd seen him before up on the ICU ward and once muttered to Ichi that all the guy was missing was a talking Great Dane, but Ichi didn't get it.

Sometimes having a brother born and raised in Japan meant some pop culture references were met with blank stares and lifted eyebrows.

Spotting me at the table, the nurse's face went grim, and he hurried across the floor toward us. I didn't like the expression he carried with him, and I liked it even less when he came up to the table and skidded to a halt.

"Mr. McGinnis? Excuse me, Doctor Branson wants you back upstairs," the nurse I'd named Shaggy in my mind squeaked. "He needs to see you about your brother."

CHAPTER TEN

FOR ME, dread and fear sat in my mouth and gut. It twisted my stomach up into knots, and my spit ran metallic and viscous over my tongue and teeth. Stepping off of the elevator, I found Ichi waiting for us, and the look on his face thickened the taste of blood in my mouth, and I swallowed, only to choke on the slide of saliva in my throat.

"What's going on, baby?" Bobby edged past me, reaching for my little brother. "You okay?"

Every inch of Ichiro thrummed with tension. It sat on his shoulders and wiped the expression from his face. He was the freest of us, always chasing the edge of the horizon, and seeing him brittle and taut hurt my heart. His black hair was pulled around his head, tugged up away from his scalp, something he did when nervous.

I was surprised he still had any hair left after the last couple of days.

"Where's the doctor? What's going on with Mike?" I caught Ichi by the waist, peering around him. He was cold, trembling under my hand. "Ichi—"

"I don't know. Maddy is still in the room with him, I think. There was an alarm or something… and a lot of people going into the ward." Ichi gulped in some air and leaned into Bobby's side. "I keep telling myself they'd kick Maddy out, yes? If there was a problem with Mike?"

We'd lost the nurse back at the cafeteria. After delivering his message, he'd scampered off to wherever nurses go after they give someone a heart attack. I was about to go hunt up a new nurse when Doctor Branson came out through the ward doors. I didn't like the look on his face, not one fucking bit, and I liked it even less because Maddy was somewhere behind those swinging doors, alone when she probably needed one of us near her.

There's a moment when fear turns all sound into a white noise. As Branson began to speak, I drowned in a sea of static, unable to gulp for air as the waves of his words crashed down on top of me. I felt Ichi hitch his breath in, and Bobby grabbed at him, dragging him close. I needed Jae. Some part of me needed Jae even as I couldn't process what Branson was telling us.

I needed to have him wrapped around me, to pin me to the earth with his serious, adorable soul so I didn't lose myself in my fear. Bobby and Ichi were there to catch me, but it wasn't the same.

It wasn't enough.

THE AIR was sharp and icy, a marble-top chill on my skin and in my lungs. I couldn't tell what time it was. It seemed like an eternity since I'd come into the dim room and sat down, waiting for something—anything—to happen.

Despite the stillness in the air, it wasn't quiet. The walls kept most of the ambient noise at bay, but the creak of passing gurneys and carts slithered through the crack of the door, and despite the gravity of the ward's patients, a murmur of laughter coming from the nurses' station punched through the beeps and whirs of the machines lined up against the wall.

I didn't know how long I'd been sitting there, but my back ached, and I'd somehow fallen asleep in a hard plastic chair with my face down on the unforgiving hospital bed. I'd been crying in my sleep, tears and snot crusted over my eyes and nose, but I was definitely aware of what jerked me awake.

Mike's fingers stroking at my hair and his raspy croaking that everything was going to be all right.

"Fuck you," I mumbled back, sitting up to scrub at my soaking wet face.

He looked like shit and smelled a little bit ripe, like five-day-old dog poop and dried blood, but his sickly gray pallor was gone, and despite the black grime left from the tape they'd put across his cheeks, Mike looked almost normal. Worn and beaten down but so fucking normal.

"Hey, brat." He tried shifting to sit up, but his injuries twisted him up in a way I so intimately knew. "Holy fucking shit, this hurts."

"Yeah, I kinda know." I took one of the pillows from the armchair they'd brought in for Maddy, then fitted it carefully under Mike's shot-up side. He gasped slightly when I rolled him up, but his relieved sigh when I laid him back down was worth it.

"Jesus, I'd kiss you if you weren't my brother." His gravel-shot voice crackled.

"Let's leave that special kind of icky at the door." I sat back down, oddly thankful for the comfort I could give him. "Lying flat pulls sometimes. You're going to want to roll up. And a bit of advice, when the doctor tells you to take it easy, take it easy. Scar tissue's a bitch and a half. The more you do, the more it grows. How are you feeling?"

"Like I was hit by a bus." He peered around him. "They moved me?"

"Yeah, deluxe private room with a sleeper chair over there." I nodded at the stretch of shadow near the partially open door. "That's one of your guys. Cops wanted to put someone on your door, but I figured you'd rather it be one of yours. And before you ask, yeah, old-timers, and no, I wouldn't let them volunteer."

"Sure you don't want to run the company?" He coughed and rubbed at his throat. "Water?"

"Ice chips." I grabbed a cup of frozen slivers from the container in the bedside table, then held it out for Mike to suck a few up. "Go easy. It'll give you brain freeze."

He didn't listen. Of course my brother, wearer of hedgehog spikes on his head, had to slurp up a mouthful of ice, then yelped when the cold began to seep through his head.

"Told you," I muttered at him, catching his spit-take before it got all over the bed.

After replacing the chips, I let him hold the cup. His hands shook a bit but held steady enough when he lifted the plastic cup up to his mouth.

"Slowly, asshole."

"Talk to me," he growled around the mouthful of ice. "What's going on?"

His voice was raw from the tubes they'd stuck down his throat, but Mike wasn't going to let a little bit of pain sidetrack him. His eyes were clear, snapping with a simmering anger. No one liked getting shot, no matter what some people might say about me, and Mike hated losing control.

Lying on his back in a hospital with holes in his body was about as far from control as Mike could stand.

In the thirty hours since they'd begun easing Mike out of the induced coma, moving him, and getting Maddy settled, I hadn't been able to do jack shit about finding Rollins. Torn between standing watch over my older brother and hunting down the man I believed to have shot him, I probably wasn't making any friends at the hospital. Jae'd been patient. So had Ichi, but Bobby was about ready to wring my neck.

I'd also lost Min-Shik. Or rather, Mike's firm had, but I'd been the one who'd shoved him under the covers and told him not to come out until I gave the all-clear.

"Frazier has Kim tucked away someplace. I figured if I moved him off the board, it'll help things." Mike's admin, Denise, arranged for the withdrawal, with Frazier periodically texting in from a burner phone. I rattled off the particulars of the job, as well as a few other things running hot in the background, and Mike listened without interrupting me... until I got to Adam Pinelli.

"So Rollins and Ben's brother know each other too?" He eyed me and sucked up another chip. Tucking it into his cheek, he looked more gopher than human for a moment as he chewed. "But—"

"How is that connected to Kim? Don't know." I cut him off quickly. The doctor warned me to let him rest, but I knew Mike. He'd climb out of his bed if he wasn't satisfied I'd covered all the bases. "O'Byrne thinks Rollins isn't after Kim."

"Who, then?"

"She thinks he's after you." Mike's eyes narrowed when I dropped that little bit of information in his lap. "You were up there in San Francisco, and Kim's driver was someone you were going to unload soon. O'Byrne thinks Derek Park was Rollins's initial in, and after the fuckup in San Francisco, Rollins shot him down here to close the loop."

"Don't know," he rasped. "Sounds shaky. Why me? And it's not enough to rule out Kim being the target."

"Yeah, I agree, but still, I'd rather cover your ass than Kim's. I've got Hong Chul asking around to see if we can connect Kim to Rollins through anything in K-town, but so far we've come up empty. O'Byrne headed down to where they've got Adam locked up, but he only gave her a few minutes, then asked to go back to his cell." In my head, I ran everything O'Byrne told me over the phone before I headed into my Mike shift, picking out what was relevant from the noise. "Apparently he's got nothing to say about his good friend, Jeff Rollins, but prison records show Rollins started visiting Adam every couple of weeks after Ben died but, a year ago, got fewer and fewer. Then about stopped cold a little while back."

"What happened a year ago?" Mike mumbled. He was tiring, sagging around the edges, but refused to let sleep take him. "Sheila. She surfaced then."

"Sheila? Maybe?" I shrugged. "Her parents have physical custody of the kids. Ben's mom sued for joint, but the courts ruled against her a few weeks back. From the looks of things, it went ugly."

"Just the mom?"

"Yeah. Ben's folks divorced a few months after he killed himself. Dad remarried about six months later, but his mom stayed single until last year. Then Ben's dad passed a year ago. Found that out while you were busy napping."

"Same time as Sheila."

"Right about then. Just another fucking piece of the puzzle from the middle of the board." I shifted in the chair, trying to get the feeling back in my ass. "I need an end piece, Mike. Or a goddamn corner."

"Chasing your tail?"

He was fading fast, slurring his words. I picked the cup out of his hand, moving it to the table, and Mike jerked up.

"Not done with that."

"Dude, you're going to turn into pudding soon. 'Sides, I'm going to get kicked out soon. Maddy's going to want some time with you for some reason."

"Love her." His mumbles were nearly a flat whisper.

"Yeah, I know." I adjusted the blankets around his torso, making sure he had enough give around his belly.

"Love you too." He grabbed at my hands. "Why Rollins and Pinelli? What's the connection? Why's an ex-cop going to see someone in lockup? Ben and Rollins that close?"

"I never saw them together, and I was Ben's best friend." There was a bitterness in my mouth, kicked up from the betrayal I nursed in my belly. "But then I didn't even know Ben had a damned brother or that he was going to try to kill me and Rick. Ben was really good at keeping his fucking secrets. Rollins could have just been another one he had tucked away from me. Now that you're awake and kicking around, I might track down Sheila and ask her about Rollins. Maybe even hunt down Ben's mom."

"Might not talk to you." Mike sighed, battling hard to keep awake. "She didn't want to before."

"Probably not going to want to now either." I adjusted Mike's side pillow again so he could rest his elbow on it. "Mrs. Pinelli's been trying to get Adam out of prison for a few years now, saying he's served enough time for what he did."

Mike's eyes drooped, losing focus. "What's he in for?"

"Beating a man to death outside of a gay club in WeHo," I said softly. "Apparently our boy Adam's got some problems with gay guys, and from what O'Byrne said, he's got more than a few choice words to say about yours truly."

WHEN I got home, there was a round black woman with high blood pressure and a pretty Filipino man dressed in red pumps, black leggings, and a McGinnis Investigations T-shirt sitting in Adirondacks on the front porch of the Craftsman. They were sipping tall glasses of what I assumed was iced tea, but with the two of them, I could never be certain. My suspicions were confirmed when I climbed the stoop and gave Scarlet a kiss on her cheek, its plump round flushed pink and warm to the touch.

Definitely not iced tea.

It was the perfect early Friday afternoon for lounging about. A crisp bite lingered in the air, warmed up outside of the shade by a soft Los Angeles sun. The neighborhood was fragrant with the scent of bread baking, either from the coffee shop across the street or the old-school Italian pizza place half a block down. Somewhere close by, someone's sprinkler was clacking away, blatantly disregarding the drought restrictions we were all in, and Honey sawed a hearty snore on a dog bed dragged out of the house for her comfort.

I didn't like it one fucking bit.

There was a ubiquitous long black sedan parked in front of the place but no sign of any stern-faced, eyeglass-wearing squat Korean guys I'd normally see within a few yards of Scarlet.

"Where's your… driver?" I was stepping carefully into a bear trap, and Scarlet lifted her chin, sniffing at me with a mocking disdain.

"Across the street." She rolled her hand and pointed, daring me to censure her for letting her bodyguard leave her. "He went to get us cake."

Our eyes met, and we had a small battle of wills, one I wasn't ready to give in to quickly. As the transvestite lover of a married Korean businessman, there'd been times when Scarlet's safety was suspect. Doubly so when she'd been a chanteuse at Dorthi Ki Seu, where I'd first met her in a Vice raid. Scarlet donned her femininity as casually as the diamond bracelet on her slender wrist, preferring to be addressed as a woman despite being insistent she was all male. She was the perfect parental substitute for my irascible lover, and Jae'd gleaned every bit of his stubbornness from her.

I sighed and gave in before Scarlet even blinked.

"How is Mike?" Claudia asked, hiding a grin behind her straw. Being a thin plastic tube, it provided very little cover for her smirk. "Your boy went to go shoot something in Venice and left us the dog. She's been keeping us company."

"Mike's good. I would have been back sooner, but he took a bit to wake up for me. Tires easily, but the doc says that's normal." I pulled up a footstool and winced at the screech of its legs on the stoop's floor.

The dog continued to snore, as if she heard nothing. I'd think she was deaf except she could hear a piece of American cheese being unwrapped in the kitchen when she was upstairs. Ruffling her short fur, I got a whimpering groan out of her. Then she flipped over for a belly rub. I scratched the healing dark sunburned patch on her stomach, and she scratched at the air with her back paw.

"Good, now he's awake and getting better, Maddy can get some rest. Girl was looking like a ghost there," Claudia replied.

She said something else, but I wasn't listening.

Sometimes my brain gives me a tickle. It's rare, but when it did, I tended to listen. And at that moment, the small import rolling up the street... *tickled.*

It was a bit out of place for the neighborhood, with its gray primer patches and dark windows, but the coffee shop's employees weren't exactly driving BMWs to work. Since the shop's bike rack was bristling with Schwinns and the outside patio was empty, I didn't think the Toyota's driver was stopping to make muffins and lattes.

So when the car slowed down and the driver's side window lowered, I wasn't much surprised to see the glint of a gun barrel raised up over the opening.

"Get inside!" I didn't wait to see if Claudia and Scarlet listened to me. As fucking drawn down tired as I was, the gun pumped enough adrenaline into my blood I could see through time. Launching off of the porch, I sprinted toward the Toyota, letting loose a raging scream loud enough to rattle the entire neighborhood.

Or at least one shocked Korean man wearing a tank top and a backward baseball cap.

I didn't recognize him. Not like I knew every Korean guy in Los Angeles, but I'd hoped to have an idea on who I was about to tear apart with my bare hands. He was flustered, either unsure about who to shoot or just surprised to see me coming at him with blood in my eye. Either way he lost control of the only two things he had going for him—his car and the gun.

He shot somewhere. Nowhere near me, but I heard the echoing cymbal tap of his Browning blasting away as he fumbled with it, his fingers squeezing at the trigger when he tried to bring it up. I got to his flailing arm before he could get a bead on me, and I grabbed at his wrist, forcing his limb back.

Everything hit me in that moment, every single second of the most terrifying week I'd had in a long time, and suddenly the young tough I wrangled with as the car slowly rolled toward the curb was going to reap what the universe'd been sowing into my fields.

If I couldn't have Rollins's blood, I'd have his. At that point, I wasn't picky.

He must have seen his death in my eyes, because he resigned himself to losing his arm to my rage and hit the gas.

The gun flew, and so did the car. Sparks burst first from the gun, then from the Toyota's muffler as the car careened away from me. I ran alongside of it, refusing to let go, and the driver began screaming at me. Since none of the Korean he spewed was something I'd heard in bed or ordered off a menu, I had no idea what he was saying to me. I did, however, take the time to punch him in the face, feeling the crunch of his teeth against my knuckles, then the hot rush of his blood over my hand just as the Toyota kicked into gear.

His arm snapped, probably somewhere in the shoulder joint, but I felt it give, much like a chicken joint did when biting down into a wing. I got in another half slap, and then the pain finally reached his tiny lizard brain because he floored it, leaving me choking down a cloud of dust and exhaust fumes.

Thrown off-balance by the car's acceleration, I hit the asphalt and rolled, scuffing up my hands and elbows. The knees of my jeans took a beating, and one gave way, splitting across the bend. Tucking in, I kept my head covered, holding my arms up over me and bearing down on the grit digging into my back as I rolled to a stop.

Oddly enough, I smelled cake, and when I slowly unfolded from my pangolin curl, I found myself nearly eyeball deep into a large chunk of *dobash* cake, pieces of its broken layers scattered a few inches from my face. A plastic container lay on its side near me, and I blinked at a pair of shiny black loafers approaching me.

Looking up, I peered at the contrite face of one thick-bodied Korean bodyguard holding a gun in one hand and a torn paper bag in the other, an odd pink syrup leaking out of a rent in the corner. He gave me a pained smile and sheepishly tucked away his weapon.

"Need help up?"

He didn't seem offended when I shook my head no.

"I'm sorry, *hyung*. I—"

"Next time you leave her alone, you don't fucking come back," I growled. "Just so we're clear. You got it?"

I didn't care if he nodded, said yes, or did handstands in a patch of broken glass. Fucker abandoned his post and all for a damned piece of cake. Even if Scarlet sent him for it, he knew better. It was going to be a toss-up if I was going to shoot him or turn the gun over to the cops when I found it.

A few yards behind him, Scarlet stood in the middle of the street, her red pumps spread apart as if she'd just laid down cover in a gunfight, and her grin was wide, an almost childlike delight sparkling in her eyes. Holding up her cell phone, she sauntered over to me, slapping at the bodyguard's hand as he offered to help her over a dip in the road.

"Thought I told you to get inside, *nuna*," I groaned, slowly getting to my feet. "Are you *trying* to get yourself killed?"

"No, Cole-ah. Most definitely not. I leave that stupidity to you." She smirked at me. "But I did get a picture of his license plate. No wonder you do this. It's very exciting. Now, where did that gun go?"

CHAPTER ELEVEN

"WHAT THE fuck is wrong with you?"

What followed was a stream of incendiary Korean swearwords and some gutter Mexican slang assuring me I would not only never be having sex again but I'd be lucky if I could pee using one of those loopy crazy straws.

"I think he's a little bit mad at you, no?" Scarlet purred at me as she picked another bit of gravel out of my upraised knee.

From the love seat, Claudia stifled a chortle, hiding it behind a cough and a clenched fist. O'Byrne wasn't so discreet. She flat-out snorted, a horsey sound husky enough to turn on Mr. Ed. Jae was not amused. Sadly, neither was I.

"Maybe you shouldn't have told him I ran towards the guy in the car," I muttered under my breath, hoping Jae didn't hear me.

"He had a fucking *gun*! Pointed right at you, and what do you do? Run *towards* him!"

A bit more Korean on the end of Jae's rant, and I winced at the heat in his eyes. I'd like to say Jae in a high rage was a sexy thing, but the truth of it was, Jae was a hell of a lot scarier when he was angry.

"It's like you're asking someone to shoot you!"

Still sexy as hell, but I'd have to wear a hazmat suit before I even dreamed of touching him.

I went through all of the excuses I'd thought up while waiting for Jae to get home from Venice Beach. They ranged from the outlandish—alien probes—to entirely rational—poltergeist possession—but in the end I went with the first thing my idiotic brain slid onto my traitorous tongue.

"I wasn't thinking," I heard myself say. It was like my brain had zero interest in prolonging our existence any further than the few seconds it would take for Jae to choke the living shit out of me.

I really was going to have to learn more Korean. Or less, because at some point in the middle of Jae yelling at me, Scarlet winced.

"Mr. Kim, just to remind you, I'm a detective. While I don't understand Korean, any and all threats of bodily injury have to be taken seriously in the presence of a law enforcement officer," O'Byrne drawled. "But I could always step outside, if you like."

There's nothing funny about a room full of amused women and a pissed-off Korean lover. Not a damned fucking thing. Sure, Claudia, Scarlet, and O'Byrne thought it was hilarious, but not so much for me. Even worse, Scarlet seemed to be digging out the road bits I'd gotten under my skin with a dull spoon, because I felt every poke, prod, and gouge.

Of course, she *was* Jae's *nuna*, and it could just be her way of getting back at me.

Apparently my blood sacrifice to the road gods was met with favorable eyes, because not more than half an hour after I'd broken Toyota Boy's arm, the skies opened up, and we were treated to a deluge not seen since Noah gathered up everything edible he could find onto his boat.

"No, I'm going to…." Jae gave me a filthy look, then smiled tightly at the detective. "You can have him for a few minutes. I'm going to go break something."

His leaving was breathtaking. A quiet stalk out of the front room, his taut ass filling out his jeans and his hands clenched tight enough to shatter steel beams as he shouldered his way past the screen door. We all watched him go.

"You, my friend, are very fucking lucky." O'Byrne perched herself on the couch's arm.

"Yeah, he's hot." I hissed at Scarlet's digging and tried to jerk my arm out of her hand. She was a hell of a lot stronger than she looked.

"No, lucky as in if it were me, I'd have fucking shot you." The detective patted the piece she had under her leather jacket. "But then you're a bit of trouble I'd have avoided as soon as I saw you."

"Good for me Jae didn't know any better." Sucking in my breath, I huffed past another pick.

"Oh, he knew better. He chose you anyway."

Scarlet slapped my arm, a slight scold to keep me still. When she picked up the tweezers again, I flinched.

"Stop that. You're making me nervous."

"I should go after him," I complained. "It's raining and—"

A chunking sound came from the backyard. It took me a second to figure out what it was, but by that time, I was already on my feet and heading to the front door. O'Byrne beat me to it. Her hand was on the screen's frame and pushed it out before my feet hit the foyer. She stopped short on the stoop, protected by the overhang, and the bemused smile she had on her face before was now a full-fledged grin.

Jostling up behind her, I peered out and saw Jae taking a sledgehammer to a pile of broken pavers we'd intended to toss out but never had. Mostly out of the rain and tucked into the broad shed where we parked the riding lawn mower, he pulled out another concrete paver and stepped back, grabbing the hammer's handle in both hands. Lifting it up with a grunt I could hear from the front porch, he brought the heavy head down on the block, shattering an edge from its side.

It didn't take a rocket scientist to know whose skull he was bashing in, paver substitute notwithstanding, and at my elbow, Scarlet sighed heavily.

"He puts up with so much from you. Is it too much to ask that you do not get killed?"

"I kinda was defending you," I pointed out. From her eye roll, I wasn't gaining any brownie points. "Sort of."

"I should go speak to him, but you need to be cleaned up." She looked up at me, a beautiful aging man weary of childish arguments, especially mine.

"You go talk to him, Scarlet honey," Claudia rumbled from the living room. "I've had eight boys. Cole's got nothing in him right now that I haven't already dug out of one of mine in the past. Cole, you come away from that door and sit your ass down here. Dell's come by to talk and probably wants to get on her way."

"Take an umbrella, *nuna*." I pulled one from the stand by the door. Her shoes were some sparkling red things with tall heels, probably shitty to walk across the grass with and in the rain, they'd be ruined before she got too far. "There's a pair of boots here."

"I'll be fine. The umbrella is nice." She slipped out, taking the umbrella with her. It unfurled easily, an enormous orange cover we'd gotten from some camera expo Jae'd dragged me to. "Go in and get cleaned up. I'll see about talking *musang* out of killing you."

I let her go, not like I could stop her, and then closed the screen door behind me, another loud chunk puncturing the shushing rain outside. My arms were sore, more from Scarlet's not-so-expert extraction methods, and my head hurt, possibly from lack of sleep. I'd been up for more hours than I cared to count, been wrung through the emotional washing machine a few times over, and bleached out my common sense by running toward a pimply faced wannabe thug driving an imported beater through my neighborhood.

And now I had to face O'Byrne's wrath while Claudia armed herself with a bottle of iodine.

It was fairly safe to say the cement pavers were getting off pretty easily, and I half wished I could take their place.

"Let him get it out of his system, Cole." Claudia pointed to the couch I'd vacated moments ago. "And let me see what she's done to your arm. Love her, but Scarlet knows nothing about patching up a hurt."

"Then why'd you let her?" I dodged her hand, but she caught the back of my leg anyway. Sitting down, I let Claudia twist my arm around so she could see what I'd done to it.

"Because she wanted to help," my adopted mother murmured. "And maybe you had it coming for doing the stupid things you seem to like doing. Dell, you'd best get your talking done, because in about five minutes, Jae's going to be done breaking things out there and will be wanting to knock a few things loose in here."

"I'm actually here on official police business. Mostly to give you an update and to tell you we're done processing the front of the house. You can reopen whenever you want." O'Byrne grimaced in sympathy when Claudia daubed the road rash on my forearm with iodine. "Bullet went wide. Tech guy found it in a tree branch. You're lucky it didn't go through your head."

"So everyone keeps telling me. Ouch! Claudia, that's my arm." I blew on the spot she'd just daubed.

"You don't get your face out of the way, it's going to be your head."

A nuclear warhead couldn't have moved me back faster than the look she gave me, and I manfully shifted my attention back to O'Byrne, trying to ignore the forest fire being set under the skin of my left forearm. "What about the guy? Did they catch him?"

"Found the car a few blocks down. Plowed into a hydrant and abandoned. Witnesses confirm your description of a young Korean man, early twenties and favoring his left arm. Requisite baggy pants and dark ball cap. Not much else to go on. Car was stolen, but since he dropped the gun, we've got his prints." Her smile was one gators would envy. "So, not exactly the smartest criminal we've come up against. Still, I want you to go through some mug shots. See if anything pops for you. Push comes to shove, we'll put you in front of a sketch artist if we can't get the lab to rush the prints through, but I don't see that happening."

"What? You can't hold the gun up to the CODIS machine and it just spits out his name, address, and next of kin?" I asked, then grinned when O'Byrne flipped me off with her eyes.

"Let me see the other side," Claudia interrupted. I held up my right arm, priming myself for the stinging I knew would follow.

I was not disappointed.

"Just so you know, we're going to be picking up Kim Ha-Eun—"

"Who?" I ran through the Korean names I'd piled up in my head. With half of all Koreans named Kim, Lee, Park, or Choi, it was a confusing, tangled mess to follow.

"Jae's aunt," Claudia remarked. "Hold still. This side's not as bad as the other, but you've got a bit of glass."

"Oh." The glass eluded Claudia's gentle probe, because she went for the tweezers. "You know, it's not too late for me to go to the ER or something. It'll all probably come out when I shower."

"Shut up and talk to the nice detective, boy," she said sweetly. "I'll be done in a minute."

I focused on O'Byrne, glad my knees were only scraped up instead of pebbled with road debris. "So, why the aunt? Think she knows him?"

"That's what I'm going to find out. I did a little digging on Kim Min-Shik, and I didn't care for what I found." She stretched her legs out, shifting on the arm of the couch. "Marriage seems... odd. Wong tells me it's normal for rich traditional Korean families but too damned cold for my blood. She's a hard nut to crack. Spoke to her on the phone about coming in, and she lawyered up immediately. That gets my back up."

"The family's not known for its warmth. You know about the oldest daughter, right?" Claudia's snort was strong enough to blow air on my abraded arm. "Killed her brother, sister-in-law, and a few others.

Auntie Kim seemed okay with it because it left her with custody of the grandson. Ha-Eun invented cold."

"She's been looked at for the attacks on her husband, but if we factor your brother into the mix, it drops down her motive. Still, I've got to chase down everything. Including the husband who's apparently gone underground somewhere, and you've got the magic key to his castle." O'Byrne glanced at the front door, hearing like I did, the murmur of soft voices outside. "I need to talk to Kim Min-Shik. Yank whatever string you've got your puppets attached to and get him in front of me, McGinnis. I want to do this without warrants, but I'll pull that if I need to."

"No, it should be okay. I don't know where Frazier has him, but it shouldn't be far. I'll tell Mike's admin to bring him in." I didn't like it, but O'Byrne was right. The net tossed into the water wasn't meant to catch Jae's uncle. It somehow was connected to Mike or possibly even me. "What about Pinelli? You said on the phone he's got it in for gay guys. Just any in particular, or do I rank up on a list he's got going in his head?"

"He mentioned you. Well, at least I think it was you. He said something about Ben hooking up with some homo. I assumed… well, you."

"Maybe. Maybe not." I filled her in on Rollins's brief time as my fuck buddy, and her irritated scowl deepened. I fended Claudia's look with a quick whisper. "No judging."

"Did you tell me that earlier? Because I think I'd have remembered you used to fuck the suspect in our shootings," O'Byrne drawled.

"Hey, never saw the guy in the Toyota before today. So not every suspect," I grumbled. "Not that much of a whore. And before you guys ask, yeah, Jae does know."

"I don't give a shit about your personal life, McGinnis." O'Byrne pushed off the couch, pacing off a few feet. "You're a fucking idiot. Why the hell didn't you tell me sooner? Rollins being… gay changes shit."

"Look, there's been so much shit going on, I just didn't even think about it. We'd talked about him and Ben's brother, and that's where my brain was at. I should have told you then." I pulled my arm away from Claudia, kissing her on the cheek and murmuring my thanks. "I'm sorry, O'Byrne. I fucked up."

"Damned right you fucked up. Great, I've been looking at women working at Kim's places for a connection when I should have been looking at men," she spat. "Shit. Okay, redirect, then. Thank God it's only been a couple of days. Not like it's the only thing I'm working on right now."

It was hard to imagine all of this crap dumped on us was only a few days old, and I tried to track back to when I'd spoken to O'Byrne about Rollins. There'd been too many short stretches of exhausted naps and stomach-twisting worry, so I'd lost track of even the day until Jae'd reminded me that morning.

"Sorry. I… fuck, I don't know where my head's at." It was stupid, and oddly, I felt like I betrayed Rollins in telling O'Byrne we'd screwed. For all I knew, the fucker was gunning for my brother, and I was feeling bad for pulling the curtain back on him. Something slapped me on the back of my head, and this time it wasn't Claudia. "Wait a second. Let's look at this. The only thing we have connecting Rollins to this is Kim Min-Shik. His initial ID, right?"

"We had security footage of Derek Park's death. Pretty clear film. I'd give it a 90 percent chance of it being Rollins, and the gun that kid dropped out on the street?" O'Byrne cocked her head at me. "Registered to your ex-partner. So Rollins definitely has a hand in this. It isn't just a mug-shot hit from Kim. We had people up in San Fran who confirmed the ID, and my guys are chasing down airline tickets in case he flew up there instead of drove. I'd just like to connect the kid today to Rollins. I'd hate to think I'm chasing after two people you've managed to piss off."

"Two? That's a good week for him," Claudia said. "Hold still. I'm putting some Band-Aids on you, and then you're good to go. Scarlet's driver's going to give me a ride home. We're probably going to stop someplace for margaritas on the way. Momma's going to be needing a drink after today. That porch of yours is deadly, boy. Might want to put some bulletproof glass or something around it."

Shit. I hadn't even thought about the porch and how Claudia nearly lost her life there before. I stood up with her, wrapping my arms around her before she got too far away. It was good to hug her, to feel her solidness, and then she squeaked, patting my back.

"I'm sorry," I murmured at her. "I didn't mean to—"

"You didn't bring this down on us, Cole."

Her eyes were wet, molasses sweet and damp, but she made no move to wipe them. Claudia didn't believe in hiding her tears. Never had. She'd weep where and when she wanted to, she'd told me once, and damn anyone who said otherwise. I got a loud kiss on my cheek. Then her thumb scooted over the spot, probably wiping away a smear of her pink lipstick.

"Now I'm going to go home, and you're going to go make up with Jae. Dell honey, you walk us out to the curb if you're done with Cole here. I'm feeling like I need someone with a gun to get me to the car."

"Of course. Can't say I blame you," O'Byrne agreed. "Anything else you want to tell me, McGinnis? While I've got your full attention?"

"Nope." I shook my head. "But if I think of something, I'll call. Promise."

"Well, I've thought of something. More than a few somethings," she growled at me. "Close your business for right now. Get your people into a hotel with security. And lastly, stop digging around for Rollins. Let me handle it from here."

"I agree with the first two." I stood firm when she stepped up into me. "But do you honestly think I'm going to sit behind some closed door while Rollins and his crew are running around trying to kill people I love?"

"No, but sometimes you should do what you're told to do," she said, stabbing my chest with her index finger. "Let me be clear about something, McGinnis. I catch you anywhere near where I am while I'm on this case, I'm dragging you in and tossing you into a cell for obstruction. If I can't trust you to keep yourself safe, then I'm going to work to keep you out of my way. Got it?"

"Got it." I nodded. "You won't see one damned hair on my head."

"Yeah, I don't know what's worse… you in my way or hiding behind me someplace fucking things up." O'Byrne sighed. "You piss me off, McGinnis. And I swear to God if I find you dead someplace, I'm going to take that sledgehammer your boyfriend's got out there and beat your body down until it's juice."

CHAPTER TWELVE

THE STORM broke away the edges of calm left in the house, stealing the last bit of light from the sky. Left alone in the living room with the dog on the love seat and oblivious to the world around her, I stood with every intention to catch Jae before he came in, but the screen door squeaked, and he ducked under the stoop's cover, shaking water off his wet black hair.

I sat back down.

It was hard to read Jae sometimes. He'd grown up hard, passed around to relatives who couldn't have cared less about raising him, then eventually ending up as a dancer in a club for deeply closeted gay men. All before he turned sixteen.

He'd fought me loving him, then battled with himself over loving me, and each damned step of the way, Jae broke my heart just as easily as he filled it.

There was no easy with Jae. Not before. Not now. Most of that was my fault. I was too headstrong, too focused on what I thought was the right thing to do without stopping to see what was around me. But in this—right now—my first thought was of him. I'd be damned if I let Rollins or whoever was hunting my family take Jae from me. So yeah, running toward someone shooting at me might not have been my finest moment, but it'd made sense at the time.

I just had to convince Jae of that.

He sat down on the apothecary chest in front of me, an achingly familiar sprawl of beauty and bone. Our knees touched, his jeans damp enough for mine to wick up some of the rainwater in them. His hands were cold when I took them into mine, and his knuckles were roughened, small daubs of blood crusting in cuts he'd gotten while bashing away his anger at me.

I kissed the backs of his fingers, tasting the blood and the rain on his skin.

Jae pulled one of his hands free from my grip, then tangled his fingers into my hair. He tugged me forward, and I leaned into him, resting my cheek on his collarbone while he cradled my head into the curve of his neck. We sat there, together, breathing in one another, and he stroked my spine, letting me draw his hand to me so I could press his chilled fingers into the warmth of my belly.

The day grew darker around us, dropping us deeper into the shadows as the sun slipped away from the city and all we were left with was the glow from the pendant lights in the foyer. I didn't care if we were bathed in the light from a thousand candles or a single remaining star in the sky, I just wanted Jae to never let me go.

Even as I feared sometimes he would.

"You drive me crazy, Cole-ah." His breath tickled and danced across my scalp as he spoke. "You're going to get yourself killed, and then where will I be?"

"I really didn't try to die today." I thought about what I said, then added, "Okay, I never really *try* to get killed. The almost killing just sort of happens."

"You are the most almost murdered person I know, honey," Jae replied softly.

Honey. He called me the dog's name. I was either really deep into the shit, or he was saying he loved me unconditionally despite my flaws.

Or it could have been both.

Either way, the dog did not budge from the love seat as far as I could see, despite her name being thrown about in the darkness.

I reluctantly pulled myself out of our curled-in hug, jostling Jae's knees when I slid forward, fitting my legs between his. My left knee brushed his thigh, a sensitive spot on his body, and I felt a tiny shiver run through him, a minute ripple of awareness spreading out under his skin.

God, I loved him.

"You don't get to kiss me." Jae quirked his mouth to the side in a rueful pout. "Not yet. Not until we talk."

"A small kiss." Bargaining, I was good at. "One thin kiss."

"No. With you, small kisses turn into larger ones, and we need to talk."

I could bargain just fine. Winning was iffy, and I conceded, "Okay. Talking first."

"*Nuna's* got a car coming for us in an hour or so." He put his fingertips over my lips, probably to stop me from asking why she'd arrange for a car when I had a perfectly good Rover in the garage sitting next to his mildly disagreeable Explorer. "Someone from *hyung's* staff is going to go over our vehicles to make sure there aren't any trackers on them, then take them over for us. She's worried, so I told her that was fine."

"Where is *nuna's* car taking us, exactly?" Relocating had been on my to-do list, but it sounded like Jae and Scarlet got the jump on me.

"She's arranging for someplace safe for us to stay while you go about trying to get yourself killed," he explained. "Not a hotel. One of the penthouses *hyung* owns. In a secure building. Bobby's going to bring Maddy there if the hospital kicks her out, so we'll have to be sure to grab the bag she brought here. We'll pack up the animals and take them with us. *Nuna* said there's a large outside space on the roof with grass. We can take Honey up there to potty."

"Huh." I wasn't sure if I liked what I was hearing, then jerked my brain back to the century we were living in and not the one where I wore a loincloth and dragged my lover about by his hair.

Sometimes, being in an equal relationship snuck up on me and smacked me in the face. It definitely was one of those times. I forget Jae was as much of a fixer of life as I ever was. He'd spent most of his life struggling to survive and still managed to send his uncaring mother money when he could. Even broken off from the family, he fretted and harangued his sisters, guiding them as best he could through phone calls and the occasional visit.

And God knew he had his hands full in keeping my shit together.

So maybe equal wasn't the word for our relationship, because when it was all said and done, he put up with my crap, and I was damned lucky for it, despite my initial knee-jerk douche-bag hackling because he'd gone and arranged for us to be safe while Claudia was picking glass out of my arm.

Sometimes, it was hard being my father's son.

"Thanks for doing that." Now I took the kiss he'd been holding back from me. It was a small one, barely long enough to do more than whet my appetite for him.

"That's all you get." Jae's whiskey-shard brown gaze measured me, searching for something. Then he shook his head. "*Agi*. Rollins—

why is he doing this? You were with him a long time ago and *now* this? What happened?"

"I don't know. Might not be connected, but let's face it, no such thing as coincidence," I confessed. "It doesn't make much sense to me. If he'd been pissed off at me, why wait so long after he's left the force?"

"And he knew Ben. Maybe something to do with Ben? Something he said or did?"

"If Rollins was mad about Ben, why wait, you know? The only thing I can think of is it's something to do with Ben's brother, Adam, because he and Rollins were... are friends. But Adam's in prison for beating a gay man to death, and Rollins, for as deeply closeted as he is and as much as he hated admitting it, is gay."

"Does Adam know that?" Jae chewed on his lower lip, making me wish I was the one doing that for him. "That wouldn't be something Rollins would tell him, right?"

"Don't know that either. Rollins could have dealt with it like Bobby deals with his uncle Robert and not say jack shit about it." There was something I was missing, and I had no damned clue how to go about finding it. "Adam hates gay guys, and I was Ben's partner for a long time. Maybe he found out I'm gay and thinks I'm responsible for Ben's dying."

"That makes no sense. He—Ben—tried to kill you. Did kill you in a lot of ways," Jae said, not pulling any punches. "It's been years."

"There's no statute of limitations for being crazy, babe. I need to find Rollins or someone who knows him," I replied. "I think Adam's the one behind this. Brother for a brother? I'm thinking that's why Mike was hit first. I'm stretching here. It's all fucking one big stretch, but the connections are there. Ben to Adam and then Adam to Rollins. But the why is off. And why the fuck is Rollins in the middle of it?"

"Take your gun with you when you go out." He puffed out his cheeks in exasperation. "Don't bother telling me you're going to be careful. You won't be. I know you. And when you go doing stupid things, take Bobby with you. I don't want you to be alone, okay?"

"Thought you didn't like me having a gun on me." I'd almost lost my mind digging Sheila up out of the gutter after she shot Jae. I'd been too tempted to blow away a woman I'd once called a sister because she'd put a hole through Jae's chest... with a gun I'd given her husband.

It was like living in one giant incestuous circle of death.

"I don't, *agi*. I really don't."

This time the kiss he gave me was hot, laden with enough promise my cock not only perked up, it began singing show tunes.

Whispering into my panting mouth, Jae said, "But I'd rather you not go chasing nightmares without something to defend yourself with."

THE PENTHOUSE was fantastic, a full fishbowl two-story spread overlooking Los Angeles from almost twenty stories up, the city yawned and stretched out in front of us.

Most people would have spent a few hours reveling in the luxury of the space. It was beautiful, elegant, if a bit too streamlined. Like the after picture on a renovation show where the before was something you'd still live in because it was a shit ton better than the mansion you lived in. The penthouse was all wood, glass, and chrome, an industrial space filled with comfortable modern furniture with a view meant to leave you breathless, especially at night when Los Angeles glittered under a stormy, lightning-filled sky.

I saw nothing but the man I was planning to undress.

We'd come in and dumped our bags in the upstairs bedroom, leaving the downstairs master suite with its soaker tub and western-facing windows for Maddy. The dog and cat went their separate ways, mostly to opposite couches in the living room space once Neko sniffed out the location of her cat box and Honey got a stinky beef chew to gnaw on. After a phone call from Bobby confirmed our suspicions that Maddy was going to spend the night sleeping on the chaise in Mike's hospital room, I was done being a responsible adult and began to focus on the one thing that mattered to me above everything else.

Jae.

It'd taken us an hour to get from our house to the high rise and then into the apartment itself. Most of it was traffic. Only some of it was maneuvering our stuff and the animals. As every second ticked past, my skin tightened on me, and I needed to feel Jae against me in the worst way.

I sat on a bed big enough to hold Henry the Eighth and all of his wives at once, a cushiony ocean of blue silk pillows set on a duvet the color of the storm outside our borrowed windows. Jae had been heading to the bathroom when I caught at the waistband of his jeans and pulled him toward me. He was silent, not unwilling to be drawn in but reserved as he stared down at me with a dash of lust in his honey-speckled brown eyes.

His back was wracked with tension, coiled and taut under my touch as I ran my hand up under his T-shirt. Hooking my arm around his waist, I pulled him in closer until my chin touched his belly. His stomach muscles jumped when I bit at where I thought his navel was, catching the thin cotton on my teeth. I'd missed, but he didn't seem to mind. Not when he raked his hands through my hair hard enough for me to know he hadn't quite forgiven me for scaring the hell out of him.

"Lie down," Jae rasped softly, giving my hair a not-so-gentle tug.

I let him push me onto the bed, but I dragged him with me, pulling him off-balance. Jae hit the bed harder than I'd wanted, and he sprawled over me, all elbows and chin. My thigh caught his knee, perilously close to my crotch, and his huff of breath was rippled with a barely suppressed laugh.

"You…," he growled as he climbed up my body, as graceful as a drunk stoat. His elbow gouged into my ribs, a half tickle with a whisper of an ache. "Are crazy."

"Like I haven't heard *that* before." I caught his knee with my hip, then slid my hand under it, guiding his legs apart until he straddled my pelvis. "Let's be careful there. No squishing the bits."

"Agreed. I've got my mouth for that." His lips held a promise nearly as hot as the one in his eyes. "Are you just going to lie there? Or are you going to finish what you started?"

"Glad to."

He slid off of me, the duvet fluffing up around his long body. I stripped hastily enough to scrape my shirt across my road-burned arms and knees. All things considered, I looked a hot mess. There were still fading bruises on my ribs from the carnival chase and more than a couple of nicks where I'd rubbed against the now shot-to-shit planter in Koreatown. Scraped to shit from the asphalt and with a couple of blown-out knuckles from a boxing match I had with Bobby the other day.

And let's not forget the scars marbling my side and chest where Ben had done his worst and I'd still survived him.

Still, for all my flaws, Jae wanted me.

"I love your eyes. Did you know that, Cole-ah?" He reached up, trailing his fingertips through the sparse hair around my navel. "I love the green in them, like leaves when the sun hits them."

"They're crappy brown with some flecks in them." I reached for his T-shirt, then wrangled it off of him. "Not even good brown, kind of like baby-food peas."

"I think you're color blind, but then look at how you dress yourself when I'm not around. They're green with some gold in them. I like how they turn bright when you're tanned."

He let me get the shirt off, then lifted his hips up when I snagged the button of his jeans.

"You're taking too long."

"So demanding," I scolded playfully, tugging his pants off. "Now let me finish what I've started here."

I took my time. I liked taking my time with Jae. We spent a too short eternity kissing, savoring each other with little nips and laving sweeps. He tasted of rain still, probably from his insane habit of tilting his face up toward the sky during a storm to catch the water coming down from Los Angeles's silt-filled clouds. The city lay on his tongue, a dark velvet filled with sweet and bitter-sharp tangs. I could taste my heart as well, pulsing where he kept it safe inside of his soul.

He moaned into my mouth, and I chuckled, then gasped when he bit my tongue in retaliation. Jae was vocal in bed, so different from his mostly taciturn, sometimes sardonic responses to my teasing. There were little sounds, gasping soft purrs and a particular hitching growl I liked to hear when I licked the inside of his thigh.

And the sharp intake of his breath with a dash of erotic, surprised moan drove me wild. I could pull that out of him with a quick bite in someplace tender and private.

Tonight, I went there first.

I licked the crease of his thigh, nuzzling his cock with my cheek. His hips rose, a slight arch of his back up to rub himself against my face and chest. Spanning my hands over his waist, I held him in place, nudging at his thigh with my shoulder so I could reach more of him. Jae raised his knees, splaying them apart in a boneless ease fluid enough to make me wonder if his joints could take what he did to them.

I didn't wonder long. His hands were back in my hair, tugging and stroking at my scalp then skimming down over my shoulders. Licking at the ruffle of his sac, I mouthed his balls one by one, wetting them thoroughly before scraping my fingers over the broken-open packet of lube I'd left on the bed. Jae hitched himself up onto his elbows, craning to pull me up on top of him. I resisted for a moment, then got up onto my knees, sliding my hand down between his legs to run my oil-damp fingers down his crease.

We weren't going to last. Both of us were riding the edge of an almost argument, passions stoked to the brink of our skin, and we needed to scratch at the burn simmering there. A slash of lightning crossed the dark, cloudy sky, drenching the room with a spill of white-blue streaks.

Jae shone under the flash, milky and strong with shadows pouring into the dips of his belly and chest. His black hair was a tousled mess around his face, sharp cuts of silk following the line of his cheekbones and jaw, and he watched me from under the thick fringe of his lashes, his mouth parted and swollen.

"Get on your back, *hyung*," Jae whispered. "I want to watch you come inside of me."

We must have made love a thousand times before, but the erotic glide of Jae's body on mine never stopped feeling so fucking right, so fucking good. His touch was intimately familiar, daring at times when I thought he'd pull back, then begging me to tease out his cries when I thought I'd taken him to the brink. He knew my body better than I did, his fingers finding the sensitive spots on my skin with an unerring ease.

Stretched out over a strange bed in an unknown room, I sought the comfort of Jae's body and soul, reaching down into him until he gasped and shivered around my fingers. He coated my cock with the rest of the lube, slicking down my shaft until I ached from my balls up. Jae moved off of my hand, pulling himself free of my fingers. Pulling the pillows underneath my shoulders, I almost caught Jae on the chin when he leaned over me. Laughing, he gave me a kiss, straddled my hips, and gripped my cock, working my tip with his hand.

"Fuck, you look hot doing that," I ground out as he rubbed his dick against mine.

The smile he gave me when he tipped forward was sinfully wicked and nearly as hot as the electricity eating up the sky. We were still a tight fit. I didn't think we ever wouldn't be, but tonight Jae sliding down onto me seemed to take forever, and he gripped at my arms while he worked himself over me.

If his smile seared me, then his body scalded me, turning my bones to ash with its hot clench.

His hands dug into my shoulders, fingernails scraping at my skin until I was certain I would be raw when we were done. I didn't care. We'd both gone past the point of pain, driving against one another in a hot slap of skin and bone. His ass held on to me, refusing to give up its prize, and Jae twisted his hips while he worked me, taking me in deep and hard.

I grabbed his waist, holding him steady so I could thrust into him. We lost our rhythm, falling into a sliding groove after a few missed strokes. Then the build began, tingling up from my ass and across my balls.

Jae was close. I felt him tremble and then shift as he found the sweet spot in his body. His nipples were hard under my palms, and I rubbed at them, catching the nubs with my fingers to pull them up. He threw his head back, gasping and mewling when I reached between us to grab at his dick.

He was damp in my hand, beaded with cum and slick from the lube he'd gotten on himself earlier. I used the wet to build up a slow friction, starting at his cock's root and pulling up until I got to his tip. A few strokes was all it took and Jae shattered around me, a hot spurting stream of seed splashing over my stomach. The scent of him, the salty milk of his body, threw me into the depths of my release.

The first wave hit me hard, tearing apart my mind and control. I'd been expecting it. I felt it building, but nothing could ever prepare me for the sight of Jae clenched up tight as he came. I never got tired of seeing him break open for me, unraveling every thread he'd wrapped around himself to keep his heart safe from harm.

In the moment—that long, precious moment—Jae unfurled in front of me, around me. He sang into my soul, gasping out tidbits of Korean and English too hot and slick to understand, but the sounds were all I needed to hear. I knew he was giving himself to me, openly and without reservation, something he'd fought against, then fought for when it looked like the world would tear us apart.

I'd be damned if I'd ever allow someone or something to come between us.

The joy of loving Jae wasn't just his slightly sarcastic teasing or his sculpted beauty. For me, loving Jae meant I could experience those slivers of time when his walls came tumbling down, and I could bathe in the sheer gold of his soul. It was being there for the tiny laughs and the long, sensual sighs when we reached our peaks.

He was free, in the shelter of our bedroom and home. Nothing was more beautiful in this world than an unguarded and open Kim Jae-Min. And I'd die or kill to protect him.

The full force of my orgasm slid over me, and the world went stark white with lightning splitting apart the darkness. My shout was lost in the thunder rolling over us, metallic crinkles of sound followed by a bone-rattling boom. I came, hard and hot, filling Jae's welcoming body. He rode me, ass up against my hips, barely lifting away while he slid over my cock, pulling out the last of my release and leaving me painfully replete.

Jae sank down into the pillows, panting and glistening with sweat. He lay there, staring up at the ceiling for a few moments, then turned his head to look at me. "You could have died today."

"I could die every day. Kinda what makes the whole living thing possible," I whispered back. "You make this whole living thing worth it, Jae. And I'm going to do my damned fucking best to keep living. I promise."

We lay face-to-face, listening to the dog's nails scrambling down the hallway toward the room as she hunted through the house for us. A second later, her weight hit the bed, then went still when she found a spot she liked. I was sure the cat would join us soon. God knows, the bed was certainly big enough.

He contemplated my words, eyes hooded and sleepy. Yawning, he rubbed at his face with the back of his hand. "Promise me one more thing?"

"Anything." I was tired. Probably more tired than I'd been in my entire life, and sleep tugged at my brain.

"Promise you'll love me. Forever, if I need it." He slurred a bit, dipping down into a cadence more Korean than English, but he was clear enough for me to understand him.

"Forever. Even if you don't need it," I whispered, nestling up into him. "Because I will."

CHAPTER THIRTEEN

THE DRIVE up to Lancaster was going to take us over an hour, and I was feeling every minute of the ride pressing against the back of my skull. I didn't like being so far away from my family, and even with a black-suited Korean faux Mafia dude shadowing my brothers, Jae, and Maddy, I wasn't feeling all that secure about their safety.

There'd been a bit of jostling about when Seong's guys showed up at Mike's hospital room, because the McGinnis security people weren't about to get dislodged by people they didn't know. It was a clusterfuck of tremendous proportions with both sides trying to assert their authority.

It took a few phone calls and a fierce sending them to their respective corners before we worked it all out. Then I'd slipped away with Bobby to drive up to face one of my previously unknown detractors.

The ride was as uneventful as any heading past Santa Clarita, and Bobby maneuvered the black Hummer one of the security guys gave us to drive like it was a tank. At some point during a Hyundai's ill-timed left-hand turn executed in front of a semi, I half expected a turret to pop up out of the Hummer's roof and a barked order from Bobby to take out the opposition.

I was going to have to have a serious talk with my brother about the video games he and Bobby were playing. Their other games, I wanted no part of. There were some things a guy didn't need to know about his baby brother and his best friend.

"Seriously, who had the brilliant idea to live in this place? It's like they're planning for the apocalypse and just said fuck it, let's move up to the 14 and experience it firsthand," Bobby groused at me. "And who the fuck taught these people how to drive? We've been sitting here for forty damned minutes and haven't moved an inch."

"Sigalert says there's a flatbed turned over on one of the bends." I held up my phone, wiggling it in front of Bobby's face. "Technology is a great thing to have. Tells you all sorts of things."

He lightly slapped my hand out of his face.

"Yeah, *knowing* why we're sitting here in a fucking cement stream of cars doesn't help any. Moving! That would help."

"Hey, we've got air-conditioning and blue Slurpees. What more do you want?" I saluted him with my Big Gulp, but Bobby kept his eyes trained on the lines of immobile cars in front of us.

Bobby being with Ichiro was like a scab I longed to pick but knew better. I'd known Bobby longer than I did my baby brother, and I still wasn't sure if I could deal with Ichi hooking up with a man who regularly kicked the shit out of me with padded gloves on. For all the flecks of gray in his short brown hair, Bobby showed no sign of stopping. Thickly muscled and quick-witted, he'd been a touchstone for me during the shit storm that'd become my life.

I felt kind of guilty giving him a hard time about Ichiro, but honestly, if I hadn't, he would have thought something was wrong.

Ichiro just blew me off. He was used to being an only child, and a rebellious one at that. He'd thumbed his nose at his traditionally minded Japanese father and took off to SoCal to find his long-lost brothers, only to fall in love and worm his way into Jae's good graces.

"Explain to me again why we're going to see Ben's thug brother?"

Bobby eyed the Slurpees when I'd gotten them, but since he'd sucked down half of his, I wasn't buying his *it's-all-sugar* crap.

"Because I'm going to be honest with you, Princess. This isn't one of your better ideas. Tell me one thing you're going to get out of him that O'Byrne didn't."

"He supposedly hates me, for one. To Adam, O'Byrne's just another cop, but me? I'm the devil." I ticked off. "So if he's anything like Ben, his mouth's going to move faster than his brain. And two, he's the only connection I've got to Rollins. Hong Chul hasn't found anyone who's even heard of Jeff, much less knows him."

"Jeff," Bobby grunted. "First time I've heard you call him that, Princess. How bad did you have it for him back then?"

"It wasn't like…." I couldn't explain what happened between me and Jeff Rollins. He'd been my partner, the guy who was supposed to have my back in a gunfight, not my ass in my WeHo cracker-box apartment with its cheap linoleum and burrito-stained carpet. "I think I was just something he used to scratch his itch. We didn't... date. He'd come over, have a few, then we'd fuck. Next day, it was like nothing happened."

"Until it happened again," Bobby rumbled. "And you didn't see him again? After he walked out?"

"Nope. I thought I would, you know? But he never came around again." I exhaled hard, drowning my rising confusion with a slurp of blue-raspberry slush. "Now I find out he was friends with Ben. Fucks with my head space a bit."

I'd been young and confused, angry most of the time in a tucked-away place deep inside of myself. Rollins stoked that part of me, the bits furious at my father and, at that time, my brother. I'd felt alone, searching for something to define me. I'd thought the badge would have done that.

In truth, Rollins walking away without looking back did a hell of a lot more for me than pinning on my shiny little tin star.

"He tossed me away, you know. Jeff. Well, Ben too, but I'm talking about when Jeff quit the force." I was trying to be as casual about it as possible, but the truth was, it'd hurt. Not heartbreakingly painful but enough of a sting to realize I'd been nothing more than meat to him. "Kind of made me realize I needed more than just settling for what I was getting. So I reached out to Mike and started looking around for someone I wanted to spend time with, not just fucking but actually doing something."

"And you met Rick."

"Yep. Then there was Rick," I replied softly. "We were good together, you know? He was a little crazy. I was a little more serious. Moved in together after I'd made detective and got Ben as a partner. He and Sheila really brought me into the family, which was nice because Mike and I were still rocky. Then, well—"

"Things went to shit."

"One-way ticket to hell in a handbasket," I agreed. "I'm not going to let Rollins do me like Ben did. Not this time. Not Jae. Not Mike, Maddy, you, or Ichi. None of you."

"And you think Adam Pinelli's going to tell you what? Yeah, I put Rollins on your ass because I'm crazy, but since I've seen you, and it's all good now?" Bobby left off staring down the traffic to give me a weighted glance. "Is that how you think this is going to be?"

"No, I don't," I admitted. "But I need answers, Bobby. Something to go on other than slinking around waiting for Rollins to pop his head up out of the bushes. I'm not going to live my damned life in a game of Duck Hunt."

"And we're going to Ben's thug-assed brother for answers?"

"Yep." I reached for my Slurpee. "And if he's got answers for me about Rollins, he might even have answers for me about Ben."

THE CALIFORNIA state prison system was a lumbering, dying elephant. It had the weight and mass to carry a fair amount of people but for the most part was broken down and rotting from the inside. Nowhere was this more apparent than standing on the outskirts of Lancaster and staring at the cement boxes prickling the city's dreary gray skyline.

We were a fair ways away from the city of sculpted beach babes and iced quad lattes with a twist of cinnamon and lemon rind curls. Lancaster, like most inland cities, was a hardscrabble, baked-down sprawl of fake adobe houses painted in various shades of pink and lizard vomit with sprayed green lawns and cracked fountains run dry from years of lean rain. The storm we'd gotten in Los Angeles hadn't been strong enough to make it over the mountains, leaving the inland valleys parched and thirsty.

Around the prison, low clumps of brush struggled to keep a grip on the dusty landscape. It was hard. The wind coming through the mountains was hot and fierce, molding the bushes and trees around the prison into troll-hair shapes.

Bobby found the Hummer a parking spot close to the gate. Not like we didn't have a wide selection to choose from, because the asphalt lot was only half-full. I wasn't surprised to be one of the only cars on the lot. Visiting hours were on weekends and holidays only, and we were eating up a favor someone high up owed O'Byrne by getting access to Pinelli on a weekday.

I only hoped it was worth it.

The prison was gray, inside and out, and there were long stretches of walking, mostly in the overbearing sun until we got to the receiving area. The sense of oppression weighed me down as I walked. There were people everywhere, hostile and uniformed, and despite being escorted to where we could talk to Adam through an unbreakable clear partition, we were glared at suspiciously by nearly everyone we passed.

"Wonder why he agreed to see you," Bobby muttered as he kept in step behind me. "O'Byrne said he'd pretty much stonewalled her about Rollins."

"I didn't say anything to the rep about Rollins. Just that I was Ben's partner and wanted to talk." The beefy guard paused at another door, going through a now familiar unlocking procedure. "Guy came back and said Adam agreed to see me, providing we could arrange for one of the private rooms."

"Still got a partition between you and Pinelli, right?" He nodded a thank-you at the guard who let us in. "Because I don't want him to take you out just yet, Princess. Your brother would have my balls for dinner."

Another man stood on the other side, shaven tight around his head and sporting a pair of eyebrows caterpillars would seduce after a drunken rave. I'd have mentioned my admiration for them, but he didn't seem like he was up for conversation.

"This way," the guard squeaked, nearly high enough to make a dog's ears hurt, and I bit the inside of my cheek to stop from laughing. "Third door on the right. They're bringing Pinelli in right now."

He continued on in his Minnie Mouse voice about the rules and pretty much what our safe word would be if we felt in danger. After reassuring us he'd be standing at the back of the room to provide us with security, he opened the door and let us in.

It was underwhelming, to say the least.

The gray motif continued, with very little attempt to soften the prison's hard edges. The room was divided, not quite in half but close to it, by a half wall made out of cinder block and steel dowels with Plexiglas inserts running from the top of the laminate countertop to the ceiling. Small holes were drilled through the clear sheets, a river of pinky-finger-sized circles running the length of the clear barrier. Despite being bulletproof, the barrier seemed scratched until I realized it was just smeared, probably with snot and tears.

Unlike the movies, there was no phone to talk to an inmate with, and I couldn't hear anything outside of the room. No prisoners asking for a good time or the rise of a mournful harmonica winding through its massive halls. The area was briskly cold and mechanically flat, although I did catch a whiff of burned cauliflower coming through the vents. There was a door on the other side of the partition, steel from the looks of it, with a reinforced glass window cut high into the thick front.

"Prisoner coming in," a speaker above us crackled.

The squeaky-voiced behemoth who'd led us in gestured to a couple of rolling stools near the counter.

"You should be seated before they'll open the door."

The seats were hard, with a vinyl cushion nearly as high-pitched as our guard whenever one of us moved. An alarm sounded somewhere close, and I got a glimpse of a sour-faced man in a guard's uniform through the access door's window. A strip of red LEDs above the frame flashed, and the door swung open wide enough to let the guard push a wheelchair through.

It was a thick plastic version of the kind they used on airplanes, narrow enough to get through an aisle yet still sturdy enough to hold a human being. In this case, the wheelchair had its work cut out for it, because the man strapped to the seat by a thick leather belt barely looked human. If Mary Shelley had seen him, she would have gasped in astonishment because some insane god brought her monster to life.

Adam Pinelli was definitely no longer as how God made him.

All of his pieces and parts were there, just not where they'd originally been placed.

His legs were tied to the chair, but I could see they were twisted and deformed, even through his wrinkled prison-issued clothes. There were barely twigs beneath his blue denim pants and chambray shirt, and his cuffs were loose, covering his wrists. His hands lay on his lap, curled in as if to protect his withered, misshapen fingers, but it was his gaunt, broken face that drew the eye.

He was definitely a Pinelli. There were echoes of a strong firm jaw, and despite the long scars running through his lip and up his cheek, his mouth resembled Ben's. I couldn't tell if he had the same strong Roman nose as his brother because it lay nearly flat against the right side of his face, a jagged line smashed as far down into his skull as anyone could get without killing him.

Adam's hair was thick but cut short, nearly to his skull, and peppered heavily with white. More scars marbled his scalp, raising thin berms under his hair. His left ear was missing, leaving a mass of gnarled skin and cartilage where it'd been. The right was only slightly better, but not by much.

What was most startling was Ben's dark eyes staring back at me from Adam's twisted face.

And the hatred burning within them.

"Like what you see, faggot?" Adam croaked as the guard wheeled him up to the counter. "Drink it in, bitch. 'Cause you've got this coming to you."

FUNNY THING about threats, I don't like them. And by not liking them, I mean I respond to them probably more aggressively than I should. In Adam Pinelli's case, my first instinct wasn't to bite back. No, instead some perverse tingle in my brain flicked a not-often used switch, and I began to laugh.

As if a three-year-old told me the best fucking farting dinosaur joke ever imagined.

Because Adam wasn't even looking at me.

Instead he'd vomited up his stew of hatred and vile right at Bobby.

Adam Pinelli didn't even know what I looked like, and Bobby ran with it, nudging me with his foot as he spoke.

"Pretty big words coming from a guy behind glass." The years of being a cop were always lurking just beneath the surface for Bobby. He'd been wearing a badge during one of the roughest times the city had, cutting his teeth on street violence Los Angeles was still hurting over. It showed in his eyes and the set of his jaw, a hardness honed during a time when the cops were at war with everyone, including themselves. "Were you that pretty coming in, or did someone rearrange your face?"

Adam didn't look good. Didn't sound good either. He battled to draw a breath, and his face was flushed, nearly beet red and cut through white where his scars sliced across his skin. Struggling to turn around, he rocked the wheelchair, twisting his neck. It took me a bit to realize he was looking for the guard who'd brought him in.

The man stood at the wall, staring off into the distance and paying no attention to the spittle-flinging prisoner in front of him.

Adam Pinelli was not very well liked; that much was clear.

"If you didn't want us here, why'd you agree to see us?" I cut in before Bobby gave Adam a heart attack.

This stopped Adam cold, and he turned his head, glaring at me. It was eerie seeing pieces of Ben there, but I had no doubt in my mind that any affection Ben might have had for me wasn't present in his older brother, even without knowing who I was.

"I wanted to see the fuckhead who screwed my brother over," Adam spat at me. Literally.

A froth of spray hit the glass, and I steeled myself not to flinch.

"We came here to talk to you about Jeff Rollins, not dredge up whatever fantasy you have about... me." Bobby sounded like he caught himself, pausing before he said my name. "If you just brought us here so you can rant, we'll leave and tell Detective O'Byrne you were a waste of our time."

"Fuck you. And fuck Jeff Rollins. That piece of shit."

Adam's eyes bugged out, and he choked, gagging while he struggled to breathe. Behind him, the guard didn't even twitch, and I worried he'd asphyxiate right in front of us before anyone did anything about it. One of Adam's hands twitched, beating against his thigh, and he took a long, shuddering breath.

"Talk to me about Jeff Rollins," I pushed. "Thought you and him were buddies."

"Buddies? He's Ben's buddy and the fucking reason I'm in this chair."

Adam spat again, and this time the guard behind him rumbled a warning, something about licking the glass clean if he continued basting it with his saliva.

"You think it's easy being back here when your brother's a cop? I didn't tell anyone shit about Ben. Then Rollins comes by after Ben's dead telling me all kinds of shit about your friend here and how it was fucking ironic that I'm in here for slapping some queer too hard and my brother's partnered with one."

If O'Byrne couldn't get Adam Pinelli to talk, she just hadn't brought the right incentive. Apparently when faced with someone he hated, Adam couldn't keep his mouth shut. Good for us and probably bad for him.

"So people find out your brother's a cop." I shrugged. Any cop behind bars had a short life expectancy, but I hadn't figured relatives would carry the same stigma. Still, with the boiler-room environment and close quarters, the stupidest thing could set someone off. "You think Rollins did it on purpose?"

"People hear shit in general visiting, and the assholes in here can't keep their mouths shut. Rollins knew that, and he blabbed anyway." Adam cleared his throat and smacked his damaged lips. "After coming by for months, he goes and lays that shit down. Up until then, it was like it'd been before I got in here. Just shooting the shit about guns and stuff. Next thing I know, he's spreading my business around. A fucking week later, some ass-chasers catch me in the laundry room and work me over. Rollins ain't been back since he came by to visit me on the ward. Stayed long enough to tell me he was a faggot like you and the guy I did."

"So you think he turned you in on purpose?" Bobby asked softly. "O'Byrne thought you didn't know Rollins was gay."

"Not until he told me. Fairies back here, you can see them a mile away. Swishy assholes who hook up with the bigger guys so they don't get the shit kicked out of them. Never saw Rollins like that. Fuck, I went camping with the guy about a week or so before this shit."

Adam's arm went into spasms, but he didn't pay attention to its flailing. It was surreal, watching it jerk about like a dying chicken as he talked.

"He and Ben knew each other from the force. They were best fucking friends. Did everything together when I was out. Thought he was an okay guy. Probably was checking my ass out the whole fucking time."

If there was anyone's ass Rollins was checking out, it'd probably been Ben's. He'd been a gym bunny's wet dream, whereas Adam looked like he'd been wrung dry even before he'd been beaten to a pulp.

But I let Adam go on thinking that. From the looks of things, all Adam had to keep him alive was his paranoia and hatred.

"So why then?" I asked. "He put up with your shit for a long time and then snapped? He decides to fuck you up?"

"It was that bitch my dad hooked up with after Mom dumped him. She handed Rollins some of Ben's stuff to give to people, but the asshole never did. Instead he comes in here all pissed off and fucks me up something fierce. Kept saying shit about how Ben deserved better than the faggot he rode with. About how he'd have loved to see me kick your fucking ass, McGinnis, like I did the queer I caught over behind my place." Adam's hands began their twitching dance again. "Kind of hard to do that from this damned chair. Something in Ben's stuff that pissed him off. That's why he fucked me over. Maybe that's why he's fucking you over now."

"What could he have found in Ben's stuff?"

This time Bobby's question was for me, and for the life of me, I didn't have an answer.

"Something of Sheila's?"

"No, something Ben wrote. Letters or some shit." This time Adam didn't stop himself, and the window between us went opaque with foamy specks. "Came in here mad as shit. Cold too. Cold, fucking son of a bitch."

The guard detached himself from the wall and stomped over to Adam's chair. He grabbed at the handles, barking for the guard behind us to buzz the door free.

"Time's up, gentlemen," he snapped at us, turning to wheel Adam off.

"Wait." I stood, slapping the glass with my hand. It stung, sending a ripple of numbness across my palm. "Where the fuck is Rollins? Do you know where he is?"

"Rollins? Yeah, check out that Korean pussy he's got stashed on 6th. Works at… shit…. *Sojuju*." Adam laughed, bitter and sour. "And all this time I thought he was talking about some hot chick. Get me my brother's shit, you assholes. You fucking owe me now."

CHAPTER FOURTEEN

THE DAY was a long one. After dropping Bobby off, I'd grabbed Ichiro, and we spent a good hour and a half with Mike and Maddy at the hospital. His color was good, and the stress lines on Maddy's face were slowly disappearing, but the worry remained. Rollins was still out there, waiting.

The drive back to Scarlet's deluxe apartment in the sky was long by Los Angeles standards. I wanted to go home, any home, and after another hour on the road trying to get past traffic congestion, I was willing to chop off my left arm just to see Jae again.

It was nearly sunset by the time we got to the building, but we'd made it home. A few swipes of my keycard got us into the parking garage, then to an elevator, which seemed programmed to amusement-park ride, because it shot us up to the roof like we were going to do battle with vermicious knids.

It made me want to throw up every time I rode it, but Ichi didn't seem to care. Of course, it could have also been the long, skinny windows on the outer wall and the whooshing scenery scrolling by like a bean-burrito purge that did me in.

Still, my manhood demanded I keep my stomach in its place despite my gasping in the cold air in the penthouse's outer lobby.

"Here, give me the key. You look like you're going to throw up." Ichi took the card out of my numb fingers. "Maybe you shouldn't have tried Maddy's kimchee milkshake."

"God, don't even talk about that." The less said about that culinary disaster the better, but Maddy could talk me into a straitjacket, and I'd taken a big slurp of the shake before my brain kicked in with its opinion that doing so wasn't a good idea. An instant later my stomach concurred, and I silently reassured every part of my body that we would *never* be doing *that* again.

"Don't eat a pregnant woman's food."

Ichi slid the card through the reader, and the light turned green. Holding it open for me, he waited for me to go by, then walked in.

"Okay, and really don't eat a pregnant Japanese woman's food. *Uni* and ice cream do not mix."

"God, you're going to make me hurl. And hey, make sure the door's closed. It doesn't latch all the way. You've got to press it shut," I cautioned. "Multimillion-dollar penthouse, and the damned front door doesn't work. Found Honey out in the hall yesterday morning."

My younger brother laughed. "Sure that wasn't Neko trying to get rid of her?"

"Nothing is beneath that cat. So no, I'm not sure." The best thing about the apartment was its sight line. I could see practically all around the first floor, right into the kitchen space, but unless Bobby and Jae were in the west-facing bedroom, no one was downstairs.

That's when I smelled meat grilling and looked up to see the second-story door to the outside space had been left open.

"Ah, I found our significant others." I nudged Ichi in the ribs and pointed up.

"Food. God, I could eat." Ichi crossed over to the stairs. "Come on. Beer. Food. And we're not in a goddamned car."

The dog gamboled out onto the second-floor landing and peered down from between the steel cables the architect decided to use as railings. Honey drooled down on top of us, then scampered toward the small flight of stairs leading to the roof. From her position on the couch, Jae's cat let out a small disgruntled meow, as if somehow I was to blame for the canine intrusion on her life.

"Don't look at me, kitten. Your dad's the one who said she was coming to live with us," I told her, scratching her ears. "Okay, I agreed, but he said it first. His fault."

"You coming up, or are you going to spend the evening with the cat?" Ichiro called down from the landing.

The door was fully open now, and the smell of grilling meat grew stronger. My stomach rumbled in response to its siren call.

"Steaks, *oniisan*. Steaks."

With that as a lure, I headed up the stairs.

The view from the top of the building was incredible. Same view as the penthouse, really, but without the windows. Los Angeles and its surrounding hills spread out around us, sparkling and colorful in the waning sun. Thing is, I'm not big on heights. Roller coasters I can do, but somehow perched on top of a cement tower twenty stories above ground level reminded me I was not issued wings.

In California, unlike Chicago, where I'd spent a lot of my misspent youth, the buildings rolled on their foundations, a safety precaution meant to prevent collapses during earthquakes. One second the building is rock solid, then it's all Black Pearl during a summer jaunt across the Bermuda Triangle the next. Disconcerting and so infrequent I don't even think about it until it happens. It was one of those things many SoCal people shrug off, measuring distance in time not miles or knowing to order extra crispy fries animal style at In-N-Out.

Scares the shit out of me every damned time.

But thankfully, Los Angeles's faults were taking a break, and the rooftop was steady as all get out.

Still... the goddamned sunset over the Los Angeles Basin. Damn.

For temporary digs, the penthouse was incredible. With the rooftop laid out like we were expecting a hip-hop video to break out filming with rattan couches with overstuffed pillows in brilliant reds and oranges, it had a raised slender lap pool and a hot tub I'd wanted to drag Jae into since the first time I'd spotted it. Bobby sat sprawled on one of the sofas, his beer set aside as he pulled Ichi into his lap.

"Hey, babe." I nested up into the curve of Jae's back, kissing the elegant line of his neck as he bravely battled a piece of chicken on the grill. He turned, and I slid my mouth over to his, licking at the corners of his lips until he laughed against my cheek.

He smelled a bit of mesquite and tasted of kimchee and Hite beer when I finally got to his mouth. It was a short kiss, probably because the chicken apparently needed the attention more than me, but I didn't mind. There was also moo-cow on the grill, and from the looks of it, I'd come home just in time.

There was a bit more kissing; then I was chased off by a pair of tongs. After grabbing a beer from the ice chest by Bobby's feet, I bumped his leg as I was sitting down. Ichi pushed at my back when I went by, nearly sending me over the edge of the sofa.

Everything was so fucking normal and domestic, it made my teeth hurt. It also made me miss the Craftsman. I wanted to go home. I wanted to trip over the cat going down the stairs and have sex with Jae in our own bed.

It was funny how being away from home—even for a few days—made me miss the life I'd been living with Jae.

He was happiest cooking or behind a camera. Even now, amid the jewel-glitter of the city around us, he smiled while he threw ears of corn on the grill's upper tier to cook. Ichi said something in Japanese, obviously an inside joke between the two of them, because neither Bobby nor I spoke enough of it to understand more than how to find a bathroom or order *katsu-don*, but what Ichi said made Jae smile.

Jae's smile—for me—tore the sun out of the sky and replaced it with his brilliant soul. I'd do anything to make him smile, to get him to give me his husky purr of a half laugh or even a murmur of silky Korean under his breath. My heart sang around him, and even the glide of his hand on my skin made me feel... whole.

He made me whole.

I was stupid in love with Jae-Min. He'd become my touchstone, a far cry from the suspicious and wary enigma I'd first met at his aunt's house. He was subtle, not something I'd been used to. I'd lived my life as openly gay as I could, embracing a lifestyle loud enough to make someone's ears bleed... no, my father's ears bleed. It was funny how after I'd been kicked out of my family for loving men, I wanted nothing more than to have my own family. And I'd found it in a sloe-and-honey-eyed Korean man with a wicked, sardonic sense of humor and an even wickeder mouth.

"You okay over there, Princess?"

Bobby lightly kicked my foot. I must have zoned off watching Jae cook, because I blinked, and Ichiro was standing by the grill, chatting with Jae while he pulled the meat off the heat to rest.

"Dozing off?"

"Nah, I'm good. Just...." I drifted my attention back to Jae, slightly envious at his easy relationship with my younger brother. "Just watching them."

"You're going to be the best man at my wedding, right?" Bobby slid over to grab another beer. "I was serious about that. Just so you know."

I choked on mine.

"Figured I'd ask you before Ichi could beat me to it," he continued, popping off the bottle cap. With a flick of his wrist, he aimed for the trash can, Bobby made a soft crowd noise gurgle when it hit the rim and flopped in. "Told him I had first shot."

"Shit, I…." My mind was left someplace in the ether, because while I'd known they were talking about it, bona fide marriage between a guy I'd called my brother and my actual younger brother short-circuited my brain.

"Is that a yes garble or a fuck no?" For the first time since I'd met Bobby, he looked *nervous* and at the edge of hurt.

We didn't touch. Not often. Bobby and I rarely hugged unless it was when I went toward him at the ring and we got tangled up into each other. Now seemed like a hug moment, and I wasn't going to let it go by without letting him know it.

As awkward as it was to hug a guy while sitting down, we made it work, and I patted him on the back before he squeezed my lungs out of my chest.

"Yeah," I murmured into his hair as he gave me one last quick embrace. "I'll be glad to, old man. You're going to need someone to hold you up at the altar when your knees give out."

"Had to get that one last shot in there, didn't you, Princess?"

He pulled away, but not before I saw the wet in his eyes.

"Don't be a shit, or I'll make you wear a rainbow waistcoat or something. Now wipe that smile off your goddamned face. The guys are coming over with dinner."

"So ADAM Pinelli thought you were Cole?" Jae chuckled, leaning against me and eyeing Bobby. "How could he not know? You don't look Japanese at all."

"With a last name like McGinnis, you think people are going to look for a half-Japanese guy?" Bobby grinned back. "It worked out for the best. Gave Princess some leeway to ask questions."

"Talked to O'Byrne before we left the hospital. About Rollins's boyfriend," I clarified when Jae cocked his head at me. "Seems like Rollins spent some time talking to Adam about a hot piece of ass down at a K-town club called Sojuju. It's been a while since he saw Adam, so I don't know if he's still with the same guy. I thought I knew Rollins well enough back then, but fuck, now? No clue. He was focused, you know? I'd have to say he was someone to stick with stuff, but he dropped his badge like it was hot."

"You say focused, and the rest of us say batshit crazy." Bobby picked at Ichi's leftovers, grabbing a slice of grilled zucchini. "He's obsessive. Kind of proved that over the past few weeks."

"I know Sojuju," Ichiro said as he pulled his plate closer to his lover. "Been there a couple of times."

Bobby's eyebrows went up. "Without me?"

"Without you. Before you. And sometimes, after you." My brother rolled his eyes. "I existed way before you came along, Dawson."

"Huh. If you want to call that existence," he said, dodging the balled-up napkin my brother flung at his head. "Think this guy would still be there?"

"Maybe," Jae answered. Stretched out on the couch, he lay with his back to my shoulder, my arm around him and my hand in his lap. He played with my fingers, having already stuffed the dog full of steak. "I've been a couple of times. Mostly with Ichi and some of the guys from Dorthi Ki Seu. Scarlet went once, but she didn't like it. Too loud. Too... grabby."

Even though Jae and I went out with our own friends a few times, it never dawned on me they'd go dancing. The growly part of me rose its ugly head, and I beat it back as I asked, "Dance club? Bar? Define grabby."

"Very Korean," Ichi answered. "Typical for K-town. Except for the gay."

"Open gay like fucking on the tables gay or wink-wink-nudge-nudge know-what-I-mean gay?" For that I got an elbow in the ribs from my lover. He mumbled an excuse me, but I didn't believe him. "Hey, it's a valid question. Vice could have some information on the place."

"Cops don't go into K-town, remember?" Jae pointed out. "Foot patrols sometimes, but they don't stick their heads in."

"No one there talks." Bobby cleared his throat when we all looked at him. "Look, it's a community thing. A lot of places in the city are like that. Usually when there's a concentration of one ethnicity, the people living there pull inwards. Cops have a hard time breaking through that. I'm not saying LAPD's done a great job at reaching out, but it's a challenge."

"Fair enough," Jae conceded. "I didn't give much to Cole when he came around to ask about Hyun-Shik in the beginning. It seemed... wrong."

"And I was there because your uncle asked me to look into it." I kissed the back of Jae's head. "It worked out."

"Mostly," he replied.

"Yeah, I love you too. Oh! Speaking of your uncle, he surfaced. Mike's guy... Frazier... brought him in. O'Byrne wanted to grill him some more." I was full, but there was an ear of corn left, and it was whispering my name. I ignored it, promising retribution later. "When I spoke to O'Byrne about

Adam and Rollins, she made some noises about taking the choke hold off your aunt. I told her not to bother. If anyone needs a choke hold, it's that woman."

"Can we get back to this damned club?" Bobby growled. "And exactly how many times have you guys gone out dancing without us?"

"A couple of times. Not a big deal." Ichi shrugged. "It wasn't my tastes, but the music's good. Some clubs play too much hip-hop, and sometimes there's too much hate in the lyrics. That shit pisses me off. In K-town, you get good beats, and none of the street slang crap in K-town."

"But this one's geared towards gay guys?" I pushed the conversation along before it dissolved into a discussion about what was wrong with the world. "Shit, things have changed since Jae and I first met."

"A bit outside," Jae agreed. "But still, gay men are behind the doors. You don't come out to your family. Or if you do, it's shaky. Clubs have always been the place to go to meet someone, even if you're just looking for someone for one night."

"Awkward." Ichi put his legs up, resting them on Bobby's thighs. "A lot of Korean guys don't know how to be gay. It doesn't fit into their world, you know? How to act and all that. There's no rules for that. Lot of fumbling around and posturing."

"It's hard."

Jae's whisper was soft, but it cut me, deep. I slid my hand into his, holding it tightly. He gave me a quirky smile back.

"Sojuju is more about the hookups. And they're like a lot of Korean clubs. The waiters get paid for booking. It's kind of why Scarlet doesn't like it."

"They get aggressive sometimes. Pisses me off." Ichiro added to my confusion.

"What the hell are you talking about? Booking what? DJs?" The two of them exchanged a look, and suddenly I felt ancient despite the sparse years between us. "Hey, while you two were out being wild, I was doing the responsible thing and adulting."

"You have never done the responsible thing," Bobby snorted at me. "Only reason you have a house is because it was a piece-of-shit crack house they were going to condemn, and you felt sorry for it."

"It had good bones. Still does," I defended. "And if people would stop fucking shooting at it, it'd be a really damned nice place to live. Booking? What is it?"

"It's when they drop the music to a slow beat or jam, and the guys up on the top deck tell the servers who they want," Jae explained. "Then the servers go down to the floor and hook that guy to take him to the tables."

"Wait, like a fucking piece of meat?" Bobby glared at Ichi. "And you do this fucking shit?"

"Cool your jets, old man." Ichi waved Bobby's ire off with a shrug. "Not like I don't know what I'm getting into when I go in. You hear something slow start up, and you duck off the floor. If one of the servers tries to book me, I tell them no. Sometimes even fuck off if they get too pushy."

"It's worse at het clubs. Those let the girls in for free, and it's kind of understood they're going to get booked to a table." Jae grinned at my incredulous look. "You, Cole-ah, are very naïve at times. You knew about the drink scam but not this?"

"Yeah, my clubbing days are way past me. When did they start doing this crap?" I frowned.

"Korean clubs have been doing this forever. It's a way for the servers to make money. But they don't get paid if the guys at the tables don't get hooked up. It's kind of like approaching a guy on the floor but with a middleman. You pick out who you want, and they go get him for you. If he says no, you don't take the hit, and the server just walks." Ichi had a grin of his own. "And if you're gay and a fob, how else are you going to get laid?"

More frowning on my part. I'd heard that before but hadn't made the connection in a long time. "Fob?"

"Fresh off the boat." Ichi held up his hand. "I am a fob. Kind of. Jae's first gen. He doesn't count. His brother Jae-Su might. It's complicated. Depends on how Americanized you are, but if you're new, it's the best way to get your dick sucked without getting the shit kicked out of you because you hit on the wrong guy."

"And Rollins's maybe-boyfriend is at this place?" I mulled over the possibilities. "Huh."

"Good money to be made at a Korean club. We like to drink."

Jae wasn't wrong. I'd been to dinner parties with Scarlet and her friends, most of whom were Korean and seemed unaffected by the sheer gallons they put away during the course of a few hours.

"So maybe a bartender?" Bobby patted Ichi's leg.

"Bartender?" Ichi shook his head. "If he's still there, he's probably a server. On a good night, those guys can pull in close to three grand, and that's just at the het clubs. More for gay guys because competition's tight. They get paid to get the guy or girl up to the table. Whether or not they stay there, that's on the guy paying."

"So if they don't hit it off, the server goes back to skimming the crowd and banking more cash." I whistled low and deep. "That's a shit ton of money just to keep your pride intact."

"Sometimes, Cole-ah, when you are gay and Korean," Jae said, brushing his mouth over my cheek, "pride is all you have left, and you do *anything* you can to protect it."

CHAPTER FIFTEEN

JOJO'S WAS always busy in the morning, but that never stopped Bobby and I from crawling out of our respective beds, donning our sweats, and going in to beat each other up. Or rather, he was ready. He and Ichi slept over, a good thing considering we put away a hell of a lot of beer, but that also meant he was knocking on my bedroom door at o'dark thirty.

I was able to stall him long enough to get a shower and coffee. There was barely enough time for a kiss from my lover, who was more interested in doing face time with his pillow than me. Dog taken care of and both animals fed, I was hustled out of the door and led into the rare, succulent air of masculine sweat and unwashed socks.

Far more bracing than coffee but less pleasant.

I'd already gone a round with Bobby by the time Hong Chul wandered in, and I waved him over to where I stood ringside, watching my best friend take a few more jabs at a cop named Montoya. Hong Chul came dressed for a workout, a worn-out tank top and loose-fitting shorts, and he caught more than a few admiring glances as he walked through the gym.

He was okay. If you liked short, beefy Korean guys with a lot of ink and muscle. Hong Chul smiled at a couple of the guys he knew, then slapped me on the back.

"You know, I used to worry I'd feel weird coming in here, but I gotta say, kinda adds to my swag." He grinned widely at me. "You up to going a few when Bobby's done here?"

"Yeah, we can go at it." My arms hurt a little bit, but it was a good burn.

I was still bruised in a few places, and from what, I couldn't even remember anymore. I knew where the nearly gone road rash on my arms had come from, but there was a bruise along my ribs I'd discovered in the shower that left me wondering where and what I'd hit. A few more taps from Hong Chul wouldn't make much of a difference.

The boxing gym was a sanctuary, especially now since Bobby wasn't letting me out of his sight, and when he did, I had a contingency of Korean shadows following me around like my own personal flock of *susuwatari*. Also kind of made me wish I had sugar stars to toss at them so I could get some breathing room.

Today it was just Bobby... and now Hong Chul, because he was eyeing the guys around us as if he expected a gunfight to break out.

"Relax. I don't think Rollins is going to jump out of the locker room and take us all out." I sighed at his sarcastic mutter of *right* under his breath. "Shit, JoJo would take the fucker down first. Do you have any idea how much of a badass he is?"

From a distance, JoJo didn't look like much, an aging black man withered from sun and a near-fatal beating, but he was fierce and protective of the guys who came into his place... his and Bobby's place. It was a bare-bones sweat factory of grunting and hard blows, frequented by cops, gays, and a few people who'd wandered in off the street and survived JoJo's interrogation.

"No, ain't arguing that. Guy can probably kick my ass with one hand tied behind his back."

Hong Chul held his hands up in mock surrender, then winced as Bobby laid a right hook across his opponent's cheek. Montoya's helmet took most of the blow, but it probably stung. I'd worn more than a few of Bobby's lightly placed kisses on my face, so I hissed in deep sympathy.

"Want to talk about Rollins? Once I had the name of that club, shit just came pouring out like a bad burrito."

"Yeah, let's grab something cold to drink and go over what you found." I caught Bobby's eye and jerked my head toward the vending machine by the front door. Montoya took advantage of his distraction and plowed his gloved fist into Bobby's ribs. I gave the cop a thumbs-up, then fell into step behind Hong Chul.

"Hope you fight as good as your boy there, Cole-ah."

Hong Chul nudged my ribs, digging into the bruise I'd found there. I winced but kept from moaning.

"I think you're going to need it with this Rollins dude 'cause from what I heard, that guy sounds kind of fucked-up."

I DIDN'T like what Hong Chul told me. Bobby liked it even less.

"So the guy we're looking for is who again?" Bobby angled the Hummer away from a tiny Toyota careening across the lanes beside us.

It was always tricky navigating Los Angeles's freeways, especially during the midafternoon when it was relatively clear in spots. For some reason, people thought it meant lanes were suggestions and turn signals were for the weak. Bobby's natural aggression, combined with a few negligent drivers, made for a fun trip to the hospital.

"Jesus, did you leave any paint on that Camry's ass? Do you want to maybe back up and check?" I held my breath as the Hummer zoomed toward an off-ramp. "Seriously, you taking driving lessons from Jae?"

"Shut the fuck up about my driving and talk to me about Rollins." Bobby slowed the beast he was driving down as we approached the light at the end of the ramp. "Hong Chul was serious? About Kim Min-Shik running drugs out of Sojuju? And this guy Rollins is hooked up with is what? A cooker? Or just distributing?"

"Maybe not Min-Shik, and this guy's probably not the cooker. His name's Darren Suh, and he's been there awhile. Maybe five or six years." I felt no compunction in holding on to the armrest when we took off again. "Mostly party shit, but a few bad tabs of E can fuck someone up like no one's business."

"Shit. I'd never have thought Rollins would hook up with someone like that. He was always... hard-nosed about chems."

"Yeah, well I never thought he'd start shooting my head off, but he seems to have taken that up as a hobby lately." The hospital loomed up over the surrounding area, a beacon of safety calling to me in the sea of craziness around me. We turned a corner and came to a dead stop, thwarted by a long line of semis blocking an intersection half a block away.

"Focus, Princess. Are we sure Rollins is still with Suh?" Bobby made a face. "Did I pronounce that right?"

"Your guess is as good as mine. I have a hard enough time with the *ch* sound in Jae's name. Give me an ñ any day of the week. I can rock *that* sound." I made myself comfortable, wishing I'd grabbed another bottle of cold water before we'd left JoJo's. "Yeah, Hong Chul said he went in late last night and talked up a few of the guys working the kitchen. Suh's not popular, and he's on and off with Rollins, who no one likes. He deals stuff out of the club, and according to a couple of pissed-off servers, he steals people's bookings. Watches the floor for someone to make their pick, then grabs them before the other server can get to them."

"That shit really weirds me out. Feels like an auction block." He gripped the wheel, squeaking its leather wrap.

"Common practice. Do as the Romans do and all that shit. Jae and Ichi didn't even blink, so... there you go." I shrugged. "Suh hooked up with Rollins when he came into the club. Details are kind of fuzzy there, but he shows up on the weekends. Mostly to watch Suh. Seems our friend Darren likes to play fast and loose with his fidelity. But any front-door guys who bounce Rollins for making trouble find themselves with a pink slip. So Suh's got some pull with Jae's uncle. There's a connection there."

"The drugs?" Bobby wrinkled his nose. "Man, I hate that more than the booking. Think Scarlet's guy knows about what his baby brother is doing?"

"Probably not, but it's not his place. Kim Min-Shik may be Seong's brother, but it doesn't mean they sit in each other's pockets. Scarlet says they barely stand each other, but I think a lot of that has to do with the shit that Min-Ho let his family pull on Jae."

"So if O'Byrne goes in, what is she going to find?"

"Probably nothing. She's a cop... and well, a she." I pointed out the obvious. "When I'm done visiting with Mike, I'll give her a call and see if she's up to letting me shake down Suh."

"You think she's going to buy that?" He gave me filthy look. "Right. Like that's going to happen."

"I've got a few things going for me. One, I'm a gay guy with a hot brother and an even hotter Korean boyfriend. I can get in the door and look around. She won't be able to." I ticked off my reasoning. "I'm not looking for Rollins. I want Suh. I find him, make it worth his while to tell me where we can find Rollins, and squeak on out."

"And what makes you think Suh's going to just cough up where Rollins is?" Bobby tapped at his horn to warn off a Honda creeping into our side. "Rollins is his fuck buddy."

"Yeah, but Kim Min-Shik is his boss." I flipped the air-conditioning on and leaned into the cold air coming out of the Hummer's vents. "While

Jae's uncle might own the club, Seong Min-Ho has K-town by the balls. And I sure as fuck am not afraid to ask him to squeeze."

BOBBY MUST have felt I was safe enough inside of the hospital, because he stalled at the cafeteria's door to call Ichi, waving me to go on when I stopped to let him catch up. From the gooey look on his face, it was going to be a while.

The guard at the door was one I recognized. Hell, I'd paid him to make the iron and wood gate at our house, so recognize was maybe slicing it a bit thin. Medium height and thick chested, Tremblay gave me a wide grin when he saw me coming down the hall. He'd left the standard McGinnis Security suit at home, opting for a black polo and khakis. His arms and hands were bruisers, rough from shaping metal and bending it to his will.

"Hey, McGinnis. Dodge any anvils today?"

Tremblay had a rich voice, a booming, melodic roll that reminded me of butterscotch and whiskey every time I heard him.

The taunting note I deserved. A roofer was onsite when Tremblay was installing the gate, and I'd somehow just avoided being assaulted by a pack of roofing shingles when they tumbled down to the sidewalk where I'd been standing.

"Day's young. Shit, not even ten o'clock yet." I checked the digital readout above the nurses' station. "Your boss still alive and kicking?"

"Yep. Maddy's gone to the hotel next to the hospital to rest. They're finally going to spring Mike later, and she didn't want to come all the way here only to just have to turn around and go back."

Tremblay opened the door for me, his eyes still on the hallway to watch for threats.

"Let me know if you need something. I've got a rookie doing secondaries today. He's earning his keep fetching coffees and stuff for the nurses."

"Great. If he trots by again, I'd kill for an iced coffee with cream and sugar." My body was aching a bit from the gym, and sitting in the car hadn't helped any.

I started for my wallet, but Tremblay shook his head.

"No, don't worry about it. We've got a tab running downstairs. Go on in. I'll take care of it."

"You going to stand there all day? Or are you coming inside?" Mike called out to me from his hospital bed.

He sounded better, garrulous as hell, and from the scowl on his face, itching to get out of his enforced medical confinement.

"Hey, Greg, can you ask the kid to grab me an iced coffee too?"

"Are they letting you have that?" I was skeptical. Last I heard, he wasn't allowed anything more stimulating than a weak cup of herbal tea.

"Fuck that. I'm getting a headache from withdrawals," he growled back. "Now get in here and shut the goddamn door. There's a hippie chick someplace on this floor who keeps singing the fucking "Age of Aquarius" and only knows the first half. She's been on repeat for the last two hours. I was about to slip her something to shut her the hell up, but they took her someplace. If we're lucky, Spaceship Ruthie will come by and pick her up."

"God, I miss that woman. She was awesome." I closed the door behind me, leaving Tremblay to keep watch for crazy ex-cops who wanted to kill me. "How are you doing? Besides stir-crazy."

"You have no idea," he grumbled, then made a face. I didn't have to remind him of my time struggling to come back from my own coma. "Shit. Just… shit."

"Ah, so eloquent." I pulled up a chair to sit down next to his bed. "So when are they springing you? That infection gone?"

"Yeah, all cleared up. Antibiotics took care of it. That and soup."

A knock on the door announced a skinny kid with jug ears in a suit way too big for him. Holding out a pair of iced coffees, he babbled for a bit, then practically tripped on himself to get out of the room. Laughing under his breath, Mike passed me one of the coffees and a straw.

"Here, take this. And don't choke to death on an ice cube."

"Funny. I'll have you know I've been murder threat free all day." I thought of the Toyota. "Okay, we did drive down the 110, but it's always Death Race 2000 there. Ichi said he'll be by later if you're still here. If not, he'll head over to the hotel to hang with Mad Dog."

"Actually, I'm kind of glad you're by yourself today."

The serious was back on Mike's face, and for a long moment he looked so much like our father it gave me chills.

"I wanted to talk to you about some stuff."

Now he even *sounded* like Dad.

"What's up?" The coffee was good, definitely not from the cafeteria if the logo on the cup was any indication.

"You're going through with chasing Rollins down, aren't you?"

It wasn't much of a question. Not with the flat finality in Mike's voice. I nodded, and his sigh was heavier than Atlas's burden.

"I guess telling you not to isn't going to make one fuck of a difference?"

"Probably not, no," I admitted. "But I'm being careful. Not going into any place alone, and hell, I'm pretty sure the Hummer Seong loaned me is bulletproof."

"Thing is, Cole, *you're* not." Mike sat up, grunting as he folded himself forward. Grabbing his side, he muttered, "Fuck, this hurts."

"Yeah, I know." I helped him up, easing a pillow behind his shoulders. "Don't overdo it. Remember? You'll make the scarring worse. Just relax and take it easy."

"How the hell can I take it easy when you're out there doing one stupid thing after another?"

"I'd have thought you'd be used to that by now," I teased. "Besides, we got a lead on Rollins, and I'm letting O'Byrne know what I'm doing every step of the way."

I filled him in on the club and what Hong Chul found out. If Mike'd been frowning at me before, he was thunderous now, but he kept quiet, letting me outline everything we knew or suspected. When I was done, his hair was in full spike mode, and he was turning his wedding ring around on his finger, chewing on his lip. It was a thinking thing for him, so I sat there, drank my coffee, and waited for him to find the end of his thoughts.

"I don't want you going in there. Not by yourself. This son of a bitch has it in for you." Mike grabbed at my wrist. "Cole, for fuck's sake. Don't...."

My brother wasn't the sentimental type. Hell, he was barely the demonstrative type. When he'd first introduced me to Maddy, I seriously wondered what she saw in him. I *knew* Mike. He was a salt-of-the-earth kind of guy, but that salt required some serious mining to get to. Sitting in his hospital bed, he was nearly emotional and a hair's breadth from being overwrought.

That scared me more than the bullets he'd taken.

"Hey, I'm not going to do this solo. Even O'Byrne thinks we'll have better luck if I go in with Wong, but it's iffy on Jae, but we might need him. The clientele is mostly Korean, Mike. The cops aren't going to get their feet in the door, even out of uniform. Not a lot of Koreans in the LAPD." I patted his hand, hoping it was more reassuring and less like I was trying to dig his nails out of my arm. "Bobby gave her some crap about coming along, but I don't think she was convinced. We'll see. Besides, I'll be wired up, and the place pats down for weapons."

"His boyfriend's a waiter there. You don't think he could get Rollins in without the bouncers noticing?" Mike scoffed. "And shit, now I've got to figure out if I'm going to cut Kim Min-Shik loose. I'm not in the business of protecting drug dealers."

"Can't say Kim's connected to that," I admitted. "We know Darren Suh is, and that's as far as anyone's found out. Kim's leery about homosexuals, for God's sake. If he knew what was going on in that club, you think Suh'd still be working there?"

"Don't know." Mike rubbed at the stubble on his jaw. "Just... be careful, okay?"

"Aren't I always?" Medusa would have envied the look my brother gave me. Prodding him on the good side of his rib cage, I asked, "So what did you want to talk about?"

He shifted under his blankets, ducking his head. If I didn't know better, I'd have said his eyes were a little bit damp. "Maddy and I looked at the tests this morning. We're going to have a little girl."

My heart stopped. I had a hitch in my chest, and something fluttered in my gut. For some reason, my mouth seemed determined to crack my face apart, because I couldn't stop smiling, and I did the first thing that came to my mind. I hugged my brother. Very tightly.

Mike yelped so loud, Tremblay came through the door with his hand on his gun.

"No, no. Shit. We're good. Just... talking," Mike coughed out, rubbing at his chest after I let him go. The enforcer shook his head and closed the door behind him, muttering something about lack of common sense running in the McGinnis family.

"Sorry." I tried to sound contrite, but it was hard forcing it past the grin I had on my face. "Shit. Damn. A girl. That is so... *fucking* awesome."

"Yeah, we really wanted a girl," Mike replied gently. "But mostly I just... wanted it to be okay. Healthy, you know?"

"You guys are both fitness freaks. How much more healthy does that kid need to be?" I settled back down into the chair. "Honestly, so damned happy for you guys. And here I was worried because you looked so deadly serious."

"It is kind of serious, Cole." Mike stared off toward the door, not meeting my eyes. "We had to really fight to fix things between us... between me and Maddy, you know? And the baby... she's just like... perfect."

"Hold up." The warmth I'd had spreading inside of me turned glacial, and icy fingers squirmed their way through my blood and into my limbs. "What do you mean fix? Dude, you didn't say jack to me about this. Neither did Maddy. What the hell? When was this?"

"Before Dad and Barbara came. We didn't want to...." My brother rubbed at his face, his palms catching on the bags under his eyes. "You were going through so much shit back then. With Jae. Hell, you were still dealing with Rick and Ben—okay you're still dealing with that crap—but it was always there, Cole. We didn't want to lay that on you. Not then."

If someone'd told me Santa Claus was real and his cold, stiff body had been found in my bed with a couple of dead hookers, I couldn't have been more surprised or shocked. Mike and Maddy were... solid. Beyond solid. Mountains looked at the two of them and envied their stability. If they'd cracked apart, what damned hope did I have of holding on to Jae?

"And what now?" I asked softly. "What the hell is going on now?"

"Now it's... good. Better than good."

Mike looked over at me, and this time there was no mistaking the dampness on his eyelashes.

"That visit with Dad and Barbara changed so fucking much, Cole. See, Maddy's more... she needed more from me than what I was giving her. More... support. More emotional connections. It's what we fought about. Hell, all the time. I worked too hard. I didn't share enough. On my side, I didn't get it. I had no fucking clue what she wanted from me."

"Until Dad's visit?"

"Yeah, until then." Mike nodded. "Dad pissed me off that day. Remember?"

"Yep, you kicked him out of your house. Hell, your life."

"And that's what Maddy needed to see. She needed to know that I *felt*, Cole. Because I'd spent my entire life walling myself up, not showing how I felt because it wasn't... manly enough. Not... I don't know. It never felt right to cry or just get angry about being hurt."

My brother didn't wipe the tear running down his cheek, but I did, catching the small dollop of salty water on my thumb.

"Maddy told me that night she finally believed I loved. Loved her. Loved you. And she was going to hang in there if I was willing to work things out."

"Shit." My gut was twisted in on itself, and there was a part of my mind still wandering around in the no-man's-land of a world without Mike and Mad Dog being married to one another. "You guys are okay, though, right?"

"Yeah, better than okay. See, you were her window, Cole. She could see who I was by how I acted with you. For you. You are the best damned thing that happened to us, and I've never been more thankful for having a pain-in-the-ass little brother than I am right now."

Mike hooked his hand around the back of my neck, shaking me lightly.

"So understand this, brat. You don't let Rollins get to you, because I need my little girl to know her uncle Cole. Because *we all* need to have you around for as long as God lets us. Okay?"

"Promise," I whispered, then smirked. "Hey, I'm so calling the baby Mad Dog Junior."

CHAPTER SIXTEEN

IF THERE was one thing I never needed to see in my lifetime, it was Detective Dexter Wong in a pair of leather pants.

Sadly, that was taken away from me the moment he stepped out of his car at the police station's parking lot, where we'd agreed to meet O'Byrne. The look on our faces must have run the gamut from astonished to horrified and everything in between, because Wong took one look at Jae and I in our jeans and T-shirts and swore at me in Chinese.

"I can't understand a damned thing you're saying to me, Wong." I held my hands up. "Seriously. If you're going to bitch me out, at least let me know it. Or do you have another round to hurl at me?"

"No, that's all the goddamn swearwords I know. Fucking son of a bitch," Wong spat back at me. "O'Byrne said to dress for clubbing!"

Wong didn't look bad. He was handsome enough and in shape, relatively, although there was a bit of a thickness around his belly, but he'd earned that after his girlfriend moved in and they started to eat healthier. Which meant he snuck around behind her back and chowed down on fast food whenever he could. Built more along a stockier frame, Wong filled out the ass of his pants nicely and probably would get more than a few looks at Sojuju, and not just because he was wearing leather during a hot and steamy Los Angeles night.

He still looked like a cop. His short black hair was nearly military in its precise lines, and his eyes scanned the parking lot even though we were surrounded by a lot of people in blue cotton wearing badges and guns.

"You look… nice."

That was Jae's concession as he eyed Wong. I envied his ability to keep a straight face, because the sides of my mouth were hurting as I strained not to laugh.

"I like your shirt. It's a good green for you."

"His shirt's gray." I studied Wong's attire. "Okay, kind of greenish."

"It's bright fucking green, McGinnis." Wong pulled at his T-shirt.

"Don't listen to him, Dex. He can barely dress himself. His world only has nine colors in it, including white and black." Jae put his hand on the small of my back and shoved me toward the door. "Let's go inside. We still have to talk Dell into letting me go."

"That's because you're not a cop, Jae." Wong fell into step behind us, which was a shame because it didn't let me see any of the cops' faces when he passed by. "I'm surprised she's letting McGinnis do this."

"I'm a consultant. Even got a card and shit." I patted my pocket. "I'd dig it out of my wallet, but you know… it's not a sight for mere mortals."

"I'm about to walk into a bullpen full of cops—real cops—I work with wearing a pair of leather pants and a parrot-green shirt." Wong snorted at me. "I passed mere mortal a long fucking time ago, *pukgai*."

"I'M REALLY not comfortable with you going with them, Kim, even if the captain thinks it's our only way in." O'Byrne was standing firm on her decision to keep Jae out of the club. "If Rollins is in there, he's going to target you first because you came in with McGinnis. He's going to know you two are in a relationship."

"How is he going to know that if there are three of us?" Jae asked.

"A rock can see the two of you are together," Wong replied from across the room. "And I thought McGinnis was the stupid one."

The tech wiring us for sound laughed under her breath, then went back to stringing Wong up. I'd already been seen to, and Jae was making his case with O'Byrne as I tried not to fiddle with the tiny black stud she'd put in my left earlobe.

"Stop fucking with that, McGinnis." O'Byrne slapped at my wrist. "I'm going to test the pickup on that thing, and I don't want to hear your fingernails scraping across the mic."

"How come I have to wear a wire, and he gets the James Bond earring?"

Wong's cry was a plaintive one, and I mocked him, pulling my mouth down.

"Screw you, dude. I'm going to lose chest hair when this thing comes off."

"You would need chest hair for any to get pulled out, Wong. And I only had one earring that's clean to wear right now." The tech fixed a slender wire to Dex's side with tape. "Now quit moving. I'd like to go home tonight."

"It's going to be hard to get inside, Dell," I pointed out. "Not that I want him inside, but none of us speaks Korean. Jae could help with that."

"You're not going to understand what anyone's saying around them," Jae insisted. "Someone could be talking about Suh right in front of Cole, and he wouldn't know it."

O'Byrne was having a hard time of it. There were lines being drawn in the sand, and the grains were slippery. If she took a misstep, she'd end up flat on her face. She did the smart thing and glowered.

Wong, however, spoke up. "McGinnis is right. The club's pretty deep in K-town. Sometimes it's hard to get into places because they don't know you. Can't imagine them just letting me and Cole inside a gay club without someone they trusted, even on the surface."

"Not that Wong isn't hot, but without Jae, I don't think we'll get in. We're not their crowd." I wasn't ashamed to admit it. Even with Wong rocking his Whitesnake, I didn't think we would fit. Not without Jae's sleekness with us. "O'Byrne, you know I don't want him in the middle of this, but unless you've got someone who can slide us past a bunch of hardass Korean bouncers, Jae's going to have to get us in. Besides, his uncle owns the damned club."

"Kim, let's you and I go outside and talk." O'Byrne pointed at me. "*You*, stay here. Wong, shut up and… shit, see if you can find a pair of jeans somewhere. You look like you should be in a boy band or something."

I DIDN'T know what Jae said to O'Byrne, but by the time they came back, she was onboard. There were doubts, mostly mine. I wanted to wrap him up and stash Jae away someplace Rollins couldn't find him. Hell, Siberia seemed like a nice vacation spot for the whole family at that moment, but from the determined set of his face, I'd lost the argument before it even began.

The ride to the club was odd. Packed in a cop van with a couple of techs, Jae and I sat as far back as we could without actually sitting on the bumper. His hand was cold, and I held it, rubbing at his fingers to warm them up, but nothing I did seemed to help.

"First hiccup, and you're out the door, right?" I whispered, leaning in close. His hair tickled my nose, and I wanted to kiss his ear, but it didn't feel like the right time. Not when I was practically begging him to abandon me to any trouble I might bring down on us.

"Only if you're in front of me," Jae purred back. "You do this all the time, *hyung*. You rush into places and things without thinking. At least this time there's cops nearby. Listening even. If Rollins is there, you grab me, we go, and we leave this for Dell to clean up."

I thought about promising I would, but if there was one thing Jae and I had between us, it was honesty. I kissed his cheek, then said, "I will try."

"*Aish*," Jae hissed. "That's what you always say, *agi*. But it's also what you never do."

THERE WAS a part of me that wanted to pay one of the bouncers to yank Jae out of the club once we'd gone through the front door, but since he was pretty much our ticket to ride, it would have looked funny. That first part was joined by a second, more insistent voice, informing me there were hungry-eyed men looking to poach on my territory, and I'd have my hands full shoving them back away from Jae.

It was much harder to fight that second inkling than the first, but I did my best. Especially since Jae'd kick my ass. I knew myself well enough to know the line between asshole and possessive was very fine for me where Jae was concerned. He could hold his own and told me that often enough. I believed him, had seen him in action, and while he was the strongest guy I knew, inside and out, I still wanted to protect him.

The literal chink in my armor, because if I had one weakness, it was Jae. I just had to not let Rollins see that if and when he spotted me.

O'Byrne doubted he'd be at the club, but she didn't know him. The Rollins I knew liked being kind of an asshole, a bit of swagger and a hell of a brag when he had a couple of beers in him. There'd always been a grit of nasty in him, something I didn't recognize until after he'd gone by the wayside. I'd been young, stupid, and more than a little naïve back then. Jeff Rollins shaped me in ways I hadn't even realized until much later, and even now, his presence cut me down to the bone—and not just because he was trying to kill me.

"Fuck, this place is loud," I heard Wong shout. "Should have brought earplugs!"

Sojuju was like other Korean dance clubs I'd gone to. They all ran loud, colorfully lit, and packed. Unlike the other clubs, however, this one was nearly wall-to-wall guys. We'd slipped a couple of borrowed Narcotics cops in with us, but they peeled off nearly as soon as we walked in, leaving our trio to wade through the treacherous waters of Sojuju alone.

It was close to midnight, a good time to get into a club on a Friday night, and the floor was packed with men. Dress was casual, and for a lot of the dancers, shirts were accessories left at the table. Big Bang was singing about apologizing, love, and lies. It was one of my favorite songs, and I shimmied behind Jae as we headed in.

"You're silly!" he shouted at me.

"Yeah, but I'm your silly!" I risked losing my fingers and pinched his ass.

Luckily the gods were smiling down on me because he only laughed and continued walking. Glancing behind me, I caught sight of Wong lingering by the door, taking it all in. Either that or he was thinking of finding the exit. It could have gone either way, judging by the lack of color in his face.

Bending down, I asked, "You doing okay, Dex?"

He nodded, but his lips were a tight line.

I didn't know how to come out and ask him if the guys grinding up against each other bothered him. Despite the growing acceptance of homosexuality, there was still a heavy stigma against gays in a lot of Asian communities. I hadn't really thought about it before I met Jae. I'd lived in a content bubble populated with other gay men as we built up our walls and kept the rest of society out, but the threat of violence still lurked. Alive, festering, and waiting.

Humans were violent creatures as a species, and there was always some unseen flashpoint waiting to be hit by a spark, an event seeming so small it could either elevate us to reach out and protect our fellow man or… as so many times before… reduce us to animals.

Inside of clubs and bars, inhibitions were tossed aside because it was safe. Safe to be attracted to another man, dance with someone hot and sweaty, and maybe even have a quick hookup in a dark corner, because nothing felt as good on a gay guy's dick as another guy's rough hand or hot mouth.

Behind walls we danced. We were fireflies doing a mating dance some might not survive to see another, because once we left our vivid, loud sanctuary, we plunged into the unknown, one ripe with hatred and violence.

The irony of being a buffer for Dexter while he navigated the hot, fast rapids of a club filled with horny Asian guys was not lost on me.

"You sure, Dex?" I was pretty sure I was blowing out everyone's eardrums in the van, but there was no getting around how loud the music was. It would be a miracle if anyone in the van heard anything but the music.

"I'm not good with stuff like this… dancing and shit. I spent high school doing homework, not going out," he yelled back. "And I think someone just grabbed my dick, but I'm not sure if I should be pissed off because some fucker touched me or flattered!"

"Go with flattered!" I spotted Jae waving at me from the relative safety of a table, so I shoved Wong his way. "Come on. We got someplace to sit."

Once we were away from the floor, the noise level dropped enough so we could hear ourselves think. The building's well-style construction meant the second-floor landing above the main space caught most of the noise, but it was still loud enough to tweak my ears.

"Do you see Suh?" Wong maneuvered himself into one of the chairs against the wall, leaving a chair on either side of him.

Jae and I exchanged glances; then I nudged Wong's shoulder. "Dude, move over one."

"Shit, sorry." He quickly shuffled over. "I forget, you know. Because… well, shit… you're guys."

Someone in the cop house felt sorry for Wong and located him a pair of jeans, but they were stiff, and from their fresh dye smell, he was going to be sporting woad on his legs for about a week. The stench of blue overpowered the sweat and alcohol aromas around us, but underneath it was a bitter, acrid thread of something chemical. It could have been poppers or something more potent, but it was hard to tell.

Jae's jeans, on the other hand, were held together by a few threads and a prayer. Mostly my prayer because I needed to focus on looking for Suh and *not* on my boyfriend's tight ass.

"No, but we can ask for him if you want." Jae sat down between Wong and I, settling into the metal-backed chair.

"Better if you don't," O'Byrne squawked in my ear. "I've got Vice floating around in there, remember? If they spot Suh, they'll pull him out, and I'll call you in. If you spot Suh, see if you can engage, but do it casually. Asking for him is going to tip our hand. Go dance or something. Scope the place out. Then engage."

"Don't have to ask me twice." I stood up and held my hand out for Jae. "Come on, baby. Let's show Wong what we've got."

"This is why I don't go to clubs," Wong huffed. "I'm always the one holding the table."

"I promise not to have any fun." I was being serious. My stomach was churning, and it all had to do with Jae being on the hot spot with me. I wanted to find Suh, isolate him so O'Byrne's guys could grab him, and then get Jae the hell out of there.

Jae had other ideas.

My dick quickly caught on to Jae's ideas, and I had to rein it in before it got me into trouble. There'd been a case I'd been on before I met Jae, and as a result, I had a crepe-skinned elderly German woman dressed in a leather getup burned into my memory. She'd been firing a shotgun at the time, unerringly aiming for my head, and the resulting combination of horror, disgust, and fear made for a powerful deterrent for any inconvenient hard-on I might get.

It usually worked. Mrs. Birkenhoff hadn't failed me yet. Until the moment my sexy, bendy boyfriend slithered out onto the dance floor and wrapped himself around me.

"You are so much fucking trouble," I muttered at him, knowing he couldn't hear me, but Jae smiled anyway, then hooked me by a belt loop to pull me onto the dance floor.

Despite the valiant effort by the dancers pressing in on each other, there wasn't a lot of room on the floor. The music reached an ear-bleeding screech, then shifted, cutting into something slow and slithery. Jae tugged, and I stumbled forward, right into his arms.

There were a lot of things about Jae I liked. I enjoyed who he was as a person, and he put up with so much of my crap. We shared the same tastes in movies, and he expanded my world in so many ways. I loved the way he laughed in low, soft tones and how he was a grumpy, ruffled mess for the first half hour or so after waking up.

I also loved the way he felt against me.

Jae fit himself into my body, his arms around my waist and his hips snugging up right under the waistband of my jeans. He was more leg than torso, and the scant inches I had on him were a definite advantage, because I didn't have to bend down very far to capture his mouth with mine.

Of all the things I loved about Jae, it was the taste of him I adored beyond measure.

I could live off of Jae's kisses.

The song playing overhead was familiar, probably something I'd heard pumped through the speakers in our house, but we'd never danced to it before. But then truthfully, I danced about as well as a penguin flew through the air. I needed a lot of help, and the landing would always be messy, but for a glorious moment, there was movement.

In this case, Jae did most of the dancing for us, and I was totally fine with that.

We found the roll of the beat, falling into a rhythm we always seemed to find. Our bellies were pressed together, hips swaying down and back while I kept my hands busy sliding over Jae's body. His face was slightly turned away, the lights flashing pink and blue over his ivory skin, but the heat of our bodies simmered and burned, setting me on fire. Jae's full mouth parted, and his tongue ran over his lower lip, laving at the kiss I'd left there. His arms went up, and he moved in closer, until I could feel the brush of his chest on my shirt, rubbing my nipples to hard points.

His back arched, and I trailed my fingers into the dip of his spine. There was a scatter of burnt-caramel freckles over his shoulder blades, and I teased him with light rakes of my nails over the spot, drawing a gasp out of him. Jae lifted his chin and stared into my eyes, holding me with a twist of his hips against mine and the delicate dance of his hands down the front of my jeans.

There wasn't a damned thing my brain had stored up that could compete with the rush I got when Jae flashed me a wanton smile, then licked up the length of my throat, only stopping when he reached the underside of my jaw and sunk his teeth into my skin.

I bent over when he let me go, intending to steal a kiss or maybe even just find a desolate corner where we could make good on the promises we just whispered with our bodies when I felt a hand close over my upper arm, then tug hard to turn me around.

There is a primal reaction to being grabbed from behind for most guys. For a split-second, the brain kicks in a fight response, and no matter how civilized we get, some base instinct curls our balls in, and something reptilian wakes up inside.

So despite my best intentions, I almost punched Darren Suh in the face.

Jae grabbed my arm before I could let fly. It took Suh a moment to realize he was about to lose his teeth, but when it did sink in, his eyes went wide and he let go of me. Backing up quickly until he was off the dance floor, he waved his hands in front of him and let loose a babble of Korean I didn't understand.

"He says he's sorry," Jae translated for me.

No wonder I didn't know what he was saying. The Korean words I knew pretty much centered around fucking and food.

"Someone wants to book you."

"I'm not for booking." I looked from Jae to Suh then back to Jae when he pinched my side. "What? Fuck. Shit. That hurt."

"Go talk to him." He shoved at the small of my back, and the lizard brain rippled back down, leaving me a little light-headed. "You *want* to talk to him."

"Crap, that's right." I closed the few steps between me and Suh, making an apologetic face, then smiling.

Darren Suh looked rough. As in roughed up and blistered. Either he was sampling his own wares and fell down five flights of stairs while stoned off his ass, or someone was using him for target practice. He wore makeup to hide the discoloration I suspected lay under the swollen patch beneath his eye, but nothing could save the bump of his split upper lip. The cupid's bow curve was speckled with dried blood, probably irritated because he couldn't stop licking at the spot. Another bump jutted his jaw out an inch, almost hidden behind a sweep of light brown hair he'd pulled forward.

"*Hyung.*" He eyed me warily but smiled back.

"Sorry. Um… habit." The molasses trickle of a song would be ending soon, and in a few seconds, the only thing I'd be hearing would be my fillings jiggling out of my teeth. "Did you want something?"

Oh, thank God I was already getting laid, because I sucked at chatting guys up. If Wong felt inadequate, I was right up there with him, choking on my own swollen tongue.

Suh tapped my right shoulder, then pointed. "Upstairs."

More Korean from Suh, but this time Jae wasn't at my back. I turned around, trying to find the one person Suh was pointing at among all the other guys moving around on the wraparound floor above us. Suh repeated what he said, then probably frustrated at my sadly lacking lingual skills, tapped my back.

"There." He nudged my chin a few degrees. "He wants you."

I knew the man looking down at me. I'd had his mouth wrapped around my dick, and his fingers explored parts of my body I hadn't even touched myself. He was older, more gray at the temples, and the years seasoned his strong face. Crow's-feet softened the hard edge of his bright blue eyes, but they were still cold, as lifeless as his soul. I was so confused to see him, torn between the infantile disgruntlement at his relationship with Ben—a friendship I had no idea existed—and rage at the senseless war he'd declared on me.

This was the man who'd shot my brother, and he stood there, a few yards away, smirking down at me as if I could do nothing to him.

And I probably couldn't. Not in time. Because as I stood at the edge of a floor full of writhing half-dressed men, Rollins pulled a gun out from the shadows and began shooting.

CHAPTER SEVENTEEN

ROLLINS WAS shooting fish in a barrel.

Literally.

With the second-floor landing wrapping around the area, he had a clear shot at anyone below, and in typical Rollins fashion, he made the most of it.

"Get off the floor!" I shoved Darren Suh farther into the shadows. "Everyone get off the floor!"

A bullet twisted through the shoulder of a guy standing next to me, a spurt of blood gushing out of the wound. Another man, an older and broader Korean, grabbed at the shot dancer, hauling him toward the shadows. He got three steps away before Rollins shot him in the back. They both went down, and then I lost them in the moving crowd.

I couldn't keep track of the flashes and barking pops above me. The tide of fleeing men was hard to fight, but the slamming flesh against me was nothing compared to keeping a hold on my fear for Jae's safety. He was in the sea of bodies, and I needed to find him.

The sound of gunfire never seemed to stop. It was one pop after another, a barrage of booms caught up on the concrete overhang and echoing through the dance club. I tried to break out of the crowd, hoping to get to the stairs, but there were too many people in the way.

"O'Byrne! Shots fired!" I screamed, hoping the mic would pick up my yelling. "Rollins is inside! Repeat, Rollins is the shooter!"

I couldn't see Jae or Wong. But then I couldn't really see anyone. My foot snagged on someone's leg, and we both went down. A knee caught my cheekbone, and I tasted blood in my mouth. Dragging myself up, I pushed at a man barreling toward me, shoving him aside before he bowled me over.

Dread gave way to chaos. I didn't know if Rollins came with more than one weapon and lots of ammo or if he was popping off all thirteen rounds in rapid succession. I *couldn't* think about it. Hell, I could barely think about anything other than Jae and safety.

Time slows to a crawl when you're gripped in fear's tentacles. Every single moment seems pared down to thin slices of jittering scents, sounds, and sights. I caught a whiff of blood first, a splash of metal on sweat. Then time moved forward, snicking off another increment of terror, and I was lost in a sea of panic.

I couldn't remember what Jae was wearing, couldn't find him in the rising tide of flesh around me. I slipped on something wet and forced myself to look down, praying with every ounce of my soul that the bleeding body by my feet wasn't my lover.

It wasn't.

The young man was barely old enough to drink, a thin, shivering boy with a straggly line of facial hair not even thick enough to use mascara on. He moaned, crying out in pain as he was trampled by a thunder-footed woman, her eyes wild and unfocused. Another shuddering jerk forward of a single second, and I was caught on the edge of a razor, balancing my soul on its dangerous edge. I couldn't stop looking for Jae. I *couldn't*. My brain twisted on the Möbius strip I'd fallen into. I could see the booted feet about to land on the young man's head, on his bloodied body, but Jae was out there in the chaos, maybe as hurt… maybe as scared… and I couldn't just abandon Jae to his fate because of a man I didn't know was bleeding out at my feet.

Time went forward again, and another foot gouged into the crying young man's side.

I picked him up. I couldn't *not* pick him up. I sent another prayer, some garbled nonsense of hoping with all my soul that Jae was okay. I *needed* Jae to be okay. I needed him to be fine because I needed to get the man I held in my arms to some kind of safety.

Because I'd brought the terror down on us all.

I got kicked in the shoulder and nearly tumbled down to the floor. Staggering, I lifted him up and let myself get carried on the moving tide of bodies. In my ear, O'Byrne was shouting about shots being fired and someone going in. I didn't care if anyone heard the tinny voice coming from my earlobe. Chances were no one could even make out what she was saying, and the screams of the wounded and dying almost drowned her out.

Hands were on my back, guiding me off the floor. I couldn't hear any more shots, but the screams continued, a strident layer of sobbing and shouts. The music continued to thump and grind out of the club's speakers, tucking in and out of the pained cries.

The club's floor was concrete, probably for easier cleanup, considering what men sometimes left behind, but in this case, I wished they'd gone with something more sturdy like Astroturf. My Converses weren't getting enough traction on the ground, and I seemed to unerringly find every spilled drink and pile of ice cubes between the dance floor and the door.

I kept swallowing my fear. My spit thickened with every step I took away from the dance floor, because I'd left Jae someplace behind me. Another jostle, and I nearly dropped my sobbing burden. Strong arms came up from the side of me, and I blinked, staring numbly at the blue-uniformed EMT reaching for the man I held.

"Give him over!" The EMT eased his arms under mine. "You get out!"

Handing over the injured Korean man was easy enough. I willingly passed him into the EMT's arms, but as soon as I could let go, I headed back to the floor. Somewhere out in the lights and pain was Jae, and I needed to know he was safe.

I wouldn't be able to breathe again—live again—until I held Jae in my arms.

There were injured everywhere. Some shot while others were victims of the crowd's panic. One man lay curled up into a ball, holding his hand and weeping while a cop dressed in body armor stood under the flashing lights with a shotgun pointed up at the second floor. There was the deep rumble of officers clearing one space, then another, boots stamping and shaking the landing above us. Even above the music, I could hear the cold, methodical brusque shouts ordering people to raise their hands and get to their knees.

Tonight there were only going to be victims and suspects until God and the badges sorted them out.

The speakers went quiet, and for a second, my brain hiccupped, unsure about the stillness and the lack of vibration in my eardrums. A squeaky purr muffled the sounds around me. Then my ears popped, leaving me with ringing echoes I couldn't shake. One of the cops tried to push at me, shoving me toward the door, but I shook him off.

"Not leaving here without my boyfriend," I growled back. It came out probably louder than I wanted it to. I couldn't hear myself, but I didn't care. The ground was littered with fallen men, and my gut was knotted up, fearful I'd find Jae unmoving among them. My ear crackled, and a tinny shout bounced out of it.

"McGinnis!" O'Byrne's voice sounded strained, a far cry from her steady, gruff purr. "Get the fuck out of there."

I ignored her. The crowd was lessening, and the cop who'd tried to shove me out turned his attention to getting someone up off the floor. It was hard to tell who was wounded and who was in shock. Perhaps everyone was a little of both, because violence was never as clean and exciting as a movie made it. It was messy and bitter, a sharp tang sitting on the roof of your mouth, and no matter how hard you swallowed, it lingered, fouling everything.

And I still couldn't find Jae. The panic was setting in, and I went from person to person on the floor, nearly shoving aside the medics as they worked, looking for that one sweet, familiar face I needed to see. One of the EMTs shoved me back, calling for the cops to come grab me, when I saw Jae walk out of the shadow and onto the lit-up dance floor.

"Cole-ah!" he said he as grabbed me, but I was faster, embracing him hard enough to make him squeak. "*Hyung*, I'm okay. I'm…."

My heart pounded and my skin crawled, nerves drawn too tight to do anything but snap back, a rubber band of tension held taut until I had Jae's kiss on my mouth. I blinked, and the world changed, dulling and peeling up, cracked under the memories I couldn't hold back.

Everything was bleached out. The floor. The lights. Even the cover of darkness under the landing paled to a grayness, and the world fell quiet. Silent except for a single buzzing note. If time stood still in the shooting, it was rolling back under the force of my fear.

It wasn't Jae I was holding. The warm body in my arms belonged to my lover, but my mind was pulling up the horror of Rick's blown-off face, the hot splash of his brains and blood on my face, then the searing agony of my sides being torn apart under a hail of bullets from a gun I'd helped my best friend pick out.

Then in a second, the sensation passed, washing away the ashes of that night with the tearful relief of having Jae, alive and breathing, pressed up against me.

"Cole. I am okay," Jae murmured into my panting mouth. "I'm here. You're okay. We're all okay."

"It's not going to fucking be okay, love," I whispered back. "Not until I stop this fucker. Because as long as he is out there, you're not safe. I can't live with that. I'm not going to stop until this fucking son of a bitch is in jail or dead. And I don't care which."

WE DIDN'T get home until nearly seven in the morning. We'd lost hours sitting in interrogation rooms, and O'Byrne's absence worried me while I was being grilled by some buck-toothed asshole who had less sense than a drowning turkey. Despite the clearance she'd gotten from her captain, having us on-scene turned out to be a huge fuck-up once Rollins was added to the mix. Everything pointed to Rollins not being at the club. He hadn't been seen there for a long time according to every source asked, but Rollins was as unpredictable as a rabid hyena and just as dangerous. O'Byrne'd planned for Rollins's presence. Even as she sent us in, she'd planned for something bad to happen.

It was a pity everything went down exactly as she'd planned.

Now Darren Suh was missing, having slipped out of the club in the ensuing chaos, and nearly everyone on the stakeout was pissed off at me for letting him go. The grumbling and concessions started once I pointed out I hadn't really let him go as much as I was avoiding getting shot. Funny how things changed once hot flying metal is brought into the conversation.

We were no closer to finding out where we could put our hands on Rollins than we had been before the foray into Sojuju, and I still had no fucking clue about why he was on my ass in particular. I'd pretty much ruled out anyone hiring him. Not after seeing the smirk on his face and the hatred in his eyes. The shit he was raining down on me wasn't about money. It was personal. And as usual, I was missing more than a few puzzle pieces.

In broad daylight, the penthouse was a sea of white and neutral. But still, it was a home of sorts, and Honey met us at the door, wagging her tail as furiously as her butt could churn. She was also happy to get outside to the roof, piss, and gambol back down, ready for her breakfast. Breakfast was out for me. My stomach was sour from cups of cop-house coffee, and there'd been a pink sprinkle donut at some point, but it was a distant, sugary memory.

Honey was still foraging her dish for kibble when I had to make good with Neko by giving her a small can of very stinky wet food that resembled regurgitated squid. She took one nibble, then went to see what I'd given the dog.

"Fuck you both."

It was a halfhearted curse, and they shrugged me off, burying their faces in Honey's bowl.

"Well, at least you get along."

"Cole!" Jae called from upstairs. "Come take a shower!"

I reeked. I was bloodied, sweaty, and tired, but Jae was upstairs waiting for me. So was the bed, but Jae was a better deal all around. Leaving the animals to their breakfast, I headed to the upstairs bedroom. There was an ungrateful pissy moment when my brain whispered a disgruntled aside about the empty main-floor bedroom, but I quickly shut it down. My nerves were too strained from the past week, and all I wanted was a cool shower and a soft bed.

I got the cool shower. And a hot boyfriend.

Jae was naked and under the rain showerhead by the time I got to the bathroom. Stripping my clothes off was a little painful. My muscles ached from being seized up in a panic, and my ears still rang a little bit, throwing me off-center. There were still bruises on my body from everything I'd done to myself, and there were still shiny pink spots on my forearms from the road burn I'd taken.

All of that went away as soon as I saw Jae standing in a pour of water, the ivory length of his body spotted with lather from the blue pouf he held in his hand. Our eyes met through the glass wall, and he smiled, warming away any chilled fear lurking in my soul.

"Hey." I slid in next to him, balls and cock swinging free and interested. I looked a mess. I knew it. He'd have to have been blind not to see it, but Jae reached for me anyway, wrapping his arms around my waist. "Fancy meeting you here."

"Almost like we'd planned it." He wrinkled his nose and turned us both, letting most of the water hit me. "*Aish*, you smell."

"Keeps the wolverines away. Like cougar piss." The water was lukewarm and soothing. I let it beat along my side for a minute, breathing in the mist and Jae's soap. "You doing okay?"

"Is this where you say I told you so for me wanting to come with you?" Jae traced around my left nipple, playing with the water trailing down my chest. "O'Byrne agreed it wasn't going to be dangerous. It wasn't… you two were going to look for Suh, and I was not going to get in the way. That's what we agreed on. There wasn't supposed to *be* any shooting. It was supposed to be safe."

"Things are never safe. Now O'Byrne's ass is a bit roasted, and Suh is in the wind. Neither of which is your fault. Or mine. I wouldn't be surprised if I lost my flashy contractor card." I exhaled out hard, hoping to lessen the pressure in my chest. "I knew we weren't going to get through the door without you. And Hong Chul... he'd already asked about Suh. He'd have been spotted, and Suh would probably have taken off. It just went bad, so very fucking bad, and now... I have no idea what to do now. Just sit and wait for Rollins to pop back up, I guess. It's the safest thing *to* do."

"LAPD needs more Koreans." Jae's fingers were doing a dance across my belly. "Maybe for things like this?"

"They'd still be cops. And before now, Narcotics didn't have enough interest in the place to run anyone with us. O'Byrne did the best she could with what she had." I rocked Jae back and forth in my arms, just enough to get his back wet. "We just weren't enough."

Jae rested his cheek on my shoulder, tucking himself into the curve of my body. "Everyone did their best. I was there, remember?"

"Babe, we are never doing something like that again. Ever." Nuzzling his neck, I sighed. "God, I was so fucking... scared."

The fatigue plaguing me hit, and I tried to hold in my emotions, lifting my head up to let the spray hit my face. Jae cupped my face in his hands and forced me to look at him. I let him. Hell, I'd let him do anything he'd ever want to do after tonight.

"I will do whatever you want, if you just promise not to do stupid things," I said.

"That is pretty funny coming from you."

"Yeah, well, I'm swearing off stupid things too. Really, anything you want. Just promise."

"So I don't have to de-head the shrimp anymore when I cook *dubu jjigae*?" He tilted his head back, studying my disgusted expression. "Yeah, I didn't think so, *hyung*."

"Eyeballs!" I grimaced and made wiggly motions with my fingers in front of his face. "And antennae. Like wiggling little stick things twitching and stuff."

"The shrimp's cooked, Cole-ah. If they're still moving when we eat, then we've got bigger problems than antennae."

"You put the heads on your fingers and wiggle them at me," I accused. "Twice you've done that."

"That's because it's funny. You almost scream."

"So not funny." Sighing, I pulled him closer. "Just like tonight. So not fucking funny. I did something I'm not too proud of tonight."

"Tease Wong about his leather pants?" Jae grinned. "They were pretty bad. No one would blame you for that."

"Took balls to wear those into a cop house," I conceded. "No, I mean, when Rollins started shooting the place up, I just wanted to grab you and get the fuck out."

"I'd call that a rare instance of when your common sense kicked in," he replied as he reached for the scrubby.

"It wasn't common sense... it was being selfish. There was this guy... and he'd been hit, but I didn't want to...." We shared everything. Or at least I did. Jae was working on it. Talking about how I felt in that moment I stumbled over the guy bleeding out on the floor wasn't going to be pleasant. "I didn't want to help him. I just wanted to say fuck it and find you. Screw everyone else. Just fuck all of them. I didn't care. Or maybe I just care about you more. But it feels like shit, you know? That I didn't just grab him without... shit."

Jae's gaze was a honey slick of concern, and he stroked my cheek with his fingertips. "But you helped him, yes?"

"I didn't *want* to. I wanted to fucking leave him there and find you." It tore me up inside to know I was willing to let someone die to go find Jae, but I knew I'd feel the same if it happened again. "It's a shitty thing to do, babe. Right there, I didn't *like* me. Not one fucking bit."

"I think right then, you were just being human," Jae corrected. "All of this shit with Rollins has a purpose, yes? We might not understand why, but it does. You're *feeling* again, Cole-ah. Maybe for the first time since you woke up after Ben, you're stopping to think instead of rushing in. You've changed in the last couple of weeks—"

"That's just lack of sleep." I broke in to lighten things between us.

"No, it is not." Jae poked my bruised ribs. "You've *changed*. And it's for the good. Instead of running to the man with the gun, you thought of us. You have been thinking of us and the family for a while now, and that's not a bad thing, Cole-ah. Tonight, you were human. Then you chose to do the right thing. Because that is who you are inside. That is the man I fell in love with. And still love."

"You're an idiot," I snorted. "At least for loving me."

"Yes, but I am your idiot." He gave me a brief kiss. "Now turn around and let me wash your back. I want to go to bed and do bad things to you there."

CHAPTER EIGHTEEN

I WOKE up draped in shadows, and my brain kicked in to a fierce panic. There was a weight on me, warm and familiar, while another small heaviness lay on my foot. It took a second for my eyes to adjust, but eventually I could see the Los Angeles skyline rise out of the gloomy dim, a universe of lights and jutting shapes beneath a film of low-lying clouds.

The small weight turned out to be the dog, who whined when I moved her. The heavier, longer weight was a passed-out Jae, one arm flung up over his head and his hand flopped over my mouth, nearly smothering me.

My bladder refused to let me lie still, and since I'd moved, the dog squirmed about at the foot of the bed, a little warning dance heralding a massive puddle of piss if I didn't move fast enough.

"Hold on, baby dog." I eased myself out from under Jae. It was going to be a tight squeeze for me and the dog. "You're coming with me."

The skin across my hips was tight from needing to pee, but the dog was boggle-eyeing me, sniffing at the air to hurry me along. I scooped Honey up and carried her into the bathroom with me, then put her in the shower. Relieving myself quickly, I checked to see if she'd held it, but she was already doing her happy kicking with her back legs and dancing in a puddle on the tiled floor.

"Shit. Well no, no shit. Do you need to shit?" I turned on the shower, flicking the water to the handheld sprayer. She licked at my face while I washed her paws, then wiggled about when I tried to towel her dry. "Okay, this would be so much better if you used the litter box."

I snuck the dog out quietly, taking her up to the roof so she could destroy the grassy beds planted above the penthouse. The evening air was crisp, smelling of rain and electricity. In the distance, lightning played through the clouds on the horizon, teasing the sea with crackling strokes. A mist dappled my face, and I blinked away a fringe of drops from my lashes, shivering in my boxers when the wind picked up.

"You could hurry this up, kiddo," I told the dog. "Unlike you, I don't have fur."

She did her business and again kicked up a storm with her back legs. Satisfied with herself, Honey trundled on down the stairs and headed to the main floor, probably to hoover up the reflection in her bowl. I followed her, fed her and the cat dinner, and petted Neko when she came over to sink her claws into my bare leg.

"Yeah, the schedule's fucked-up, but you still got breakfast and dinner." I unhooked her points from my skin. After I patted the blood away with a paper towel, I nudged her bowl across the counter. "This is kind of where I came in last night."

My teeth were furry, and I longed to go back to bed, but Jae would be hungry and probably a little grumpy when I crawled back into bed with nothing but cold feet and a frozen nose. He and Neko shared a lot of the same traits. Both were prickly for a few minutes after they woke up and when hungry, could strip a cow in thirty seconds.

Knowing this, I brought up two mugs of Vinacafe and toasted brown-sugar Pop-Tarts with me when I invaded the bedroom. He was lying facedown, his head buried under a couple of pillows, but I would have sworn I saw his butt twitch at the smell of caramelized sugar and silky strong coffee.

"Mmfel cofgur?" he mumbled from under his cave. Since I had become fluent in Jae-speak, I sat on the edge of the bed and held a mug out until he grudgingly sat up.

A half-awake Jae was probably the cutest thing I'd ever seen. His rumpled hair flopped down into barely open eyes, catching on his lashes, and his mouth was always slightly swollen because he bit his lower lip in his sleep sometimes. Since he couldn't stand to sleep with a shirt on, his pale skin prickled with goose bumps, and I knew he was almost sentient when he rubbed at his right arm to warm himself up. There were other smaller things he did, quirks that changed from day to day. Some days he'd rub at his ear or fiddle with his belly button ring or scratch his chest. But his wake-up fumble always ended with a lengthy rub along his arm and then a sweet, beautiful smile.

He'd told me more than once he only smiled in the morning when he saw me. I could melt glaciers with the soft, warm burst his shy, barely there smile gave me.

It also meant he was ready for coffee.

We had our rituals in the morning. Jae would either be up and gone by the time I woke up or lie in bed until I brought him up a cup of hot, strong, and sweet brew. Waking up at six in the evening, our calm torn to shreds by Rollins's fuckery, and sleeping in a strange bed did odd things to our rhythm, but it was Jae's smile that brought everything back into place.

I climbed into the bed behind him, putting my legs on either side of his body. He lay against me, sipping the coffee, and we both watched Los Angeles dress itself in lights and prepare for the encroaching storm. A minute later, the mug was half-empty, and Jae was mostly awake, carding his fingers through his hair and grumbling about the stickiness on his teeth.

"Coming back," he warned me. "Don't drink my coffee."

I drank it anyway, leaving my full cup on the nightstand for when he came back.

"That was mine," Jae huffed, padding back into the room. Most of his grumpy had been peeled off with toothpaste and soap, but a bit of grit remained.

"No, this one's yours. It's even full." I grinned and held up the cup off the nightstand while he climbed into bed, sitting across my legs.

They'd go numb perhaps, but it was worth having his thigh up against my crotch. It also meant his hands were pretty much able to touch any part of me he wanted. I could always count on Jae's incessant need to touch.

And he didn't disappoint me.

"I never did get to do naughty things to you this morning." Jae looked at me over the edge of his cup.

"Nope. I think we both passed out midkiss." I rested my head against the tufted headboard everyone and his fairy godmother seemed to have in their bedrooms now. "Actually, I think I was midnibble, and then the next thing I know, I've got your fingers up my nose."

His horrified look was epic, and he slapped my leg when I laughed.

"You're a dick, *agi*." His tongue made short work of the foam smeared over his upper lip, and I chased it back into his mouth with a kiss. When we finished, he handed me the cup and said, "Put that on the table."

I stretched over, fumbling the cup and nearly dropping it on the floor, but Jae was waiting for me when I leaned back. He turned, getting on his knees between my legs, and pressed me into the headboard. Its small fabric-covered buttons dug into my back, and I hissed at the scraping pull on my skin.

"Hurt?" Jae sucked my lower lip into his mouth.

"Uh… hrrr."

It was my turn to mumble, but Jae seemed to understand me anyway, because he slid his hands into the waistband of my boxers. My body sang under his fingers, and he cupped me, stroking at my shaft in its cotton prison.

"I kind of like you like this, Cole-ah."

He'd let go of my lips but moved on to my neck, nipping at every sensitive spot he could find. Jae soothed the sharp stings from his teeth with gentle kisses. Keeping me trapped against the headboard, he continued to explore my body as if he'd never touched me before.

Odd how he found every single one of the places I loved to be stroked.

I reached for Jae's hips, intending to shove his sweats down, but he pulled back, pinning me with his hands on my shoulders. Shaking his head, Jae held me still. He was strong, lithe and muscular despite his lanky frame, and there was a dangerous glint in his golden-brown eyes.

Jae nuzzled my ear, then bit my lobe. I yelped, and his knee bore down into my crotch. The pressure was steady and light, but there was no mistaking Jae's intent. I was meant to stay put and, more than likely, be quiet.

I didn't do quiet well.

But then neither did Jae.

We tangled into each other, awkward elbows and knees banging into ribs and legs. The tension building in my gut broke, spooling out into a desperate aching need for him, and I clawed at his sweats, finally getting them free. I had him on the bed, on his back and staring up at me. My unshaven face left scrapes along his chest and collarbone, slender red welts marbling his pale skin. His nipples were flushed and tight, drawn into hard nubs, and I bent my head, tonguing one up against my front teeth.

He gasped, pushing up into my belly, and I tugged at his nipple, worrying it until the skin was bright and sharp tasting on my tongue. Letting go, I licked at the spot, and Jae slithered away, sliding out from under me.

"Too much?"

I slid a hand over his ribs. He sat on his haunches and stared back at me.

"What?"

"Can I have you, *hyung*?" He trailed his fingertips over my mouth, and I kissed them. "This time? Now?"

"Yeah. So long as you're sure." I cupped his face, and he leaned into my hand, pressing his cheek into my palm. "Because if you don't want to... don't think you have to because of... me, babe. I...."

Loving Jae was sometimes complicated. No, loving Jae was easy. How to love Jae was complicated. We both had our broken strings and banged-up souls, but his pieces were more tightly wound around things I could never hope to understand. I tried. God knows I tried, but there were so many bruises on his soul I couldn't make heads or tails of because they were so far outside of my own experiences.

I also couldn't even begin to imagine how anyone... how his family... used him, peeled him apart and left him torn into pieces to wither away in a very cruel and unforgiving world.

In all of my pain, I had Mike and Maddy. There were others along the way. Ben, Rick, Bobby, and Claudia to name a few. I could even plunge myself into the senseless hedonism of being a gay man in Los Angeles if I'd wanted to, free to bathe myself in satisfying my own needs.

For Jae, his family came first. They were his needs. Everything he had, everything he was, went to keeping their lives and traditions going. And with every breath he took, he died more and more because he wasn't truly living. Never truly loving and always alone.

Until he asked me to catch him if he fell. Until he asked me to love him with all of my heart and every thread of my soul.

He'd hated being gay, hated wanting a man to love him, and the thought of sex with another man, penetrating another man, scared him. If fear was the right word. I couldn't grasp it. It was too slippery, a will-o'-wisp of an idea too foreign for me to comprehend, but when he felt safe, he would sometimes ask—tentatively, as if he thought I could ever refuse him—if he could be inside of me.

I always said yes, knowing it was important for him to make that step across the chasm he'd dug and hoping that one day he'd accept I'd give him anything he wanted. Take anything he gave. Because I loved him. And I wanted him to be happy.

There was also the sheer pleasure I got knowing Jae was filling me and I could make him lose his mind, clenching tightly around his cock and kissing him senseless as I brought him over the edge.

"Baby, please…." I rubbed my palm against the head of his dick. "I love it when you fuck me."

WE WENT slow. Or at least he insisted on going slow. Jae needed coaxing, reassuring he was doing all right. His touch was tentative, feeling me out carefully. Despite the time we'd spent together and the pleasure we'd made, there was still some small part of Jae's mind I couldn't touch… a sliver of apprehension because someone at a point in the past hurt him.

He never spoke about it, but it was there. A hesitation, mostly because he was afraid he'd cause me pain.

It hurt me more knowing Jae was willing to take me inside, risking his own pain instead of finding that pleasure in me.

So we went slow. Because Jae needed it.

Sometimes, it just killed me. Because damn, I wanted him in me.

The lube we'd brought with us was something I'd tossed into the bag. I hadn't been thinking clearly. Obviously some part of my brain equated Jae and a suitcase with lube, because I'd grabbed a sampler pack we'd picked up at a pride festival. It had a range of scents and alleged flavors, none of which proved to be anywhere close to realistic when we'd opened them up.

"This is supposed to be green tea." Jae sniffed at the open bottle. "It smells more like honey."

"Honey the dog or the bee vomit?" I propped myself up on my elbows and grinned at his long-suffering, exasperated sigh. "Valid question."

"From bees. Not the dog." He kissed me, a long, smoldering glide of his mouth on mine, and I moaned, opening my lips to take his tongue. "Can we *not* talk about the dog right now, *agi*?"

"What dog?" I ran my hand down his belly, then grasped his length. "Just you and me here, babe."

The lubricant smelled sweet and was a touch cold when Jae drizzled a thin line of it on my balls. I gasped at the chill, more surprised than anything else, and he gave me a wicked grin.

"Sorry."

He didn't sound sorry. I didn't expect him to be. I'd gotten him more than a few times with still chilly lubricant, so reaping what I'd sowed wasn't a surprise. It lightened the heaviness between us, and the tension uncoiled out of his shoulders. Pressing against my entrance, he toyed with me, spreading me apart slightly so he could dip the tip of his finger in. I slid my hand around the back of his neck, pulling his head down. Our kiss was as slow as his tease, savoring the taste of our bodies and how we fit.

We fit *very* nicely.

I used my thumb to circle around Jae's head, smearing the damp spot at his tip. He shivered under my touch, his cock trembling in my palm. The light trail of hair on his belly tickled the back of my hand, a butterfly sensation on my skin. Our kiss lingered, the taste of coffee on his tongue a sweet brush on mine when he slid in past my teeth.

His fingers delved in deeper, smearing the now warm lubricant into my hole. It was wet and messy, a soft gliding smack of oil and flesh as he worked me. My balls were tight, anxious for the long, hard cock about to slide over them, trapping them into the hollow of my thighs. I felt the kiss of his palm on my ass; then Jae pulled back to begin again.

"Driving me crazy, Jae." I scraped my lower teeth along his collarbone. He liked getting bit, and I enjoyed leaving purpling slivers on his skin.

"Do you want me, *hyung?*" He teased me again, another dip, then a swipe along my balls, the crinkled skin slick with its drizzle of lube. Jae slipped his cock out of my hand, laying it along my sac. He ground his hips down, coating himself with more lube.

"Now would be good," I gasped. It was hard to breathe. I wanted him that badly. My belly clenched when I thought of him pushing past my oiled ring. My knees were parted, my legs spread wide to take him, and still Jae teased me with a rub of his cock. "*Jae.*"

He laughed, then murmured something in Korean, probably about my impatience, but then he leaned forward and kissed me.

It burned when Jae slid into me, when he stretched me, and then my body surrendered to his cock's insistent slide. Seated up against my legs and balls, Jae gave me a gentle kiss, and we both sighed into each other's mouths.

Then he began to move.

The sky outside of the stretch of windows was growing dark as the storm clouds I'd seen off over the ocean began to roll in. Los Angeles's tequila-sunrise-tinted lights were tamped down by the rain-heavy gray sheets covering them. It was never truly night in the City of Angels, but a storm could wash much of the glow from its light-polluted sky.

But what the storm did leave caught on the strong planes of Jae's beautiful body and filled the hollows with gold-kissed shadows.

Jae took my breath away. With a smile. Or a touch. And now, moving in me, slowly sliding his cock in and out of the clench of my ass, he let go of everything he wrapped around himself and let me see his raw and naked soul.

"Love you, Cole."

Jae thrust harder, and I cocked my hips in time with his. He lost his English when I bore down on him, refusing to let him go on one stroke and throwing him off.

I probably used every bit of dirty I had in me to coax him along, urging him to slam into me. My body throbbed and burned for his flesh. The push and pull on my ring caught my attention, and I wasn't willing to break free from its whispering sparks of ache and pleasure. I tried to grab at my dick, but he was already there, working at my shaft in long, torturous strokes.

My cock head was tender and tight, bristling with the promise of cum every time his palm slipped over my ridge, but Jae held me back, slowing his thrusts when I got too close. He played with me, drawing me to the edge, then reeling me in until I nearly begged for him to finish me.

I couldn't think anymore. My entire existence was centered around the man inside of me. My hands clutched at his shoulders, then at his hips, urging him to go deeper, to split me apart. We were caught up into a frenetic pace, challenging the storm outside to match our fury.

Jae pulled me open, trembling under my grasp, his cock harder than I'd ever felt. My balls were pulled in, churning and roiling in time with his fingers on my shaft. I laid my hand on his, working myself with him. I was so close. My mouth was dry, wanting to taste the salt in the air when we spilled. Then Jae caught my lips in a savage kiss, and I felt my body give.

I didn't hear the storm outside, but I felt it in my bones when I came. Power surged through my blood, bleaching out my senses until I could only ride the glut of stars pouring down from the sky and into my body. I went rigid, jerking and flailing under Jae's body, and when my ass tightened down on his cock, he joined me.

There was no greater sensation than the hot of Jae's cum filling me. He licked at my insides with his release, an intimate lave so private, so soul-wrenching I couldn't find the words for my exultation. We were giving something of ourselves no one else would ever see or touch, a moment of cloistered joy unseen by the world and shared only between our joined bodies.

He was mine.

I was his.

In the middle of the pleasure of our flesh were kisses and touches as sensual and fulfilling as sex. He touched me everywhere, both inside and out, pushing into the dark places I'd buried when I hurt and holding me together where I was broken.

And now he spread me open, splaying out my soul so the lightning could lick at and fill me as he found his release.

The world tilted and stayed that way for a long while. I could still see the stars floating in my vision where they burned me when I came. Jae slowly slipped out of me, easing himself away, then lying down next to me, panting heavily, nearly in time with my own gasps. Outside thunder rolled, a furious churl of a storm moving in around us, but it couldn't touch. Nothing could. Not as we lay against one another, sticky with sweat and cum but boneless with satiation.

Jae's hand found mine, and I threaded my fingers into his, our heartbeats erratic and pumping. He sighed and stretched, moaning a little when I kissed his shoulder.

"I love you, Jae." It was something I said every day. He should have been used to those words coming out of my mouth, but they never seemed to grow stale for him. His eyes still lit up, and a smile always tugged at the corners of his generous lips. "*Saranghae-yo.*"

"I love you too."

I waited a skip of a beat. Then another. But there was nothing else, just Jae catching his breath and the clash of clouds battling outside of the penthouse's windows.

"That's it? No snappy rejoinder?" I turned over onto my side so I could see his face. "Just *I love you too?*"

"What else is there to say, *agi?*" he teased. "Isn't that all we need?"

CHAPTER NINETEEN

I WOKE up alone.

And in daylight. Such as it was.

I was getting kind of sick of waking up alone.

The storm was in a lull but still held the city in its grip, stealing the sun from the sky and coating the penthouse in an ashen light. It felt uneasy, too off and chilling, and the stillness around me was unsettling. I missed Jae's warmth. Hell, I even would have loved having Neko smeared across my face. Anything to take away the cold off-kilter shards building up in my gut.

I barely remembered a mumbled conversation with Jae about Scarlet, scouting a site, the dog, and someplace with rusted metal dinosaurs. There was a small tickle of a bulb going off in my head while I was brushing my teeth, ribboning in bits of information I'd tucked into the folds of my brain.

"That diner on the way to Vegas. With the dinosaur park," I informed the cat, waving my foamy toothbrush at Neko lounging on the toilet bowl tank. "He went to go look at them because… something something fashion shoot, maybe? Well, fuck, they'll be gone all day. That's like three hours from here."

I had faith they'd taken a driver. Where Jae drove like a bat out of hell, Scarlet was about as wonky as a miniature golf course. They'd take a driver, not just because her lover insisted, but because Rollins was still out there.

Rollins was *still* out there.

Leaving Neko to her contemplation of travertine tile, I discovered Jae'd taken the Dr Pepper T-shirt we seemed to be sharing now and dug through his clothes to find something of his. I dressed in sweats and a beat-up Crossroads Gin T-shirt, then headed downstairs in search of coffee. I got to the open landing on the second floor and ran against a wall of hot air. The downstairs heater was on, full blast and pumping out the stagnant air left in its ducts since the last time it was on.

There was also a sickeningly sweet, rank smell.

A smell I knew all too well.

There was blood in the apartment, cooking in the overwhelming heat, and enough of it to fill the air with its metallic burn.

The landing's painted concrete squeaked beneath my bare feet, and I took the stairs two at a time. My heart froze when I spotted the spill of limbs, black hair, and blood in the middle of the living room area. I couldn't see his face, but I knew the body was male. A limp ball sac and the remains of a cock peeked out from under a slender thigh, and the crack of the man's rear was dark with fine hair. His body was riddled with long gashes, his asscheeks nearly crenulated with stab wounds. I kept telling myself the skin tone was wrong, there was no ink on the naked man's body, nothing to tell me it was Jae lying facedown with his guts spooled out around him in a Medusa tangle of intestines and bile.

My brain wasn't listening to any of my shit. It needed to see for itself... needed to turn over the body to make sure Jae's gold-flecked brown eyes weren't dulled and filmed over. Even when everything in me screamed it wasn't Jae, I still had to see for myself.

Milky shadows played with the room, filling in crevasses and corners I didn't know the space had. The stark monochromatic furniture was now marbled with drying brown splatters and lines, shapes made of blood and swipes of something flat. Death had been brought to the apartment. It hadn't come here of its own volition.

But its victim lay at my feet, a not-Jae body spread over the remains of my sanctuary.

"No touching the body, Mac."

One of the shadows spoke, and I jerked my head up, staring into the grayness beyond the living area.

"Crime scene and all that fucking shit. Or have you forgotten?"

Tucked under the landing was a sitting area Jae and I used once for breakfast, feeding each other an omelet I'd failed to turn over perfectly. We'd laughed as we ate, using garlic naan to scoop up the eggy mess. We'd left the half-eaten food and tumbled onto the couch, where I'd made love to Jae until he screamed.

Only to come back and find the dog'd eaten our breakfast and the cat was sitting in our basket of naan.

It was wrong for Rollins to be sitting there. Wrong for him to be sprawled in the same chair I'd been sitting in when Jae sat in my lap and shoved a strawberry into my mouth. He was an abomination, a cancerous tumor growing on the life I'd nursed into being, and he'd brought Death with him.

Then I saw the gun he was pointing at me.

"You look good, Mac."

Rollins stood and took a step toward me. His smirk was so familiar, one I'd seen a thousand times before, usually at the expense of others, but sometimes in the dark of our patrol car, he'd use it on me, a lick and a promise for what would be a long, drunken night of sex and rage.

"Door was open a little bit. Thanks for that. Made things a fuck of a lot easier."

"Yeah, well you look like shit, Jeff." Killing wasn't good for the skin, because Rollins's was stretched tight and sharp over his bones. "And no one invited you in. I thought assholes needed to be asked in before they crossed a threshold. Oh no, wait, that's vampires."

There was a craziness in his eyes, a dead flatness I'd seen at the club before he shot the place up. Blown-out fine veins turned his nose and cheeks into a tapestry of pink lines, and gray skin and the bags under his bottom lashes were thick and swollen. His body was still powerful but too lean, and his jeans hung down on his hips, baggy across his thighs and crotch.

Rollins was sick in the head. He always had been. The possibility of it dawned on me. I'd been so far removed from him during the years, I'd not thought about his lifestyle and arrogance. He'd been a small, violent bump among other larger, catastrophic events. I hadn't given Rollins *any* thought, not until he'd intruded on my life again.

"So now *I'm* the asshole? When you're up here like a damned king?" He shrugged. "We can't all live off the department, you piece of shit."

The gun remained on me, and his finger was firm into the trigger well. There was a lot of room to move in the apartment. The designer'd gone minimalist with the furnishings and décor, which was great in a penthouse made up of windows and the Los Angeles skyline but shitty if you needed cover from gunfire. I was beginning to sweat from the overwhelming heat, and it was getting harder to breathe, my nose ripe with the stink of the dead man a few feet behind me.

"Who did you kill, Jeff?" I kept to his first name, trying to maintain some intimacy between us.

"Really, Mac? You don't know it's that bitch I'd been fucking before he started whining too much?"

"Suh." The last time I'd seen Darren Suh, I'd been trying to stop him from getting killed. Apparently I was just delaying the inevitable.

"Because he was going to tell you where I was. You know that. As soon as he got away, he was going to spill his guts to the cops." Jeff smirked again. "Now he's spilling his guts all over your fucking floor."

"So you killed him? None of this makes any sense, Jeff." I was getting under his skin, literally. A pink flush rose over his cheekbones, and his eyes narrowed. "Suh was probably the only person you had on your side, even if he'd come to his senses and kicked you out. He still did what you told him to do. And you went and killed him."

"I was getting tired of him. It was time to get rid of him anyway. At least now he can't tell anyone where I am. He was just a piece of ass."

"Like I was?" I prodded.

"Mac, you were never stupid. Naïve as fuck but never stupid. You were a piece of ass I had a hard time walking away from. But there's no way in hell I was going to get caught in the shit you were calling down on yourself. Everyone in the department knew it wouldn't be long before someone capped you. No one wants a faggot sitting next to them in the car. You were going to catch a cop's bullet at some point. Didn't you know that?" Jeff cocked his head at me. "Or did Ben shoot you in the head and no one told me? That what happened? Stray bullet?"

"No, just the body." I touched my chest where Ben's bullets had torn into my flesh. "And no matter how fucked-up the department was then, there's no way in hell they'd want a blue-on-blue happening. Especially if it meant two cops dying while on duty."

"Yeah, heard you went flatline on the table a few times." Another step closer, and Jeff could have reached out and touched me if he wanted to. "See any white lights? Heard the voices of your loved ones calling to you? Did Mommy call you home, Mac?"

"She might have still been alive when I was shot." I tried to remember when Ichi said she'd died, and I caught the wide-eyed spark of shock in his face. "Yeah, come to find out she was alive the whole time. Died afterwards."

"It's like a fucking soap opera with you, Mac," he chuckled. "Nothing's ever easy and straightforward."

"Probably not," I agreed. "Kind of like my ex-partner showing up and trying to kill my family."

"You didn't see that coming?" He mocked me, pulling his mouth out into an O and gasping lightly. "Come on, Mac. It's a classic move. How could you not expect someone to come around and finish what Ben started?"

There it was. That thread. However thin and unraveled, there was something almost obsessive connecting Rollins and Ben, something I had no way of knowing because neither one of them ever let on they were buddies when Ben'd been alive. Whatever it was, I'd picked at, trying to find the end, but just ended up back at the beginning again, as ignorant as I'd been from the start.

"What do you think Ben started?" This time I was the one who closed a bit more of the distance between us, but Rollins wasn't having any of it. "Because you've never finished a damned thing in your life, Jeff. You walked out on the badge. Because of what? They hurt your feelings?"

"Fuck off, Mac. The department turned its back on *me*."

He took a few strides away from me, going past my left side and toward the dead man he'd left on the floor. I tracked him, turning as he walked to keep him in front of me.

"And here you are, living off of Ben's dead body. The department paid you in blood money and you go off with your life like Ben meant fucking nothing." Rollins spat, his face flushed red and screwed up tight with anger. "He loved you. You were his damned brother but he hated your guts because you couldn't just be gay like everyone else...like me. Cops hide that kind of crap. You know how much damned shit he had to put up with because he had this faggot in the car with him? You had to put it into everyone's damned face and expected everyone to be okay with you bringing your *boyfriend*around Ben and his kids."

"Ben hated himself. Don't put this on me," I countered. "He's the one who brought the gun that night. He's the one who pulled the trigger."

"Being around you pushed him too far," Rollins shook his head. "So yeah, I don't blame him one bit for pulling that trigger. After what I read in Ben's letters to his loser brother, I knew I couldn't just let it go by without finishing up what Ben started. You should have fucking died that night. Along with that homo you called a boyfriend. Ben should have done it and walked away. Your entire damned life should get wiped away, like Ben's was."

"The department hid that Ben was fucked-up." I tapped my head. "Something was going on in his mind, and no one did jack shit about it. He killed his fucking doctor, Jeff. Shot me and Rick, then killed *himself*. Now you're coming around saying you've got to *finish* things? Ben fucking *finished* things. He fucking finished them when he chewed on his own damned gun!"

One thing about Rollins, he loved to hear himself talk. He'd spent a lot of our shifts going on about things, usually commentary about society and the assholes out on the street with guns waiting for cops to drop their guard. I could always depend on him going into an eye-bulging rant with just a few well-placed words.

Or ill-placed ones as well. Like right now. Something about Ben triggered him off, and for me, Rollins's rage couldn't have come at a better time.

I jumped him. Old-school, Chicago-hard brawling. The beatings I'd gotten growing up a half-Asian kid in a couple of bad neighborhoods was nothing compared to what I intended to give Rollins. I couldn't even see straight anymore. In the heat and the convoluted nonsense he'd flung at me, I'd become mad, unreasonably and irrevocably enraged.

He shot me.

I felt the bullet hit my arm. Felt its sting and then the sear of blood on my skin. I didn't know if he only creased my bicep or shot me all the way through. Hell, I could have been bleeding out by a struck artery, and I would have kept going. My hands itched to feel Rollins's blood on my knuckles, and I plowed right into him, slamming his face with everything I had.

He broke.

Literally broke. His jaw or nose gave way. Something did at least, because I heard the bones in his face bend and snap under my fist. Then the fucker bit my hand, and all bets were off.

We went down, stumbling over Suh's body, and the chill of his dead flesh on my foot gave me the shivers. Rollins gave no sign of stopping, and somewhere on our trip down, he'd lost the gun. I couldn't see it. Couldn't really look for it because I couldn't risk letting him go. Not when I had him down on the floor.

His fingers scratched at my face, digging deep into my cheek. Punching him on the jaw got him to let me go, but he was back again, shoving his stiff hand into my Adam's apple. I lost air, sucking on the tight feeling in my throat. Pulling my head back got me some breathing room, but Rollins was too quick. Jerking his head forward, he smashed me against the temple, and I saw stars.

The hit was a good one. Too good, because the back of my head ached as much as the front, a sure sign I'd bruised what little brain I had left in my skull. We were both on our knees, but he had a better reach. Everything on the steel and glass coffee table was something he could use against me. Even without a gun, there were enough heavy items around we could use on each other. He must have been thinking the exact same thing, because I saw him stretch his arm out as I struggled to get to my feet.

Suh's arm tangled around my left leg, and I was trying to shake it off when Rollins grabbed one of the little silver freeform sculptures the designer thought was a good idea to litter about the living room and used it to bash me across the face.

I tasted blood and choked on the river of it coursing down my sinuses. The pain was sharp and hard, with a swelling across my nose moving too quickly for me to do more than hawk out what was in my throat and hope to breathe through my mouth. The sculpture was in pieces, a plaster-of-Paris piece of crap covered in a shiny plastic, but for all its fakery, it still did damage. I couldn't breathe, and Rollins was dusting the remains of his weapon off his hand while looking for something else to hit me with.

Or maybe he was looking for the gun. Either way, I wasn't willing to let him arm himself.

I swung out, scoring a punch somewhere on his chest. He floundered back, thrown off-balance, then landed on the glass table. There wasn't enough momentum in his fall for the glass to break, and he skidded over its polished edge, landing in a heap on the floor.

"Why'd Suh toss you out, Jeff?" My brain was scrambled and my mouth was off and running, its filters pulled out and the stupid flow of my thoughts pouring out of me. I didn't give a shit if Rollins was sick or just overstressed. "Couldn't get it up?"

When it was all said and done, men fight with stupid weapons… childish taunts and underhanded sucker punches. There was a huge difference between what I did in the ring with Bobby and what Rollins and I were doing to each other on top of Suh's inert body. One of us was going to die. There was no walking away for one of us, and I was damned and determined to make sure it was going to be him lying next to Suh.

"Got it up enough for you, bitch," he snapped back.

His punch went wide, a glancing blow on my arm, but it stung, landing too close to the spot where he'd shot me.

"You probably miss my cock so fucking—"

Talking always got Rollins into trouble. Even when we'd been partners, he couldn't shut up. Thankfully, my right hook did that for me. I hit hard, following through as much as I could while on one knee. He went down, and I got up quickly. The heat was getting to me. I was sweating out of every pore of my body, and the blow I'd taken to my head threatened to undo my guts. I was shaky on my feet, a steep vertigo swamping my senses. I didn't know if I had it in me to stay up, but I didn't have a choice. Rollins had to go down. He'd never let Jae or Mike go if I died. He wouldn't stop until everyone connected to me lay dead at his feet. Something had dug down into his psyche, and somehow I'd become the dragon he had to slay.

Knowing why didn't matter. Not with Rollins still grabbing things off the table while I fought off the blackness creeping in on the edges of my vision.

Fuck, he must have hit me harder than I'd thought.

A salver went by my head, then another sculpture. I ducked instinctively, because that's what stupid gut reactions make someone do, and Rollins came after me. We went down again, rolling around on the floor and punching. Everything spun, a dizzying churn of colors and shapes I couldn't track. I kept hitting, hoping to score a good blow somewhere on his body, but nothing seemed to faze him. His hands kept moving, jabbing and punching the air out of my lungs, leaving me gasping. The heated apartment swam around me, undulating while I tried to find oxygen in the steamy mess I was pulling in.

Something sharp scraped into the small of my back, and Rollins shoved me hard against it. I flailed, slapping my hand on the peninsula at the edge of the kitchen. My fingers found the rungs of a bar stool, and I tried to grab at it, but Rollins kicked it out of my reach. I was on the ground looking up when he stood. He cocked his leg back and struck hard, slamming his foot into my balls, then down on my face.

I couldn't roll out of the way. Trapped against the cabinet, I threw up what little water I had in my guts when he kicked my crotch again. My balls were up past my stomach, and my throat was closing, the tingle of my guts losing hold threatening the back of my throat.

Dry heaving, I gagged and struggled to catch my breath. I couldn't find Rollins in my line of sight, and I panicked, wondering where his damned gun'd gone. Grabbing anything within my reach, I hung on to one of the tall bar stools and tried to pull myself up. I got to my knees when Rollins came out from around the peninsula, holding one of Jae's knives in his right hand.

"Going to carve you up and feed you to that fucking stepmother Ben's got."

Rollins's lupine grin was bloody, and his front tooth was missing. I counted that as a small victory.

"Bitch wouldn't give me all of Ben's stuff. Said it was for you. Like Ben wanted you to have it. The fucking perfect Cole McGinnis. God, how he fucking hated you in the end. Pity you won't be around to see how she squeals when I'm choking the shit out of her."

I couldn't breathe. Or what I was getting in me was too hot for me to get anything out of. Tasting the green of my stomach's spill in my throat and my blood on my tongue, I kicked out at Rollins's legs, needing to get some distance between us. The bar stool skittered away from me, and I couldn't grab the countertop in time. My legs gave out from under me, and I hit the stone ledge with my arm, sending shock waves of pain through my system. There was more blood seeping out from my wound, muddying Jae's gray shirt with a slow crawl of red.

Rollins lifted the knife up over his head. It was a thick-bladed curve, kept sharp by a few strops on a whetstone Jae stashed in a drawer near the stove. I'd cut myself more than once on his blades while cutting things, not even realizing I'd been sliced open until I saw the blood dripping down on the counter. The pain always came later.

Not this time. This time it would be instant and hurt all the more because he was going to kill me with something Jae took very good care of. For the first time since I'd known Jae, I wished he'd been a little less diligent with his things.

"I'm really going to love fucking your guy's ass when he gets home." Rollins sneered at my attempts to grab the stool. "Right on top of your dead—"

The gunshot scared the fuck out of me. I felt its boom in my jaw and scrambled to move. My hands were too sweaty and bloody for me to get traction on the stupid trendy slick floor, and I twisted around, gouging my knee into the cabinet as the top of Rollins's head exploded.

He fell, slamming down on top of me. I had nowhere to go, and he landed hard, bouncing on my shoulder and chest. I shoved as hard as I could, getting him clear of me. I didn't want to be trapped under his weight and bathing in his blood. The knife skittered across the floor, bouncing and arcing up once like a stone skipping across a still pond. Rollins's body twitched as he died, gurgling sounds slithering out of his open mouth, as if he couldn't go out without cursing my existence one last time.

Laughing, I recognized the leather Converses coming around the peninsula before I saw who was wearing them. New York City graffiti on white, I'd teased Jae about wearing them when he was clearly a SoCal kind of guy. He liked the style, he'd said. And now they'd be smeared and stained with the bloody floor he was crossing to get to me.

I found Rollins's gun. Not before Jae had, obviously, and he carefully placed it on the counter, then bent down to give me a kiss. Running his hand over my overheated body, he clutched me to him, ignoring my protests of getting our shared shirt filthy with sweat and blood.

"Oh God, Cole. He's... shit, I killed him." Jae's face was stark white, and I was scared he was going to pass out. "I killed a man, Cole. But he was going to... fuck. I forgot about the door. The damned door."

"Hey, you're back," I mumbled.

He shouldn't have been. Not if he was heading to that diner. I shouldn't have seen him for hours... never would have seen him again if he hadn't come through the front door. He stunk of gunpowder and fear, his hands shaking as he touched me.

"Fuck, I'm glad to see you."

"I had the driver turn back around. I couldn't remember if I'd shut the door all the way. It doesn't close. I told Scarlet to wait. I wasn't going to be long. She's in the car and...." He sighed. "God, *hyung*. What... oh God. I *killed* him."

"Yeah, but if it makes you feel better, he's been trying to kill us first." I sat up all the way and nearly fainted. "It's too fucking hot, and I'm—"

"And you've been shot." Jae frowned, smearing the blood dripping down into my eyes with his thumb. "Goddamn it, Cole. You told me you weren't going to get shot."

"I'll work on it, babe," I promised heartily, catching his mouth in a kiss as hot as the air around us. "I really am going to work on it."

CHAPTER TWENTY

"ARE YOU sure you want to do this, *hyung*? I know I keep asking you that but… well, so long as you're sure."

Jae carefully steered up the winding road, heading to a ranch tucked into the hills. I may or may not have been gripping the Rover's armrest from sheer panic, but I was passing it off as leaning against the door and enjoying the brisk air coming through the open window.

"She could have mailed it to you. You're just now feeling better."

It'd been a rough month. After the shooting, we'd been put through the ringer with the LAPD, and the seemingly meat-only shot I'd taken went south, putting me in the hospital for a few days while they pumped me so full of antibiotics I glowed under a black light. Jae'd been by my side the entire time. Except when the cops were questioning him in a small, puke-inducing room about the madman who'd tried to kill us.

He'd been trying to talk me out of driving up to the mountains to meet Ben's stepmother, Elizabeth, since the first time she'd reached out to us. Rollins's rampage made the news. Between the constant news broadcasts and well-meaning phone calls from the cops to check on her, she'd IDed Rollins as the man she'd handed Adam's letters to and then rebuffed when he wanted the rest of Ben's effects. O'Byrne didn't tell Elizabeth she'd been on Rollins's wall of targets he'd put up in a garage he'd been squatting in. Sometimes ignorance was bliss, but the detective was pretty certain there wasn't anyone else looking to put me and mine into the ground.

I'd spoken to Elizabeth on the phone, and she offered then to send me the letters and journals Ben'd left behind. After a bit of back and forth, I told her I'd go up and grab the package. It seemed odd to me that he hadn't planned on killing me, intending me to be handed the package of papers if something happened to him. Or at least that's what the note on the package he'd left in his safety deposit box said.

It was a cold comfort knowing he hadn't *meant* to kill me.

But he'd done it anyway.

"I'm good, Jae. And we're almost there. I just want to get this over with, you know?" The Los Angeles canyons were long past us now. We were up in the wilds above the city, a few miles under Solvang, where we could get fresh pretzels, handmade sausages, and wooden trinkets while quaffing down beer strong enough to put hair on our chests. A tricky feat since neither of us had any to begin with. "Kind of like a Band-Aid. Just rip it off, and it'll be over in a minute."

"I just don't want you to tear your skin off with it."

Jae reached over and patted my thigh. Since I always panicked when he didn't have two hands on the wheel, he laughed when I stiffened.

"I don't know why you're scared. Not like I've ever hit anything. And between the two of us, who's gone through the most cars?"

I didn't deign to answer. Instead I sniffed and pointed out the turnoff ahead of us. "There. Tabray-Collins Lane. She said turn left at the horses, and we'll see the house through the trees."

THE HORSES were barely larger than Great Danes. Coming up over the ridge, they were a tiny herd of thundering hooves and tossing manes seemingly ready made to make a horse-mad little girl convince her father she could have one in the backyard. Since I was about to have a niece in a few months and an older brother to torment, wee dog-sized horses were a Christmas gift waiting to happen.

"Don't even think about it." Jae's scold jerked me back to the present where logic and reason ruled. "Put whatever it is that you're thinking out of your mind. And don't bother saying *nothing* because I can see it on your face. *No.*"

Shit, it was like he knew me or something.

Jae turned left at the horses, and the road became a pair of ruts on a mostly grass road. The house appeared as she said it would, a ramshackle ranch with a wraparound porch, an old-fashioned triangle dangling from a support beam to summon everyone to a meal, and fifty dogs of various ages, breeds, and drool-splatters.

Maybe twenty, but with all the tail wagging and booming howls, it was hard to keep an accurate count.

The woman sitting in a rocker on the broad porch was older, a slender, pleasant-faced lady dressed in a very practical pair of old jeans and a snap-button shirt. She set a mug of something down on a rough wood table next to the chair, much to the disgust of a humongous marmalade tabby spread across its top. The cat's fluffy tail twitched, but its ears remained pointed forward, a good-humored feline despite the pack of hellhounds baying us in.

Jae parked. Well, Jae left the Rover in the middle of the dog pack, and we got out, slowly working our way to the house. The dogs followed, a merry, happy chorus probably chattering to us about tennis balls, squirrels, and probably the orange cat that ruled the roost. Honey would have fit right in. It was hard going, weaving through the excited throng, and the woman laughed as she came down the stairs to greet us, gently nudging a mastiff aside with her knee.

"Hi, I'm Elizabeth."

Her hands were dressed in hard calluses from working outdoors, but she wore her years well. The lines on her freckled face were more from laughter than sun, and the touch of silver to her short brown hair was slight. She gave me a strong handshake, then moved a beagle mix out of the way to get to Jae.

"Come up to the porch and sit if you like. I'll be getting what you came for and be right back out. If you've food on you, don't let any of these beggars con you into anything. It'll spoil their dinner."

I wandered out to the fence where the miniature horses were nibbling at something grassy in a trough. One sauntered over, obviously the Aramis of the bunch, and stuck his head out to be scratched. I obliged, finding a sweet spot on his dainty forehead because he leaned against the fencing and made a very unhorselike noise.

"Screw Mad Dog Junior," I muttered at Jae. "*I* want one."

"You already have a dog and a cat," Jae reminded me. "You can't have a horse too."

"The cat is yours." I touched his palm with my fingertips, tickling him. He drew back, laughing. "And she has *you*. Not the other way around."

"Isn't that the nature of a cat?" Jae turned at the sound of a screen door banging into its frame. "She's back. Come on."

He walked away from me, lithe and self-confident. We'd held one another in the dark after the shooting, quiet with patches of crying and murmurs. He'd taken a life. Even in the middle of the horrors Rollins brought down on us, Jae never once thought he'd have a man's death on his conscience. We'd survived Rollins. We'd survive anything the universe threw at us.

It wasn't anything we questioned anymore. After everything we'd gone through, we were *together*. Would stay together. No matter what.

"Are you coming?" He paused, caught in a maelstrom of happy hounds. "Or do you want me to get it for you?"

"No, I'll grab it." I brushed the tiny horse's mane out of his eyes one last time, then headed over to where Jae waited for me. "I'm ready to put this whole thing behind us. Once and for all."

WE ENDED up in Goleta at a treelined state park. I told Jae to follow one of the outer loops, swinging the Rover around to a pair of picnic tables and BBQ pit seldom used by anyone but the locals. A brisk ocean wind kept most of the people off the beach, and it gave us a bit of solitude, a ring of palms and evergreens at our backs as we stared out over the ocean.

With the Rover parked out of the way, we sat side by side on the picnic table's top, resting our feet on a bench. The package sat between us, a manila harbinger from my past. A small fire burned in one of the square metal BBQ racks California thoughtfully erected for its park visitors. I'd gotten briquettes and a starter box at the convenience store near the park's entrance, thinking we could maybe toast some of the marshmallows Jae'd tucked into the basket.

Now I wondered if the crackling, cheerful fire was going to be a pyre for my past and memories.

Salt stung my nostrils, and the tall cup of dime-store coffee I'd gotten sat lukewarm and forgotten between my feet. A woman in a red bikini tossed a ball to a mutt who scampered after it, then left off chasing the ball so it could bark at a mound of kelp. A couple off in the distance walked hand in hand near the waterline, foam churning at their feet as the waves tumbled low on the sand.

And still the damned package sat there. Inert and as explosive as a grenade with its pin pulled out.

"You don't have to read what's in it, *agi*." Jae touched my hand, tracing the tops of my fingers. "It can wait. Forever if you want."

"Nah, I'd rather spend forever with you than this." He meant well, but I was carrying ten tons of shit on my soul, and the one question I'd had throughout all of this was... *why?* Now my biggest problem was if I truly wanted to know.

"You are so... *aish*," he scoffed. "Cheesy. I'm just saying, it's waited. If you want to wait too, it's okay. Whatever you want."

"You know what's weird? I'm glad she didn't give this to Rollins when he came by." I watched the dog play tug-of-war with its owner's towel. "Ben's stepmom. She said he pushed her for all of it when she gave him Adam's letters—"

"Which he probably read. Well, we know he read because whatever was in them made him crazy." Jae picked up my cup and took a sip, making a face at me when the sour black coffee hit his tongue. "Ben's mother, she should have given you those letters when they were found. His father too. It's a pity his step-mother had to wait until you reached out to her."

"I think reading Adam's letters before he could is the least of Rollins's crimes. He was insane, babe. Squirrel-fucking-nuts off his rocker. And he liked his secrets. Jeff told me jack shit about what was in Adam's letters. He was more interested in killing me because...what? I survived Ben? He wanted to wipe me, you and my family out because Ben's life fell apart? That is not the mind of a sane man," I said. He took another sip of my coffee and shuddered. "I didn't put cream or sugar in that."

"I know. I just need something to keep my hands busy, or I'm going to open that up *for* you." He saluted me with my cup. "I have no patience with things like this. I worry about things. Worry for you. I want to read what's in there so I can tell you not to fool with it. And I know better, but still...."

"But still...," I echoed. Sighing, I picked up the padded envelope and opened the flap. Its adhesive was long stuck to the paper, and it tore slightly as I worked it loose, exposing a bit of the bubble wrap beneath. Apparently I'd found the magic strip of glue, because everything came tumbling out, five brown paper-backed notebooks like the kind we used when we'd worked together and a stack of letters wrapped with a few old, stretched-out rubber bands.

There was also a single white envelope, nearly pristine and marbled with faint blue lines, a security precaution to prevent someone from seeing an enclosed check or even a confession letter written to a best friend.

The envelope had my name written on it, strong bold letters in black ink. Ben's handwriting. My name. Like all of the fucking notes he'd slip into my locker at work to tell me what time to get to their house that evening or what to get the kids for their birthdays if I was stuck on an idea.

I needed to breathe.

And I couldn't.

Fuck if I didn't get a damned paper cut opening the fricking envelope.

It was a single piece of paper, nearly covered with Ben's blocky writing, front and back. My heart did a skip when I saw my name at the top, and then it stopped beating altogether when I read the date at the top.

He'd written me the letter nearly a full week before he'd gunned us down in West Hollywood. An entire week I'd spent nearly every waking moment with him and Rick, going about our lives doing mundane things like picking up dry cleaning and making dinners while Ben festered something dark inside of his soul.

"I'm right here, *hyung*. If you need me."

Jae's hand was on my forearm, squeezing me tightly, anchoring me to the now.

"I want you to know something, babe," I said softly, turning to face him. "This isn't about Rick. This isn't about me loving him more or less than you. I—"

"I never once thought you love me any differently than you loved him," Jae whispered. He stroked at my mouth, playing with my lower lip with a push of his finger. "I *know* you, Cole-ah. You love fully. With everything in your soul. I don't think about how he and I compare. Or who you love more. He's gone. And I'm sorry about that. Because he shouldn't have died. But I am glad for two things. He was loved by you while he was alive and that I am loved by you now."

"Just don't forget that, okay?" I kissed his finger. "Because when I fall apart here… I might need you to put me back together."

"What do you think I've been doing since the day I first met you?" Jae laughed. "I am always saving you from yourself. First thing you did was try to poison yourself with raw bitter melon."

"I thought I was being suave." I'd tasted it since then, cooked and vile. I couldn't even imagine putting the disgusting vegetable on my tongue in its raw, unadulterated malevolent form.

"You would have puked all over the kitchen floor. Now, read your letter, Cole, so we can get out of the wind and someplace warm." He nodded to the BBQ. "The fire isn't going to last very long."

I knew what he was saying. If I was determined to plunge into a ghostly bloodbath from my past, I should do it quickly and soon. The sun was falling fast into the ocean, tentatively brushing the sky with a daub or two of rose and lemon. With the wind threatening to chill my veins with its icicle bite, I shook out the page and read Ben's final note.

If you're reading this, Mac, then I've gone and fucked our lives up. Shit, I don't know what I'm going to do about you, but I know what has to get done. But you're not a part of this. Not really. And I'm really fucking sorry for what's going to go down. Because as much as I love you, I love him more, and I can't fucking deal with this shit any longer.

First thing I should say is I hate you so much. Because until I met you, I was happy with the wife and kids. I was the guy I knew I needed to be, and then you came along and took that all away from me. Faggots are supposed to be pathetic, whiny assholes. Needy, you know? Because no matter what they did, they weren't ever going to have a real life—like a house and kids kind of life—and that's what I wanted.

I told the Captain I'd be your partner because I didn't think a gay guy would last long. We had bets on how long you'd wear your badge, and fuck me if you didn't turn out to be a good cop. And a really fucking great guy. I paid out so much cash because I bet against you making it past a month, the guys started calling me ATM.

Yeah, that's why they were calling me that. Not because Sheila kept buying shit for the house and I was complaining about it. It was 'cause you didn't quit. And then you went and became my friend. My fucking brother. I liked you, Mac. Loved you because my own fucking brother is a damned asshole. He's in jail for killing a guy he found sucking me off. Beat the guy to death because I was getting my rocks off.

There was nothing left in my lungs, and I gasped, forcing air past the pain growing in my chest. Jae rubbed my back, and I shuddered, thankful for him bringing me back to the present. There was more. I didn't want more. There were too many scabs being pulled off, leaving me raw and open. Ben would bleed me out one last time, and then we were done. So I kept going, even though I'd already seen the outcome of Ben's anguish.

Back then, that's when I knew I had to get married and be straight. Because I didn't want someone killing me like that. Adam beat that guy to death with his fucking bare hands, and then he kicked the shit out of me. I was a kid. And it scared me so fucking straight I hooked up with Sheila.

I was doing okay, you know. I had you, the kids, and Sheila. My parents were happy, and Adam's never getting out, which all things considered, is fine by me because I don't want him around my kids.

Then you brought Rick into it, and I fucking lost my mind.

I knew he'd been out there. You told me you had a hot boyfriend, but when it got serious, when you and Rick went and played house, it was the beginning of the end.

Not because I was jealous of him. Because I wasn't. I was jealous of you. Because I met him and wanted him so fucking much. Not like I'd ever wanted anyone before. And he was sleeping with you. Loving you. Watching you guys kiss made me sick to my stomach, and every damned fucking time he hugged you, I wanted to blow your brains out.

I can't do this anymore, Mac. I can't deal with watching him with you and then going home and being with Sheila. I can't be gay, not if I want to keep the kids. No fucking judge is going to hand the kids over to some faggot when there's a mom around. No matter how many pills she pops in the back bathroom when she thinks no one's looking.

Rick turned me down, you know. That one time we all went to Cabo and got wasted off of that crappy tequila and you passed out? The two of us were lying on the beach, naked as fuck because we'd gone for a midnight swim, and I couldn't stop from wanting him. I grabbed his dick, and he told me no. Because he loves you. He fucking loves you, Mac, and I can't deal with that anymore.

I don't know what I'm going to do. No, I do know, but I just don't know if you're coming with us. If you're reading this, then I'm sorry. I took him from you the only way I know I can. And I'm probably not coming back from this either. I love you, Mac. No matter what, with all this shit and hate inside of me, I love you.

All of the other letters were addressed to Rick. Ben'd written them and never sent them. Instead he professed his love to a man I'd shared my bed and life with, while Ben called himself my brother. I couldn't read them. My eyes were already stinging with tears, some anger but a lot of regret. Holding back the thick emotion threatening to break my soul, I got off of the picnic table and slid all of it into the fire. The edges caught first, blackening, then flaring up to be consumed by the hungry, licking flames.

The horizon bled crimson, roiling in oranges and golds, much like the fire crackling through my dead best friend's worshipful letters to my murdered lover. I turned and found Jae standing there, the sunset reflected in his dark, concerned eyes. The tears came then, hitting hard and fast, but Jae didn't mind my jerking sobs.

Instead he did what he always did for me. He wrapped his arms around me and held me together until my heart could heal from being broken.

EPILOGUE

THE WEDDING went to shit nearly as soon as dawn broke. If something could go wrong, it did. The rental shop sent over the wrong tuxedoes and didn't have the right ones available. Then we got a call about the church's water main breaking, flooding the place so badly Moses couldn't have parted the waters so we could get to the altar.

Well, so we could get Bobby and Ichi to the altar.

To make matters worse, the caterer's truck caught on fire, and the enormous cake Bobby ordered slid out of its box while it was being moved onto the elevator, but the wedding went off without a hitch.

"It's like *you* fucking planned this damned thing, Princess. It's all gone so wrong," Bobby growled at me as I adjusted one of the black kilts I'd gotten from the rental shop on Hollywood Boulevard. "Tell me you have the damned rings."

"I have the damned rings," I promised.

And I had them, right up until the moment when I passed one over to my best friend and then to my baby brother so they could be joined together in the eyes of God, a sobbing black woman with a zillion kids, a beautiful Filipino transvestite, and the rest of the crazies we called a family.

I might have gotten a bit teary eyed, especially when Bobby slammed his elbow into my ribs when the minister got to the part about anyone having any objections, and Ichiro narrowed his eyes at my gasp.

The reception was held later that evening under the stars, or as many as we could find in the Los Angeles night. Fairy lights sparkled overhead, strung up on poles we'd erected on the rooftop where Bobby and Ichi lived. The building was big enough to hold the fifty-some-odd people who'd been invited to celebrate their wedding and then the thirty or so more who came by after their shifts ended or wandered up from downstairs.

A drag queen in a red beehive and sparkling green sequined dress regaled a cluster of geriatric women about the joys of moisturizing while my brother Mike balanced a plate of Chinese food on his very pregnant wife's stomach. We'd turned the west portion of the rooftop into a dance floor, digging out two banks of disco lights from Bobby's storage unit and setting them to a frenetic cycle of rainbow flashes in time with the music coming from his apartment's sound system.

Champagne flowed freely from the bar, as well as a few microbrews Bobby and Ichi argued over. In the end, they toasted one another with different IPAs and fed one another pieces of flourless chocolate torte we'd gotten from a Korean bakery on Wilshire.

Claudia snuck up on me as I watched Jae from across the dance floor. His head was bent down while he flicked through the photos he'd taken of the wedding, Scarlet looking over his shoulder. They were animated, laughing between them in a burble of Korean and Filipino. He'd sacrificed his own tuxedo so Ichiro had something to wear and eschewed one of the kilts, choosing instead to wear a dark gray suit. Somewhere along the way, he'd lost his tie, and his loafers were replaced with black Converses, but he was sexy as hell.

And all mine.

"I'm glad you found him, boy," Claudia said as she slipped her arm into mine. She'd gone bright for the wedding, an orange suit jacket and skirt combination only topped by the matching hat she had perched on her loosely curled helmet of hair. Claudia smelled good, like fresh linens and love. "He's good for you. Like you're good for him."

"Pretty sure I got the better end of the deal." I kissed her powdered cheek, and she slapped at me, playfully reminding me she could hand me my ass at any time.

"Don't argue with your mother," Claudia cautioned. "You're not so big I can't beat your ass."

"Yes, ma'am," I teased back.

Scarlet must have felt us watching them because she looked up and waved, nearly drowning out the blanket of lights above us with her smile. Dragging Jae with her, she slowly crossed the rooftop, heading to where Claudia and I stood, chatting as she walked, but nothing stayed her course.

"Come on. No sense letting them do all the work." Claudia heaved a sigh. "God, I wish I had that woman's body. If I didn't love Scarlet, I'd kill her, she looks that good."

"She's got nothing on you, Mom," I whispered into her ear. "Even if she's got the love of my life on her arm, you're the prettiest one here."

"I like you in a kilt, *dongsaeng*," Scarlet said to me when they drew near. "You've got nice legs. Now here, you take Jae and go dance. I'll hold on to the camera. Maybe take a few shots. It's not right if there's no pictures of Jae here. He was... the *other* best man? *Aish*, too confusing. Go. Go."

Relieved of his camera duties, Jae took my hand and led me out to dance in the ring of paper lanterns he and Ichi strung up that afternoon. The song turned maudlin, something about love, sin, and silver. The words didn't matter, not when I had Jae in my arms.

We danced, shuffling around in a tight circle, because when it was all said and done, I danced as well as I stayed out of trouble. Bobby and Ichi swayed back and forth nearby, their heads drawn together, and their low laughter tolled wickedly sweet. A few feet away, Mike was doing his best to coax Maddy to get to her feet for a waltz, and from the looks of things, he was winning. She handed her plate to one of Claudia's grandkids and let herself be waddled over, her hand on her ripe belly and her bright smile wide and only for my brother. If she went into labor at the wedding reception, it wouldn't surprise a single damned person there.

"Scarlet *nuna* is right, you know," Jae murmured between us.

"She usually is." I realized I had no idea what he was talking about and wrinkled my nose. "What is she right about?"

"You've got nice legs." He laughed at my snort. "You've got nice everything."

"Mostly I've got a nice... no, fantastic boyfriend." I looked around as we slowly turned. "You ever want this? Well, something like this?"

"A dance?" It was Jae's turn to look confused.

I kissed the corner of his mouth and shook my head. "No. Getting married."

"You and me?" He tilted his head back to stare at me.

"You know anyone else I could be talking about?" I teased back. "Seriously, have you ever thought about it?"

"Sometimes," Jae sighed. "Because... I don't know. I guess it is because it's a step in life. Like getting a car or buying a washing machine. It's a declaration of existence, I think. Marriage, yes. Children, no. The cat is enough. And now the dog. We have more than enough responsibilities with them."

"I'd be offended that you compared me to a washing machine—"

"You broke the last one."

"*We* broke the last one," I reminded him.

"*Saranghae-yo*, Cole-ah. Together, we're all that's important. If we live in sin for the rest of our lives, I'm okay with that. If that's what you want." Jae returned my kiss, laughing when I spun him around. "Because I know you love me."

"I do love you, baby. With all of my heart and soul." Stepping into the shadows just outside of the dance floor, I tightened my arms around Jae and murmured only loud enough for him to hear. "So what do you think? Want to stop living in sin and marry me?"

RHYS FORD admits to sharing the house with three cats of varying degrees of black fur and a ginger cairn terrorist. Rhys is also enslaved to the upkeep of a 1979 Pontiac Firebird, a Toshiba laptop, and an overworked red coffee maker.

Rhys can be found at the following locations:
Blog: www.rhysford.com
Facebook: www.facebook.com/rhys.ford.author
Twitter: @Rhys_Ford

Also from Dreamspinner Press

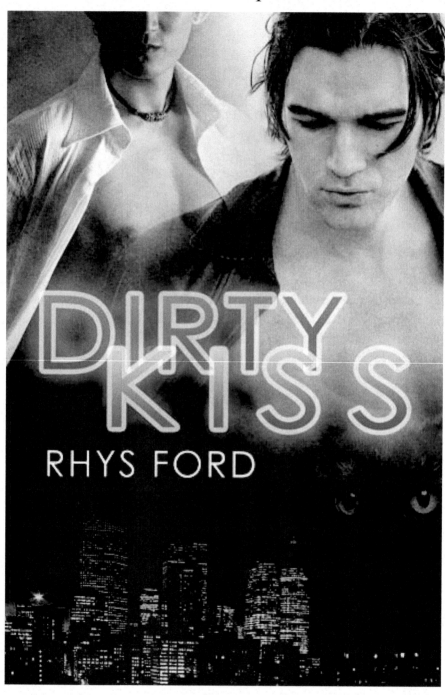

DIRTY KISS

RHYS FORD

www.dreamspinnerpress.com

A Cole McGinnis Mystery

Cole Kenjiro McGinnis, ex-cop and PI, is trying to get over the shooting death of his lover when a supposedly routine investigation lands in his lap. Investigating the apparent suicide of a prominent Korean businessman's son proves to be anything but ordinary, especially when it introduces Cole to the dead man's handsome cousin, Kim Jae-Min.

Jae-Min's cousin had a dirty little secret, the kind that Cole has been familiar with all his life and that Jae-Min is still hiding from his family. The investigation leads Cole from tasteful mansions to seedy lover's trysts to Dirty Kiss, the place where the rich and discreet go to indulge in desires their traditional-minded families would rather know nothing about.

It also leads Cole McGinnis into Jae-Min's arms, and that could be a problem. Jae-Min's cousin's death is looking less and less like a suicide, and Jae-Min is looking more and more like a target. Cole has already lost one lover to violence—he's not about to lose Jae-Min too.

www.dreamspinnerpress.com

Also from Dreamspinner Press

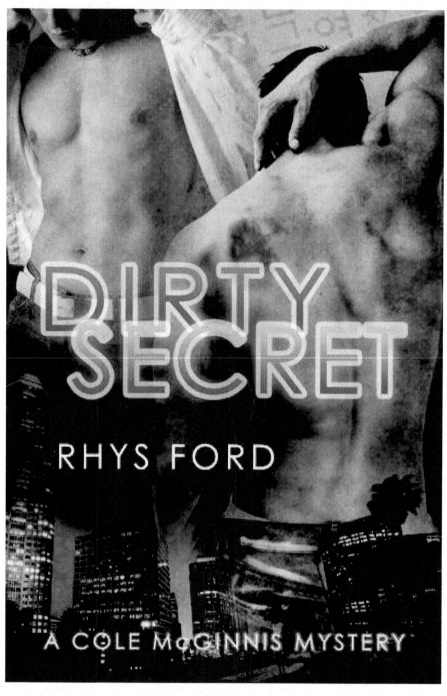

DIRTY
SECRET

RHYS FORD

A COLE McGINNIS MYSTERY

www.dreamspinnerpress.com

Sequel to *Dirty Kiss*
A Cole McGinnis Mystery

Loving Kim Jae-Min isn't always easy: Jae is gun-shy about being openly homosexual. Ex-cop turned private investigator Cole McGinnis doesn't know any other way to be. Still, he understands where Jae is coming from. Traditional Korean men aren't gay—at least not usually where people can see them.

But Cole can't spend too much time unraveling his boyfriend's issues. He has a job to do. When a singer named Scarlet asks him to help find Park Dae-Hoon, a gay Korean man who disappeared nearly two decades ago, Cole finds himself submerged in the tangled world of rich Korean families, where obligation and politics mean sacrificing happiness to preserve corporate empires. Soon the bodies start piling up without rhyme or reason. With every step Cole takes toward locating Park Dae-Hoon, another person meets their demise—and someone Cole loves could be next on the murderer's list.

www.dreamspinnerpress.com

FOR

MORE

OF THE
BEST
GAY
ROMANCE

DREAMSPINNER
PRESS

dreamspinnerpress.com

CPSIA information can be obtained
at www.ICGtesting.com
Printed in the USA
LVOW01s0410150316

479141LV00017B/62/P